The Ghost of Mary Morgan

Amanda Aubrey-Burden

The Ghost of Mary Morgan

The Ghost of Mary Morgan

DEDICATION

For Mary Morgan and her baby

The Ghost of Mary Morgan

CONTENTS

The Ghost of Mary Morgan

ACKNOWLEDGMENTS

My heartfelt thanks to everyone who has supported me on this extraordinary journey. You kept the faith, not just in me, but also with the idea that Mary Morgan suffered a great miscarriage of justice. It is my hope that this book will go some way in challenging the misconceptions that surround her case; and by doing so, clear her name. We did it for a young girl whose tragedy took hold of our hearts and refused to let go. We did it for Mary. We did it for love.
Special thanks to: -

The Venerable Karen Lund, Archdeacon of Manchester, for her unstinting support.
Rebecca Eversley Pgdip, BA (hons) for all of her brilliant research.
Demelsa Hopkins for having belief in her gift that became integral to the story.
My best friend and Chief Cheerleader, 'the Madonna'!
The Reverend David Thomas and his wife, Davina, of Glasbury.
The Reverend Andrew Perrin of Holy Trinity Church, Llandridnod Wells, and curate, Lisa Morgan.
The Reverend Stephen Hollinghurst of St. Andrews Church, Presteigne.
The Very Reverend Geraint Hughes.
Prys of the 'Seven Stars' pub, Aberedw.
Margaret Morris.
Glenys Millichamp
Roger Millichamp.
Lynne Traylor.
Kay Hughes.
Les Pitt.
Henry and William!
Janet Matthews of the Dukes Arms.
Lorna and Martha of Lorna's Sandwich Shop.
Jeremy Price.
Belynda Johnson Carranco Maclean.
Betty Creed.

Nicky Evans.
Hilary Marchant.
Bernadette.
Ceri Evans of the National Library of Wales.
Mari James, Librarian at St. David's Cathedral.
Liz Smith and Gill Deacon of the Anthony Family, Clyro.
The Morgans of Painscastle, Derek, Brian, Iris and Nerissa.
Heather and Phil Bufton of the Powys Family History Society Amanda Jones of Powys Archives.
Andy and Sally Williams of The Harp Inn, Glasbury.
Madelline and Tony Goodwin of Glasbury.
Janet Gardiner.
The team st Judge's Lodgings.
Mr and Mrs. Kendell of Bradshaw Manor.
Diana Powell and her brother, Nigel.
Jerry and Allyson Davis of Rock Woodcraft, Llanddewi.

My thanks, also, to the wonderful people of Presteigne, who are a legend unto themselves. Kind-hearted, down to earth, and unfailingly courteous. They have watched as this story developed, shown interest, and assisted when needed. They have been, and they remain, the salt of the earth, and I am proud to count many as friends. And to those who wish to remain anonymous, thank you for trusting me and for keeping Mary Morgan so close in your hearts. I salute you all!

And last, but not least, Cousin Mary, and the rest of my lovely family, including my mother, Suzanne Edwards, for their contributions and for having confidence in me to tell Mary's tale with respect and integrity.

Special thanks to Pete Rawlins for proof-reading, editing, and cover design.

FOREWORD

Venerable Karen Lund – Archdeacon of Manchester

It is one act of Love that gives me the privilege of writing the foreword to this book.

The whole story of how I came to be in Presteigne on an afternoon in August 2021 is filled with beautiful moments of divine intervention.

The first whilst I was on holiday staying at The Bleddfa Centre in Wales founded by the late James Roose-Evans and founding Director of Hampstead Theatre Club. I had written a review of his book Inner Journey, Outer Journey and just prior to travelling to Wales as part of my priestly sabbatical, I received a beautiful thank you card from James, and then discovered his connection with the Centre. On my arrival at the cottage in Bleddfa, a book on trees awaited me sent by James, [trees were my sabbatical study theme] and from then on, he befriended me, supporting my study during my stay in Wales right up until his death exchanging cards, emails and old-fashioned long mail correspondence but mostly sharing spiritual wisdom with me. It was truly an act of Love.

God is Love and those who live Love, live in God and God lives in them. 1 John 4.

So that is how I happened to be in Wales and whilst there on a day out, I decided to visit the next village of Presteigne where more love was awaiting me.

How I love! Love! On the streets of Presteigne High Street, the love and friendship with my dear friend Mandy, the author of this book was birthed out of love for the truth and a deep compassion. This book and the love contained in it will have the potential to share love across all nations and for all those who read this story of Mary Morgan.

It is the Love that is stronger than death that has revealed mysteries. Perhaps love was intended to be forgotten and buried with the death of Mary Morgan hanged in Wales in 1805 for the murder of her bastard child, but Love has proved its power in her story.

The same Love that raised our Lord Jesus Christ from death for Love's sake, is the same power of Love that that has resurrected the story of Mary Morgan and the words that follow in this book are shared through the calling and obedience of Mandy an intuitive and sensitive to the beautiful things of the Spirit. It is her Love that has brought this into being, and her Love that has permitted me to share my experience of the generous portion of Divine Love bestowed upon me and my participation in the story which is very small.

So, I do feel enormously privileged to take up the invitation to write this foreword and in doing so I have the opportunity to express the way in which Love weaves its way through the hearts of everyone who is open to it. Love has a way of making loving connections where there is desire and breathes new life into dry bones.

I am writing this in the period of Holy Week in the Church, when we remember the Passion of Our Lord, recalling his suffering and crucifixion leading to renewed life and his bodily resurrection.

It is clear that the seventeen-year-old Mary Morgan suffered in her young life in ways that are incomprehensible to modern ears in parts and would drastically fail our contemporary standards around employment and age discrimination laws. Mary too endured her own passion in the short time she had on this earth.

There is also an infant in this story, who also carried pain to death. It is a tragic story.

But just as Jesus reaches out of the pain of his own dying, he leaves a universal model for each one of us, so that the words in the bible in Revelation 21 is true for all, *that death is never the end*, death can never be the end.

Some may believe that those words are true for us just at the moment when our physical death comes, but this story, Mary's story, Mandy's story and my participation in the story comes to bring the comfort that Jesus gave to his disciples that we are never alone and that the Holy Spirit stands alongside us as our guide. That our daily experiences of brokenness and death, does not ever lead to a finality.

The story of Jesus is everyone's story – the story of the power of love overcoming darkness, deceit, wrongdoing, failure and even murder is a love able to reach us right where we are. Love is able to bring together past and present, different tribes, religion and faith, transparency and goodness and is able to sift and sort until we arrive at the place of resurrection.

Similarly, the story of Mary Morgan has brought together a new community of people. What we have in common is Love.

In this 650th year of the shewings [the visions] of Julian of Norwich, we recall her speaking out the voice of the Holy One, that 'love was his meaning'.

So, the vision of Mary in the video footage I saw, was and is for Love's sake.

Meeting a woman stranger in the High Street of Presteigne in 2021 was and is for Love.

This book will lead you to know the necessity and the power of Love to transform relationships and to bring truth from the dead. Jesus speaking of the death of Lazarus [John 11] that his death would somehow bring glory to God. In other words, bring attention to God who is Love and spotlight the power of love once again.

And God has done it again in the story of Mary Morgan. So that all that was buried in 1805 brings glory to God today through the hands of the author Mandy.

And for those unfamiliar with scriptural language or for whom it feels a little distanced, 'Glory to God' I think mean – we have an opportunity to give fresh meaning and understanding to the power of Love.

Something lovely continues to happen in the world of the dead and something lovely continues to happen in the world of the living and that might begin in Presteigne High Street or wherever you find yourself in this vast universe we are blessed to inhabit. Whether as far back as the nineteenth century or in the context of the twenty-first century, matters not. All we need remember is that God is Love.

This Mary Morgan experience encourages me to pray without ceasing, that is to be spiritually open to the leading of the Holy Spirit where I have been taken beyond my imagination, my denomination, beyond religion, beyond my inevitable limited understanding of the truth of Christ and the meaning of his life and death.

I am overwhelmed with joy and gratitude that Mandy has been able to release the spirit of Mary in writing her story, so that she may truly rest in peace. Though I have a feeling and I have experienced that she is not only resting in peace but speaking and participating in her own story through Mandy and her writing, and through her spiritual connection with me.

I feel very blessed as I write these words that the presence of the spirit of Mary is strongly with me, urging me to express this, to encourage all those who want to enter the depths of profound love, divine love, and unconditional love.

Let the story of Mary Morgan add a sobering reminder that anyone who chooses the journey of faithful, unconditional love will encounter much suffering, unfaithfulness, rejection and untruths, but will always be held by one act of indivisible Love.

But there will be days and days of glow and light as the Divine Spirit takes you higher and higher to unknown places and Christ will always turn up to be with you at every moment.

We shall often find ourselves bent out of all recognition, but we shall never be infinitely broken.

To Mary Morgan: May you Rest in Peace, May you dance freely and May you Rise in Glory.

CHAPTER ONE

I was born in the Spring and died in the Spring. Accused and condemned by the highest in the land. I was sentenced to hang at the end of a rope. Damned to shame for all eternity. To be remembered, always, with innocent blood upon my hands. Stained forever to the depths of my soul.

I, Mary Morgan, little more than a child myself, condemned to death in the year of our Lord 1805. Hung by the neck on Gallows Lane. Cut off in the bloom of tentative youth at just seventeen years of age.

And my crime?

Infanticide. Murder.

I killed my baby.

They said ...

Guilty.

They said ...

But who were they? And who was I?

For all those who know my story and have stood quietly at my grave, I've listened to your murmured prayers and felt the judgement in your heart. I've watched as eyes traversed the graven words that herald my ignominious fate.

But they are not my words. The sentiments expressed thereon far from my own. My tongue had been well-bound before the Judge even laid eyes upon my wretched state. My fate sealed as soon as the first breath was drawn by that tiny life. Her life, cruelly taken, they said, by my very hand.

Guilty, they said . . .

But was I?

Pray, before you raise your voice in protest, I bid you heed mine first. For I was there, remember.

I was there.

And I do not rest.

I've not rested since terror held me in its grip and all that had been promised fell by the way as death looked me in the eye and the noose tightened around my neck.

What chance had I? A poor, serving girl, against the might of a powerful class.

I've lain within the cold dark earth for over two hundred years, far from all I once held dear. All that is long ago to you, seems like yesteryear to me.

So, tarry here with me awhile. Bide with me back along that treacherous path that led me to my doom.

I, Mary Morgan, whose day of reckoning has come to pass. Look beyond the testimonies of what 'they' said and hear 'me' from beyond the grave.

Listen with an open heart and then be the judge of me

CHAPTER TWO

This is no ordinary book. But then, this is no ordinary tale.

American civil rights activist Maya Angelou was quoted as saying, "There is no greater agony than bearing an untold story inside you." She never spoke a truer word, not least because this story opens with a voice that hasn't been heard in over two hundred years. A voice that was sealed into silence by scandal and subterfuge.

So, just to be clear, the words in the opening chapter are those of Mary, not mine. Her testimony, not mine. A declaration that took three weeks to write. Discerned and dictated from a place of great pain and unrest.

Her words.

This is her tragedy, her story, and it leads on a journey from which there is no return. For what I discovered on this 'treacherous' path will challenge, forever, the accepted narrative of her fate.

So, buckle up and settle in. Suspend disbelief and hold your peace as I tell it as it all unfolded. All I ask is that you read between the lines, above them and below them, and then, as Mary said . . . be the judge of me.

As for my part in all of this?

Why, I'm just the messenger . . .

When I came to Presteigne at the end of 2020, I'd never even heard of Mary Morgan. Despite a love of Welsh myth and social history, the drama of this young girl's demise had completely escaped me. Fate had other ideas however, but it wouldn't be until some months later when a chance encounter in the local churchyard saw me introduced to her grave.

It was a beautiful summer's day in late July. Like a lot of people, after the rigours of lockdown I walked often and would usually find myself drawn to the precincts of St. Andrew's. The church sits on the edge of the town just yards from the river Lugg that marks the border into England. Despite serving the Welsh populace of Presteigne, St. Andrew's is actually part of the Herefordshire Diocese, a handsome building that dates back to Anglo-Saxon times.

Its main entrance is flanked by two benches and here I would often sit soaking up the sun.

On this particular day as I came into the churchyard via the Scallions, I espied a man with a dog, talking to another as he gathered up grass cuttings. Presteigne is a friendly place, where people will almost always acknowledge you, even if you're a stranger in town. Well, I was certainly that and eager to know more about its history.

After the usual good morning greetings, I paused to chat. I had a question about the area but first, were they local?

As the one man turned back to his cuttings, the other nodded.

Yes. What did I want to know?

'I've heard that Presteigne lies on five ley lines,' I said. 'Is this true?'

He scratched his chin as the dog scampered between us.

'I'm not sure,' he said, 'Why do you want to know?'

I replied that I was a writer and had a life-long interest in esoteric matters.

'Ah,' he fixed me with a keen look, 'Have you heard the story of Mary Morgan?'

Now it was my turn to be mystified.

'Follow me!' he said and promptly led the way over the newly cut grass to a cluster of well-aged headstones.

Stopping before a rectangular slab of stone he pointed to the extensive script.

"To the Memory of Mary Morgan, who young and beautiful, endowed with a good understanding and disposition, but unenlightened by the sacred truths of Christianity became the victim of sin and shame and was condemned to an ignominious death on the 13th April 1805, for the Murder of her bastard Child.

Rous'd to a first sense of guilt and remorse by the eloquent and humane exertions of her benevolent Judge, Mr Justice Hardinge, she underwent the Sentence of the Law on the following Thursday with unfeigned repentance and a furvent hope of forgiveness through the merits of a redeeming intercessor. This stone is erected not merely to perpetuate the remembrance of a departed penitent, but to remind the living of the frailty of human nature when unsupported by Religion."

After reading this extraordinary script, I was struck by two things.

Firstly, a sense of sadness that was followed through by the thought, 'Why would anyone want to erect such a stone?' Not to mention such a patronising message!

I just found it a bit odd, particularly as it had been commissioned by a member of the aristocracy. Thomas Brudenell Bruce, Earl of Ailsbury, no less! But why?

My attention was then drawn to the sun-faded bunch of plastic flowers that nestled at the foot of the grave.

'Someone also leaves fresh flowers here. But no one knows who it is. Have been doing it for years.' offered my guide helpfully.

'Interesting.' I said, still taking it all in. 'Thank you for showing me. And your name is?'

'Henry Fisher, and my dog is called William!'

I thanked him again and as he wandered off, I remained at the grave to take a few pictures. At that point I wasn't aware of the second smaller headstone that sat opposite at Mary's feet. I was just intrigued at the whole spectacle, but no more than anyone else seeing it for the first time.

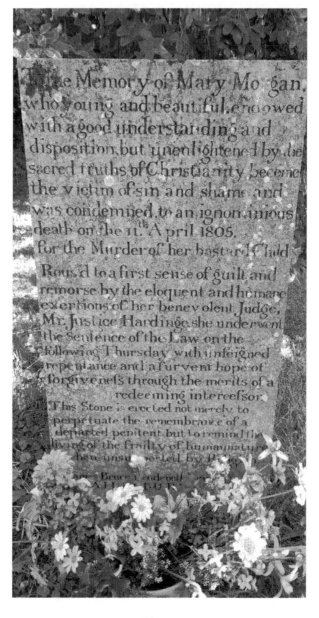

Summer went by, and I remember showing my mother and a friend the grave when they came up to visit. Upon reading that sanctimonious script my mother muttered something unintelligible tinged with disapproval. My friend, who I call 'the Madonna', however, was much more vocal and didn't hold back. She was disgusted at the judgemental tone and for someone who is usually the epitome of calm, this was quite out of character.

One thing we did have in common however, was compassion for Mary Morgan; indeed, every person I encountered when the subject came up, expressed only tender words. If anything, the local people of Presteigne were very protective of this young girl's memory, and I found that touching, to say the least.

Immersed in my own affairs, Mary faded into the background until I received a phone call from my mother late one evening.

I'd actually turned in early and so was on the cusp of sleep when her excited voice pulled me back into the present.

'What! Seriously?'

I could hardly believe what I was hearing. You couldn't make it up!

When the call finished, I lay back and stared at the ceiling, my mind struggling to absorb the news that she had just told me.

In fact, it was a long time before I was able to go to sleep, and when I got up in the morning, knew exactly what it was I had to do!

Just to be clear, and I feel that this is most important, I am not religious. Spiritual, yes, but not of 'the flock' and certainly not a churchgoer. Yet, the very next morning I found myself hotfooting it down to St. Andrews in time for morning service.

Why I felt the urge I have no idea and as the bells pealed out, first I went over to Mary's grave with a strange feeling in my heart. I just felt compelled to go to her.

What do you say to a girl who's been dead for over two hundred years that you've just discovered is your kin!

Mary Morgan, the tragic figure of Presteigne's history was family. How on earth do you get your head around that!

Oblivious to the curious stares of those making their way into the church, I stayed at the graveside until the bells fell silent.

It was time to go in.

I couldn't remember the last time I'd been to church, and the timing couldn't have been more significant. It was All Hallows Eve and with this bombshell of a revelation, the veil had truly parted and no mistake!

As I stepped inside, I was met by a masked member of the clergy seated behind a small table with pieces of paper. Because we were still in the middle of the pandemic, I assumed it was just another system of registration and presented myself accordingly.

To my pleasant surprise it was an opportunity for those who wanted a prayer said for loved ones past and present.

Even better!

I don't know the last time someone asked for Mary Morgan but judging by the widening of the eyes above the mask, it had been some time. I quickly explained the connection and why I was there. She wrote Mary's name down on a fold of paper and I took a seat at the back.

As I lowered myself down on to the hard pew, I was aware that my presence had drawn a few looks. I was a new face after all, so their curiosity was understandable.

As the service got underway, I hummed my way through the hymns and followed the lead of the congregation for cues. If I'm honest, I felt a bit of an imposter and still wasn't sure why I was there.

It was a bright but cool day, and quite chilly in the cavernous church despite the wall heaters. As a shaft of light beamed in through the stained-glass window and alighted on my pew, I took it as a sign I was welcome and felt grateful for the extra warmth.

The sermon was read by the Reverend Michael Tavinor, the former Dean of Hereford Cathedral, and I listened intently.

It was about life and after death, a most apt subject under the circumstances.

I have my own beliefs about what happens when we die, so to

hear first-hand the view of the Church was of particular interest.

It's worth mentioning at this point that my mother, Suzanna, is a fervent born-again Christian and has been for well over forty years. She's a very proactive Elder at the Pantygwydir Baptist church in Swansea with a penchant for dressing up as a pirate for the children's holiday club!

I've always walked my own path, but I find religion fascinating. Indeed, it features heavily in two of my books, 'The Devil's Messiah' and 'The Journey of Jonas Llewellyn', where I readily confess, I took untold fictional liberties!

But back to that morning and the all-important moment when prayers were said for the selected. I felt lifted when Mary's name was read out and when I stepped up to the front to light a candle, all became clear.

I'd watched as a cluster of parishioners had gone up before me to light their candles and couldn't help but notice that they did so in silence. Whether this was procedure, I didn't know, but as I took the taper and lit the flame I suddenly spoke out and in Welsh.

Before the surprised faces of the three clergy before me, I claimed Mary Morgan as my own. It was an unplanned moment but immediately felt appropriate. As I walked back to my seat, I could sense a slight ripple amidst the congregation. Guess no one was expecting that. Me included!

As the service concluded and the Reverends stood outside to greet their flock, I was the first one out the door. The lady who had taken the prayer requests introduced me to the other two ministers. Of course, I didn't know their names at the time, but it since turns out that the lady was the Revered Debbie Venables, and our Rector, Steve Holinghurst.

I complimented the Reverend Tavinor on his sermon and no sooner had I left the church, than another chance encounter sent me off on the next stage of this strange odyssey.

I'd popped into the shop on the way home and bumped into Demelsa who runs a business on the High Street with her partner. Both were already known to me and would go on to play a significant part in the project.

Excitedly I told her about the family link to Mary and that I'd just come from Sunday morning service. She looked suitably bemused before asking if I'd been up to Gallows Lane.

Gallows Lane?

I'd never heard of it.

'It's where they hung her,' she told me, 'The tree is still there.'

Whaaaaat! I could scarcely believe my own ears!

'The execution site is still there?'

She told me how she'd visited as a child as part of a Girl Guide's outing some thirty years ago. The small shiver she felt when the hanging tree was pointed out with the rope marks still burned into the bough.

It's the second tree in, she told me.

Wow!

I had just had to see for myself.

As made my way back home I still couldn't quite get my head around it.

The hanging tree is still there!

Gallows Lane, Gallows Lane, my mind kept repeating those words like a mantra.

Just the name pulled up a certain imagery. A mysterious and darkling path, tainted with the air of death echoing with the final gasps of long-forgotten lives.

Except for Mary's, of course.

I was going to see where she died. I was going to revisit the ground where she took her last breath. The sense of the surreal was strong as I went to get the car. What a morning this was turning out to be!

Gallows Lane sits just outside Presteigne, and after parking up in the layby I was presented with three paths.

The one to the left was a farm track that led up to a field. The second, a narrow footpath was bordered from the field by a brook and very overgrown. And the third had a modern metal gate accessible to walkers. A public footpath sign pointed that way but which one to take?

I opted for the middle one little knowing that it was the original path. There were still enough brambles around to make my passage thorny, but I persevered. I was trying to get a feel of the land, how it would have been, what she would have felt.

I kept going until the path brought me out to a low wooden footbridge. A clearing with two large trees lay beyond an old-fashioned stile.

Was this it?

I had no idea, but something made me pull out my phone and start recording.

I'll be honest and admit I'd already been chuntering away to myself. Battling through, the brambles had heard more than the occasional expletive, but I was also noting what I was feeling and the sense of being inexorably drawn to know more.

I'd hit the ground running with all of this and wanted to record my thoughts for reflection later. It all just seemed so bizarre.

I clambered over the stile and made my way over to the two trees. As I swung the camera between them, I openly said, 'Which one?'

Both were sturdy with strong branches that waved slightly in the gentle breeze as though inviting me to choose.

I didn't have a clue.

So, I reached out with my heart instead. My inner nous. The sixth sense. My mojo. Call it what you will, but with the absence of a sign, I had nothing else to go on.

The second tree, to my right, had the most elaborately gnarled roots that bulged out from the earthen bank that kept drawing my eye.

As a feeling of sadness swept over me, I can be heard saying, "It's this one, it's this one. This is the tree!'

Still filming I called out as I now focused up into the branches.

'Mary Morgan . . . Mary Morgan!'

I don't know why I was calling out. I suppose I was just trying to acknowledge the moment and the tragedy. How many people had perished in this place, kicking out into thin air as the life was slowly choked out of them.

Then the sun broke through, and I expressed the wish that she, too, was in the light and had hardly finished the sentence when suddenly, the wind blew up, and I don't mean in a brisk or even moderate fashion.

It blew up like a hooley that threw up the leaves and lashed the branches with a latent fury. Not quite the reaction I expected, but it was exhilarating and captured fair and square on my camera. As this strange phenomenon tore torridly at the tree, I continued to call out, for I knew deep in my heart that this was Mary.

And, oh boy, was she angry.

Very angry!

As the wind died down, in that instant I also knew something else.

It was no coincidence that I was related by marriage, as it was also no coincidence, I was a writer. A self-published author with no less than six books under my belt, three of which deal with the paranormal.

Well, it wasn't going to get any more supernatural than this and on the ancient Celtic festival of Samhain! You couldn't make it up. Thank goodness I had pulled out my phone and started filming.

Before I left, I did two things. The first was an assurance to her that I would write her story. If ever there had been words in the wind, it was in that moment. Unspoken, granted, but as strong as the call of a siren, as meaningful as the softest murmur and I had heard it.

Loud and clear.

She wanted to have her say and by God, she was going to get it!

And the second thing?

I sang to her.

Taking up position on the small footbridge I turned, and I sang.

But not just to her.

I also sang for the other little life that had been lost in all of this.

The baby.

The little baby girl that had once lain tender in the womb of Mary Morgan.

Her baby.

My kin.

As we say in the boxing world; I'm in your corner. Only in this case, I would be getting in the ring and putting on the gloves because something told me one hell of a fight lay ahead. A fight for what really happened. A fight for the truth.

The rage in that wind wasn't for nothing. Her fury not without cause.

At this point, I had absolutely no idea of the whole saga, much less the finer details of her conviction. But what I did know was that there was a sense of frustration borne of thwarted recourse and an unheard voice.

So, what was the story? Why the drama? I intended to find out!

As soon as I got home, I did an internet search for 'Mary Morgan of Presteigne' and was surprised to find that there was quite a bit out there about her. Indeed, there is so much, for now I'm going to start by taking it down to the basics.

In short, in the early 1800's a young girl goes to work up at the big castle in Glasbury-on-Wye called Maesllwch (or in some versions spelt as Maeslough). Her employer is Walter Wilkins, who made his fortune with the East India Company, and he is the MP for Radnorshire. At sixteen Mary gets pregnant by some young beau yet manages to conceal her condition until secretly giving birth in her room. She kills the baby by slitting its throat and hides the body within the mattress. She is discovered by her counterparts and finally confesses, before being put under house-arrest.

Two weeks later she's well enough to be transported to Presteigne Gaol to face trial at the Great Court Sessions. Six months later she stands before the Judge who, together with the Jury, find her guilty, and the sentence is death.

That's it. That's the tail end of it. The official version, tightly packaged, sealed, and stamped. No more to see here. Only there's more. Much more, and what of the poor baby?

Sadly, back then, infanticide was not uncommon. Look and you will find a trail of desperate women committing desperate acts, but by the 18th century, with a shift in social consciousness, many were spared the rope. Indeed, by the time Mary stood trial, it had become standard for the death sentence to be reprieved as a matter of course.

So, what went wrong?

Only the week before in Brecon a young woman, Mary Morris, had been tried for the very same crime, yet had escaped the gallows. Mary Morgan, however, would receive no such stay of execution and herein begins the rub. The logic. The questioning. The reasoning as to why.

She was just a young servant girl, remember? Just another unfortunate who had dallied or been forced to submit, before finding herself in a position where often the only option was to destroy the evidence of an ill-fated tryst. Deny, conceal, and pray that her wretched act would escape detection.

Well, I think it's fair to say that Mary's plight certainly didn't escape detection. If anything, her case attracted considerable attention at the time and remains of interest. Rather a lot of fuss for a mere servant girl, don't you think?

So, what made Mary Morgan so special? What was it about her and her demise, as tragic as it was, that should warrant poetry, remorse, and not one, but two, dedicated headstones!

Was she guilty?

Did she really kill the baby?

And more compelling yet; why did she have to die?

It's said that patience is a virtue, and in the forthcoming months I certainly had to have a lot of that. At the time, I was already to committed to another project and working to a deadline. For any writer discipline is key, and any kind of distraction can prove dangerously disruptive. So, as much as I wanted to dive into the saga of my kin and her terrible tale, slow and steady would win the day.

I did allow myself to make some enquiries, however, and the most obvious place to start was The Judge's Lodging on Broad Street. This grand old building is the jewel in Presteigne's crown and could tell a tale or two. Once the seat of the County Assizes for Radnorshire it is now an impressive museum of Victorian splendour – unless you lived below stairs or were housed in its cells!

Many visitors who know of Mary Morgan's story mistakenly think that this is where she was tried and convicted.

It is not.

A lot of people also believe that she was imprisoned in one of the cells there.

She was not.

The current building wasn't built until 1826. Mary's trial was in 1805.

I'm specifically making the point here for Gabby, head curator, in the hope of addressing this misconception. Mary stood trial in the Old Shire Hall that is now Lorna's Sandwich Shop on the corner of High Street.

Yet, the Judge's Lodging is not without interest and is built on the site of the old County Gaol where Mary was kept! I've a lot more to say about that, and so does Mary, but after the great revelation and my stint in church, with the Judge's Lodgings closed for the Season – the next port of call was the pub!

Namely, the 'Dukes Arms' that sits further up the street. Family-owned and very friendly, it is the oldest pub in Presteigne, full of ancient beams and unabashed character. It also has the loveliest beer garden out in the back – and if anything's worth knowing about town, this is your gaff!

It was here that I first learned about Jennifer Green who had written about Mary's tragedy some thirty years ago. The book was entitled, 'The Morning of her Day' and after a quick search I found a copy and couldn't wait to get stuck in.

Jenny had come to Presteigne in the seventies and had quickly immersed herself in the local community. She was particularly active in theatrical events, and had been drawn to the story of Mary, little knowing her quest would create a whole drama of its own!

That she was a talented and rather formidable character is not in doubt. Unfortunately, her robust approach made her as many enemies as it did friends, but she didn't shirk in pursuit of the truth, I'll give her that. Indeed, her efforts to tie up loose ends was indefatigable considering she didn't have the benefit of the internet. All searches were a painstaking process that had to be undertaken manually in various archives. Not an enviable task by any stretch of the imagination, and she'd certainly done her homework!

It was an interesting and informative read, and the more I immersed myself, the more I too, began to question the 'official version' of events.

So many questions and not enough answers, but it soon became clear to me that Jenny had no qualms about who she suspected put his seed into Mary. As was her belief that this young girl had been well and truly set up. By the time I finished reading her book, I was of a same mind. Seems I wasn't the only one.

Since coming to Presteigne in the Christmas of 2020, the first few months were marked by lockdowns and social distancing, so I didn't really get to know anyone until the early Summer. I was a new face about town. The new kid on the block. People were still wary of getting too close, but I soon merged into the community in a strange kind of way and became known as 'The Boxing Lady'!

So, imagine the surprise – no, make that shock, when I informed people, I was the walking, talking kin of Mary Morgan and intended to write her story from her perspective once my current project was complete.

This disclosure was something they weren't expecting from the 'Boxing Lady', and for that matter, neither was I. My plan had been to write a follow-up to one of my books that had been sat waiting for two years with 10K words already on paper.

Murder, mayhem together with the machinations of an obsolete justice system was the furthest thing from my mind, believe me!

So, as I dropped the gentle 'bombshell' on the good folk of Presteigne, even after two hundred years the tragedy is still a sensitive subject that incites the odd ripple. That soon became apparent, but what I hadn't expected was the protective air towards Mary that I found most touching. An unspoken pact of empathy between the town and this young girl whose legacy still echoes with her much-maligned fate.

So, was she guilty? I asked. What did they think? Had there been foul play with her conviction?

There has never really been any kind of hesitation when I asked those questions. If anything, the general consensus of opinion among Presteigne's born and bred, is that she was almost certainly stitched up. No smoke without fire, I'm thinking, and you don't have to look back far to find absolute bonfires in the history of our judicial system.

Take the Cardiff Three, for example, back in the eighties. An elaborate set-up that fooled the law and the courts into the wrongful imprisonment of three innocent men. Despite their sentences being overturned two years later and the real killer caught via DNA, the damage was insurmountable and already had been done.

And let's not forget the last innocent man to be hung in Wales, Mahmood Hussein Mattan, who hailed from my very own Tiger Bay. Many people have gone to the Gallows with the cry of innocence still on their lips. Derek Bentley, George Kelly, Raphael Rowe, Timothy Evans, to name but a few, and all of them, each to a man, one too many.

I guess one young serving maid wouldn't present too much of a problem . . .

I couldn't do much more at this point, but I wanted to do

something for her as a gesture of love and support. With my birthday just weeks away I thought it would be nice to include her as part of the family, and who better to join us than my mother and the Archdeacon of Manchester!

This lovely lady of God is the first black Archdeacon to be appointed to the Church of England and has held this prestigious role since 2017. She is the Venerable Karen Lund, and I am proud to call her my friend.

We crossed paths on Presteigne's High Street one sunny afternoon in 2021 and ended up going for coffee. When I asked her what she did, she told me she was a reverend and was on sabbatical just down the road in Bleddfa. I had absolutely no idea who she was, but we hit it off immediately and had lunch together a couple of times before she returned to Manchester. We stayed in touch and indeed, she was one of the first people I confided in when the Mary Morgan connection emerged. So, imagine my delight when she offered to come back for my birthday weekend and perform a little ceremony for Mary and the baby. In fact, I couldn't believe it and my mother was no less thrilled at the thought of meeting Karen.

By this time, I knew she was an Archdeacon, and the fact I'm not a Christian has had absolutely no effect whatsoever on our friendship. She accepts me as I am, and I, in turn, have massive respect for her position and refer to her affectionately as, 'The Rev'!

So as not to step on the toes of our incumbent one, Karen asked his permission first, and he granted it without further ado. I'm sure there have been many words and makeshift ceremonies at Mary's grave over the years. But perhaps not quite like this.

For the purpose, Karen had brought with her a beautiful clay moulding of a baby curled up asleep. There was a groove into which to place a tealight, and after lighting the candle in the cold stiff wind, we placed our offering carefully on the grave.

Beyond that, nothing had been planned although I knew Karen had prepared something. I suggested we link hands and just go with

the flow. I'd never done anything like this before, and there was no set sequence of events, no script.

Karen spoke first. A beautiful eulogy that spoke of love and compassion. I don't remember the exact words, other than that they were meaningful and powerful. We weren't there to take note and record. We were there for Mary.

And the baby.

Mum went next and talked about forgiveness and finding peace. By the time it was my turn to speak, the significance of three women stood on the grave of a long-lost girl did not escape me. I may not be a churchgoer, but I am aware of the Holy Trinity, and that this representation of 'Mind, Body and Spirit' was as potent as it was unusual. And yes, in case you're wondering, it all felt a bit surreal, yet strangely comfortable and somehow familiar.

Again, I don't recall what was said exactly, but I do know that I told her something along the lines of, 'It's okay, Mary, you're no longer on your own. You have your family now.'

From the cold earth I felt a warmth that rose into the circle of love we'd created above her.

'Do you feel it?' I cried excitedly, 'Can you feel the heat?'

I think we each felt something as our heartfelt vigil came to an end, and for me, at least it marked the beginning of an incredible journey that would take me all over Powys and to the very core of myself.

As I've previously mentioned. I'm not religious in any shape or form. Indeed, at one time the Church would've probably seen the likes of me off tied to the stake! For I am what's known as 'a sensitive'. Or to be more precise, I'm Clairsentient; a feeler.

I've also been known to have precognitive dreams and just so you don't think I'm well away with the fairies, I have been documented and given evidence in a Coroner's Court. Everyone who knows me, knows this is my bag. I don't make a secret of it, but I don't shout it from the rooftops either. I am what I am, and I've got a track record to prove it. Yes, I get it wrong sometimes, but overall, I'm pretty much on the money.

I have to tell you this because this aspect of me is integral to the story, and the moment that wind came through the trees on Gallows Lane, I knew it to be Mary, as I felt her rage. At this point, I had no idea of the magnitude and why, but I'd got the message loud and clear. Yet, in order to take the story forward, I need to rewind a little and share with you the sequence of synchronicities that brought me to Prestiegne. As I do, my fervent belief that not only did Mary know that I was coming; but that also she was waiting for me.

That last assertion is quite a statement, isn't it? But as I said in the foreword, you'll need to suspend disbelief and just go with the flow because things are about to get interesting!

The first quirk was my pre-destination. In early 2020 I had actually moved to Glasbury amidst the Pandemic following some life-changing decisions. I was there for several months, with absolutely no idea that Maesllwch Castle was just up the road, never mind any inkling of Mary Morgan.

Like a lot of people at the time, I was struggling to deal with the sudden World-wide pestilence and the rigours of lockdown. It was a crazy year, and when the owners of the house said they wanted to sell, I needed to move on. More importantly still, I needed to find a job. But thanks to the Pandemic, openings were scarce, and my options limited.

Then, a friend living in Ludlow threw a lifeline. Their place of work were looking for staff. But no sooner did I find a place to live than I was pipped to the post.

Thwarted or re-directed? Either way, with no other accommodation available I widened my scope. Places were going so fast. People were moving out from the cities and had the means to pay top dollar, so as quickly as rentals were listed, they were rapidly snapped up.

It was a frustrating situation, but Presteigne kept coming up in the searches like a homing beacon calling me in, and eventually I turned my attentions there.

I knew nothing about the town, much less the surrounding area, and as the ticking clock grew louder, I figured I had nothing to lose. A one-bedroomed cottage had come up for grabs. I was the third in line for a viewing, and with at least a dozen other people interested, I didn't rate my chances.

My bestie, 'the Madonna', said she'd come up and keep company. She lives on the Monmouthshire border, so we arranged to meet somewhere in town. But where?

I did a search and for such a small town there were a multitude of places to go, but we opted for the Wine Bar. I even called ahead to check if they did lunch, which they did. We were all set!

I arrived first but after walking up and down the busy main street couldn't find the wine bar for love nor money. But I did spot a cosy little café called 'The Hat' so I dived in there and texted the change of venue to my friend.

This next quirk of fate was to prove nothing less than remarkable. After a brief chat, the owner put me on to her neighbour who had just bought the property next door. Turns out to be Catherine of David Parry Estate Agents, daughter, and co-owner, and what's more, they were looking to rent out the flat above their office!

I moved in with my little cat, Kizzie, just days before the Christmas and the next lockdown. It had all been so effortless. I couldn't believe my luck! Especially as I didn't get the other property anyway. To conclude. the wine bar was directly across the road all the time. I just didn't see it. Talk about a quirk of fate. Go figure! But it sure felt as though the Universe was smiling down on me. It was all good, I was incredibly grateful, and all was tickety-boo until it soon became apparent that I wasn't alone.

Before I elaborate any further, I just need to tell you a little bit about the flat. It was a rambling, two-bedroomed affair that ran the length of the building. It was also jam packed with character from the uneven floors to the age-old doors. Granted, it would creak and groan as these old places do, but I wasn't expecting to be woken up on the first night by the sound of someone walking around above me!

Slightly alarmed and still somewhat fuggy with sleep, I was immediately aware that it was coming from the attic.

Just what the hell! Or in this case, who on earth was moving about above my bedroom and how did they get in? Because, yes, in the first instance, I'm thinking it's a person, right? A neighbour, perhaps? But not a good neighbour, I'm thinking, because why else would they be creeping around unless they had a sinister agenda? And as I switched on the lamp the noises quietened and the air became still as if whoever was up there had paused and was listening. As the hairs came up the back of my neck, I looked at my cat whose eyes remained glued to the ceiling.

I wasn't just dreaming then. In fact, I knew I hadn't dreamt it because the bloody sound had woken me up!

The noises didn't resume which mystified me even further, and I spent the remainder of the night with the lamp on as I tried to envision the lay-out of the building. A quick reccy the next morning established that there was a separate building at the back that conjoined the attic. But you'd have to have been very small to have been able to walk about upright. Indeed, the roof space was so low, only a gnome would have managed – and that was pushing it!

I was extremely reassured by this, and thought it highly unlikely my neighbour, who turned about to be a very nice chap called Dean, would have dared to venture into such cramped and dodgy territory.

Which left the only other possible explanation, and at this point, with the stress of trying to unpack and settle in for Christmas, I really wasn't in the mood for any seasonal ghosts, past or present! That is, until the second night when once again I was woken up by the distinct tread of someone walking around.

This time I didn't turn on the lamp. I just lay there quietly and listened. Once again, the mystery mover came to a halt just above my head, and as the cat and I stared up into the ensuing silence, I could 'feel' a pair of eyes looking right back down on at me.

Okay, I thought, we have company and they're obviously moving about to get my attention, but they're going to have to bloody well wait! I'm just too tired for this nonsense now.

As though by some unspoken accord, there was no more disturbance, and I managed to go back to sleep. The situation had to be dealt with, however, and before I turned in the following night, I sat on the end of the bed and tuned in.

It was a girl. A young, servant girl, and she definitely wanted me to know she was there.

'Listen, love,' I said kindly, 'I know you're here, and that's fine. I don't mind sharing the space with you, but please can you stop walking about and waking me up. I'm absolutely knackered, and I need my sleep. Please can you do this for me?'

There wasn't so much a creak, but I had the sense I had been heard and understood and passed the night undisturbed.

The trend continued but she was still about and determined to make her presence felt and in no uncertain way. It was like she was saying, "Ok, I won't walk about in the attic, but I'm still here and you're going to know about it."

Suffice to say, I lost count of the number of times I heard activity out in the hall with its long, wonky floor. Occasionally I got up thinking it was the cat, only to find her curled up in the living room where now she slept once we were settled.

Settled?

If only!

Knocks, bangs, strange shuffling's, all the signs of a good old-fashioned haunting. She was relentless. I wasn't too fazed. I'd had worse. I just didn't know what her problem was, and she especially didn't like it when I'd have the music on loudly. Then, I'd get a groan in my ear as if to say, "Why are you making this awful racket? Please stop ..."

For the most part I ignored her and her hyper-activity. I had a lot going on and no time for pesky ghosts. Fortunately, I had a witness to this phenomenon whose possessions, namely a cigarette lighter, would be moved around on a regular basis.

The friend from Ludlow wasn't dealing well with the lockdown and had come over to stay for a while. I got used hearing expletives coming from the other end of the building when things became lively, and once the initial shock wore off, the shenanigans of the unseen but noisy visitor became something of the norm.

I wondered if something had happened in the building. As the former County town of Radnorshire, Presteigne had seen its fair share of action on its borders. Indeed, word had it that Owain Glyndwr had fired the street during the fight for Welsh Independence. Could this noisy spirit be a leftover in the fabric of past tragedies, and why hadn't she moved on?

When lockdown lifted, curiosity saw me make a few enquiries and my first port of call was an interesting-looking shop across the road. All the buildings on High Street are quirky and historical, so my guess was that I wouldn't be the only one with an uninvited guest. Or so I hoped!

The business in question used to be one of the many pubs that filled Presteigne, and it was here I first met Demelsa and her partner. Yes, they told me, they too, had experienced inexplicable happenings in the building, usually upstairs. It was good to talk about my ghostly visitor and how disruptive she was being. We speculated whether she'd died there or was just attached to the house. An unconventional topic of conversation for a first encounter, I admit, but I know they believed me, and both specifically remember this conversation and how I described the ghost as a young servant girl.

Looking back and knowing what I know now, I have no doubt that this energetic and persistent spirit was Mary. Because once I started to trace her story, the activity began to subside. She didn't need to jump through hoops to gain my attention anymore. I was on the case. Mission accomplished. She just began to manifest in different and more peaceful ways.

Interestingly, and on reflection, as these things often are, the view from my kitchen took in the tower of St. Andrews, as it did a direct channel to Mary's grave, the significance of which was not lost upon me. Indeed, it was a friend (the Madonna) who pointed it out, which neatly brings me on to another friend of religious connotations, only of a more official nature!

At this point, the footage I'd taken at Gallows Lane had only been shared with family and close friends. I knew what I'd captured was extraordinary, and if you were lucky to be trusted, I forwarded it on.

One of those people was Karen Lund, and I could hardly believe it when she told me what she saw. Quite clearly, and to her eye, within the footage was stood a figure of a young girl with long, fair hair, one arm raised as though she was pointing at something.

What the ...?

I couldn't fathom it; I was supposed to be the psychic one! Yet, despite Karen providing me with a breakdown of timings I paused, and I looked, I watched, and I paused, and quite simply, I just couldn't see it!

> ← Karen Rev
>
> This video is so beautiful Mandy. On my second view I notice the figure of a woman at 1.10, 1.34. 1.56, 2.12 (the best pause) and 2.20 (another clear image for me) See what you think. From such stillness to strength in the wind is absolutely amazing. You must tell her story and be a voice for her x

It was so frustrating, but also absolutely and totally incredible! This venerable lady of the church, my lovely friend, the Archdeacon of Manchester could actually see the spirit of Mary Morgan on film! I mean, let's face it, who else is it going to be? It took that line from the movie, 'The Sixth Sense', 'I see dead people', to a whole new level!

This is a high-ranking member of the Church of England, a well-respected figure in her own right. It was nothing short of miraculous!

Obviously out of respect for her position I asked if it would be okay to write about this. I know that the Church hasn't always had an open view on these things, although during the course my investigations, I have found quite the opposite to be true. If anything, the clergy have been tremendously supportive throughout this project. An aspect I hadn't anticipated, and their quiet acceptance of me and what I'm about, has been as heartening as it has been unexpected.

But this . . .

Despite checking the footage again and again, I still could see nothing. But other people have reported seeing different things, that suggests another famous line, only this time from Hamlet: "There are more things in Heaven and Earth, Horatio, than are dreamt of in your philosophy."

Well, you could say that again, Shakespeare was on the money and no mistake! And so, it would seem, was Karen.

I had absolutely no reason to doubt her word. Besides her high-ranking role, it wasn't as though she had anything to gain from this, other than a kind of spiritual epiphany, perhaps. And let's be honest, I – or rather Mary – couldn't have chosen a better person of good standing and integrity. Understandably, for some, this disclosure may come as something of a surprise. So, for authenticity purposes, here is a section of the transcription that shows the date.

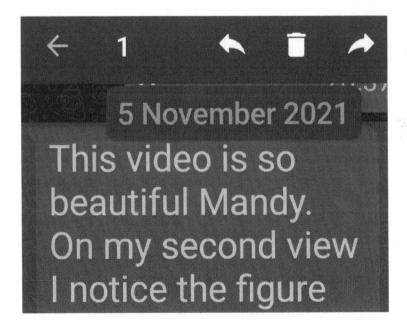

This was an endorsement like no other, and, to my mind, an affirmation from the very top. God, Our Father, the Goddess, the Universe. I wasn't about to argue. I'd seen and felt enough in my years to know that Hamlet was right and that there's more out there than just the Milky Way. Interestingly, throughout this project it has been the clergy who have proven to be stalwart in their support. With such controversial subject matter, I wasn't sure how they were going to react to this two-hundred-year-old story with suspected foul-play. But to be fair, the people I have dealt with have been open-minded and supportive and have my life-long respect for that.

Top of the list was the Reverend David Thomas of Glasbury-on-Wye, and as soon as I was free of commitments I got in touch. I left a voicemail requesting a meeting and informed him what it was about. Within a few days he got back to me and there then ensued a conversation about Mary, her story, and the availability of church records.

He didn't really have anything on the latter, he told me, but I was welcome to come along the next time he was holding Sunday Service in Llowes.

He seemed okay and willing to help, and at this point I needed all the assistance I could get.

There's very little known about Mary's family and her early beginnings. We know her parents were called Rees and Elizabeth Morgan, and that Mary was baptised in Llowes. Apart from testimonies, court records and the musings of the Judge, she represents as a very shadowy figure, and I needed to know more.

So, one damp morning in early spring, I drove via Gladestry to St. Meilig's church and took Glenys with me.

Glenys Millichamp is a well-known figure in Presteigne. Just a few years shy of one hundred, she began her life in Evenjobb, but Presteigne has always been her home. Sharp as a whistle and fiercely independent, I admire her spirit and we've become good friends.

'How do you fancy church this Sunday, Glenys?' I asked her, 'A run out to Llowes and lunch at the Radnorshire Arms, afterwards?'

As usual, she was well up for an adventure but when we rocked up the service was well underway. For some reason I'd messed up the timings, but it didn't matter. A rattle at the doorknob soon announced our arrival and we were welcomed in by a curious parishioner.

As we took our seats near the back, a lady in the pew behind greeted us with a warm smile and gave us each a book of hymns.

The congregation was small but intent as the Reverend Thomas, held forth in his melodious Breconshire accent. I hummed along, bowed my head, and said 'Amen' when required, and watched as Glenys took Communion.

A few heads turned as I remained in my seat, but the last time I'd taken the bread of Christ I must have been about six years old.

As soon as the service was over, I turned to the lady behind us. Besides wanting to say thank you for her thoughtfulness, there was something about her and I just had to know more. It turned out she was one of the church wardens and a retired headteacher by the name of Margaret Morris. She had taught in Rhosgoch primary school for many years before its closure in 2013, and as soon as I explained the reason for my visit, her face lit up.

'Oh,' she exclaimed, 'I used to tell the story of Mary Morgan to the schoolchildren. Shame you weren't about then, you could have come into class and given a talk!'

Her obvious interest in the subject delighted me, and I gave her my card with the hope we could talk again at leisure. Next up was the Reverend who introduced me to his wife, Davina.

The vibe was upbeat and friendly, but time was of the essence as is the lot of many rectors these days. There were other services to conduct in neighbouring parishes and the clock was ticking. It was good to put a face to the name, and he promised to put me in touch with a local historian who lived in Glasbury.

Before we left, I took some pictures, with particular interest in the old stone font where Mary had been baptised all those years ago. As my gaze swept around the little church it seemed hard to believe that Rees and Elizabeth had once stood within its shadowy interior and pledged their only child to God. A tiny, innocent scrap of humanity fated to end her short life at the end of a rope. It just didn't bear thinking about.

Left: The font in St. Meilig'where Mary Morgan was baptised.

As Glenys and I drove back over Brilley Mountain there was much food for thought, but not much interest from my companion. Glenys had been one of nine and raised on a small holding where life was simpler and often a struggle.

The shenanigans of a young servant girl was not something that particularly concerned her. But there were plenty out there who were interested, however, and our paths were yet to cross.

Now that Mary had my full attention, I lost count of the times she'd draw me out of the house and down to her grave. Here I would stand and lean my back against the bigger headstone, above her head, if you like, looking down towards her feet.

We have no time, or respect for Brudenell's slab of sanctimonious script. She prefers, as do I, the smaller stone and not without the good reason. This was erected some years after her death, and that of the judge – again, with good reason. It reads:

"In memory of MARY MORGAN who Suffer'd April 13th 1805
Aged 17 years
He that is without sin among you
Let him first cast a stone at her.
The 8th Chapr of John, part of ye 7th vr

Obviously due to space restriction, some of the words have been abbreviated. But it is a direct and meaningful nudge to the bystander to read between the lines.

The other stone, however, has no such constraints and is almost gung-ho in its eagerness to press home the message that truly at the heart of it, Mary was a bad girl! Irreligious, ignorant, with the implication she had brought it all on herself. Rather a lot of trouble to go to for a mere servant girl, don't you think?

So, anyway, there I'd be and with me would be Mary, still suffused by emotions and keen to offload her absolute fury after over two hundred years.

As I'd stand quietly above her, she'd rant and I'd listen, or in this case, 'feel'. Her frustration was boundless and at this point I thought I understood. She'd fallen foul of the trappings of love and had paid the ultimate price. Strung up and strangled in the bloom of her youth, as the father of her blighted child, had walked away a free man. That her side of things had been shelved and silenced, buried forever in her pauper's grave.

She wanted to have her say. To present herself. Explain her reasoning, and why she took the life of her babe.

Or so I thought . . .

At this point, like everyone else I believed she had done it. I was labouring under the impression she was mad at her life having been taken. Her name besmirched. Her reputation never to be forgotten as an ill-fated lover and child-killer.

"He that is without sin among you. Let him first cast a stone at her." Remember?

But things were different back then. The law more badass than an ass, especially if you were poor. But that she had been hard done by, I didn't disagree. There was nothing I could do to change an age-old tragedy, but I could be a channel and give her a voice. It wasn't the next project I had in mind. If anything, after writing for other people for the past three years, I was looking forward to writing for myself. Immensely! Guess the Universe had other ideas, though, eh?

The good folk of Presteigne have seen me stood at that grave many times in passing. Wind, rain, or shine, there you'd find me, a silent sometimes shivering witness to her anguish. And when Mary put out the call, she had no qualms whether it was day or night, often pulling me out after dark. For the most part I didn't mind, St. Andrew's is a peaceful place, and I never saw another soul during those nocturnal visits, until one cold Winter's night.

On this occasion as I made my way to Mary's grave, I don't mind saying I was less than happy. It was absolutely freezing and not knowing how long she'd have me by 'the ear' I'd taken a detour in a bid to warm up. Instead of coming in via the main entrance, I'd gone around the back before taking up the path that led past the Memorial Garden. This runs alongside the main body of the church and brings you out to the front. So, imagine my shock as I came round the corner to find a figure sat on the bench.

At first, I thought I was seeing a ghost. The figure was so still, the face frozen in profile as it stared ahead as though fixated.

I think I yelped; such was my shock. But as I swept past and turned fully to look, I quickly realised it was a man. I apologised, not least because I'd come out of nowhere and had probably surprised him as much as he'd startled me. And then, of course, there was the fact I'd been caught talking to myself – or rather to Mary!

Indeed, I'd been in full chunter, grumbling at being dragged out late at night when I should have been at home abed! I don't embarrass easily, but it felt awkward to have been caught in such a private moment.

I needn't have worried. Turned out the mystery-man was our local psychotherapist by the name of Jeremy Price. He too, had been having his own private moment and seemed completely unruffled by my sudden appearance. We went on to have many a chat at that very same bench – during daylight hours, I hasten to add! – but it was some time before I addressed our initial encounter and his thoughts about that.

The view from 'the favourite bench' that looks across to Mary's grave.

So, did he think I was a ghost making its way towards him that night, or some raving lunatic out on patrol?

'Neither', he replied, 'I just thought it was someone passing through and that they were singing.'

Singing?

'Yes,' he said, 'and my actual thoughts were, how lovely! Who am I to judge people? You were doing your thing, as I was doing mine. Who is to say what's wrong or even odd behaviour, if that's what drives them at the time.'

An interesting and empathetic answer and one I wasn't expecting. Not least because my Welsh accent had rendered my mutterings musical, and I couldn't help but be delighted by that! As I was by his own little nugget of family history, when his Great

Uncle had caused a scandal by eloping with a beautiful gypsy girl. No big deal, you're probably thinking but for the fact his ancestor was a man of the Church. A Rector, no less, and proof that sometimes not even the power of God can compete with the love of a wild woman!

Another time Mary pulled me out of the flat, I hadn't long got out of bed and was just easing into the morning when I got 'the call'. I can't describe this other than an irresistible urge from within. So, with a groan, I finished my coffee and jumped in the shower.

I got ready in record time all the while wondering what on earth she wanted with me so early! Still somewhat pie-eyed I emerged from 'Fagin's Alley' onto the High Street just after eight and the first person I bumped into was local Lynne Traylor. She's looking at the houses in David Parry's window as she waits for Presteigne to wake up and we greet each other in bemusement.

Lynne is a well-known and proactive figure about town. When she's not in the Spar (where she's worked for over 30 years!) on Saturdays, weather permitting, you'll find her on the High Street raising funds for Cancer Research.

It's not that I'm surprised to see her. I just wasn't expecting to see her so early. And she, it turns out, was equally as surprised to see me. I'm usually not seen until mid-morning at best!

With no one else about we began talking as I tried to explain away my early appearance in a vague manner. Not everyone is receptive to calls from beyond the grave, and even though I'd chatted with Lynne on many an occasion, she knew nothing about my mystic tendencies. Yet somehow, I found myself telling her about Mary and the family connection and before you knew it, Lynne also began opening up about her experiences.

Now, you're probably wondering why I'm going off piste with this, but believe me, I'm not. This chance encounter was to be extremely significant, especially towards the end.

It is with Lynne's permission that I will share her experiences with you, because the second story is really quite extraordinary.

Suffice to say, she swears by both events, and I have no reason to disbelieve her.

The first concerns her father who passed away when she was fourteen. On the night he died, she suddenly woke up to see him stood by her bed, and the reason she was so certain was because she saw the sleeve of his herringbone jacket! The second was when she saw the ghost of a Highwayman up on the Knighton Road. At the time she was about seventeen and travelling back to Presteigne with her friend. It was early evening but dark as they made their way over the winding heights before the road brings you down into Norton. They were chit-chatting when suddenly in the headlights Lynne saw a mounted figure at the side of the road looking straight at them. She is absolutely and unequivocally sure of what she witnessed; a masked man in a cloak and tri-corner hat sat on a dark horse beneath the tree. Unfortunately, her friend didn't see it, but Lynne had no doubts and to this day, can still see half of his face and his eyes, a man, she told me, of about forty.

That she should share something so personal on two counts was really meaningful, and as we continued to talk, the conversation came around to Jenny Green.

As mentioned previously, the impact of Jenny's book had rattled a few people in Presteigne, and Lynne, it turned out, had been one of them. Finally, I would get to hear the reasons for her unpopularity, and straight from the horse's mouth!

'She upset a lot of people,' Lynne said, 'Brought cameras to the town. Made money and when she was on TV, said that the people of Presteigne were secretive. We're not secretive!'

Her voice rose indignantly on the last statement and having lived among the good folk of Llanandras for the past two years, I had to agree. If anything, the people here are friendly and direct, and take a pride in their community.

A picture was emerging, and I could see how this portrayal by Jenny would have been deemed offensive. As we talked on and the street got busier, Lynne would stop people intermittently and introduce them to me. These were Presteigne people, born and bred, and as she touched on my connection to Mary, it was akin to an endorsement, and I was grateful the gesture.

That the subject of Mary Morgan could still be contentious after all these years was evident, but I was family and that made it okay. And besides, I'm going to write this book in her words, I told everyone. I'm going to write it in the first person, as though it is Mary telling the story, because at this point, that is what I thought she wanted. Her thoughts, her feelings, and why she killed the baby. To my mind, she was absolutely desperate to have her say, and I believed that, I really did. Why else was she so insistent? From the moment I felt that angry wind, I just knew, as my assurances on tape clearly state.

'They might have strung you up from one of these trees, but by God . . . by God! They will not quench your story or your spirit! And if I've got anything to do with it, your tale will be told from your side, my love . . .'

And I meant it. In the meantime, I discovered another book entitled, 'Mary Morgan of Presteigne. Victim or Villain of Infanticide', penned by a chap called Peter Ford. I ordered a copy and couldn't wait to get stuck in, but first there was the business of moving house. It was time to say goodbye to the quirky, old flat and my lovely landlady, Cath Parry. That it was meant for me to have been there I had no doubt. It had been interesting tenancy tinged with sorrow, when after sixteen years I had to say goodbye to Kizzie. She left this world poignantly, on the same day, October 6th, when Mary was transported to Presteigne Gaol.

Of course, Mary was still about. and although I wasn't sure she'd follow me to the new abode, as it transpired, she did not. I guess there was no need now. She'd got my attention, work was in hand, and besides, her grave is not that far, and I visited often.

It was time to get with the living, and thanks to Reverend Thomas, I finally contacted Sheila Leitch, the Glasbury historian. Intrigued by the project and my family connection, she invited me over one gloomy Sunday afternoon. Unfortunately, she'd had a bad fall, so was hobbling around on a walking frame. But she was bright and inquisitive and had lived a remarkable life as an academic and a mountaineer. She was also passionate about history and a keen member of the 'Radnorshire Historical Society'. Indeed, a whole room at the top of her house was devoted to tome after tome of parish records.

After a few directions I was sent upstairs to find those relating to Glasbury, but on my return I only managed a quick flick through as chit-chat took over. Unbeknown to me at the time, most parish records are online these days, but it was lovely to meet Sheila and hear her stories.

Before I left, I took her dog, Mandy, for a short walk with the promise I would stay in touch. It had been an interesting afternoon, and for future reference she gave me the number of Phil Bufton, Chair of the Powys Family History Society.

(Just weeks from completing the book, I learned that Sheila had passed away. She had been the first person I'd spoken with in my investigations, so it was with no small sadness when I received the news. My namesake has a new home with a neighbour, and may the mountains be many where Sheila is now, and that all her questions be answered).

Shortly afterwards I contacted Margaret Morris, who I'd met at the church in Llowes. She invited me for coffee at her bungalow in Cusop. I was intrigued to know how she knew about Mary and her tale of woe. Turns out it was after a church visit to Presteigne during her time as a county councillor. Local officials had shown her the grave, so she took the story back to share with her pupils and did so for many years. Mary had been a local girl, after all!

Margaret proved to be another fascinating person, and no stranger to tragedy herself. As a teenager she'd contracted TB and at one point was so poorly she was earmarked for the Sanitorium on Sully Island, South Wales. An absolutely terrifying prospect, because once you went there you never came back. Thankfully,

Margaret recovered, as did her father, who was also struck down. The strain on her mother with two other daughters to support, must have been immense. Yet, she rallied through in her role as headteacher and the main breadwinner. A remarkable feat in itself!

There was little Margaret could add to my investigations, but just the fact that she had passed the story on to future generations, was, to my mind, reward enough. She did, however, provide me with some names of local families who had history in the area. Everyone had been so helpful, Willing to open up their homes, and their lives, quite remarkable considering I was a complete stranger! And all in the name of a young girl who had played with fire, and yet was now rising from the ashes of her catastrophe like a phoenix determined to fly. It was as though the Universe was saying, as you have pledged to help to her, so we will help you.

A fanciful notion, perhaps, but stranger things were yet to come.

CHAPTER 3

I'd kept in touch with the Reverend Thomas and asked if it would be possible to meet with the current owner of Maesllwch. I was coming at this project organically, and with so much ground to cover, it just seemed natural that this should be the next stage.

The castle was where it all began, and I really wanted to meet with them and get their side of things. To avoid confusion, it is worth mentioning at this point, that the 'Wilkins' reverted back to their old name of 'de Winton' (de Wintona) by royal license in 1839.

Whether this was to distance themselves from the Mary Morgan scandal, or their links to the East India Company, who can say – but just so we are clear, I will be referencing them as they are, and were at the time.

The vicar invited me to attend the next Sunday Service he would be holding at All Saints in Cwmbach. The church sits on the edge of the Maesllwch estate and Mr de Winton is church warden there.

Perfect! Neutral ground and in a House of God, I couldn't ask for anything more apt!

On this occasion I decided to leave Glenys behind. I had no idea how things were going to pan out, and I needed to be focused. It was a beautiful day, and as I drove over, I wasn't apprehensive in the slightest. Yet there was a palpable tension in the car that got stronger and stronger as I came over Brilley Mountain.

Mary?

Oh, she was with me, alright, and I was in no doubt as to how she was feeling. Just another surreal moment in this ongoing saga and perfectly understandable. Finally, she was going to come face to face with the descendent of a family who had stood by as she went to her doom. Whose name would always be linked with hers, manacled forever like Prometheus chained to the rock. She was far from happy.

Glancing across to the empty passenger seat I could all but envisage her there. Eyes front, body tense, her smooth brow pinched with anger.

'Cool head, Mary,' I said, more as an assurance as anything else. Because let's face it, stranger things have happened, and I would never forget the power of the wind that day. What if she decided to have a Calypso moment again? Only this time in the church, right in the middle of the service! Immediately I could all but envisage that scene too. Hymn books and pamphlets going flying as Mary unleashed her age-old fury on the former land of her former masters. People panicking and diving for cover as a bewildered Reverend appealed for calm. The scene was like something out of a movie and of course it was just that. But it crossed my mind enough to concern me, so I spoke again.

'I understand this is big for you, and that you're as mad as hell. But you have to remember that this isn't the 'Walter'. Yes, he's of the family but we can't blame this man. He is merely the descendent, so don't be going off on one, Mary, okay?'

There was no answer, of course, but it did make me feel a bit better. There's nothing like laying down the law to an errant ghost!

Although in this case, maybe she had good reason . . .

As always, as I drove through Llowes, I thought about Mary growing up here as a girl and wondered what her childhood was like. My thoughts then swiftly turned to Walter and what his reaction would be when we came face to face?

I would soon find out.

I turned off for Glasbury and then up into Cwmbach before a sharp right took me to the carpark in front of the church. As I pulled up, the Reverend Thomas was at the door talking to one of his parishioners. Not wanting to interrupt, we acknowledged each other discreetly as I slipped in through the doors.

All Saints Church built by the de Wintons.

I took my place, once again, at the rear of the church and looked around. There were no more than about half a dozen people scattered among the polished pews, but my arrival had not gone unnoticed as necks craned around to check me out. They had no idea why I was there, of course, and to ensure an air of niceness and serenity, I had worn my favourite top. A lovely sky blue, the colour of peace and communication and totally in keeping with the reason for my visit.

I wanted no ruck with the current de Winton. Just a chance to chat, with the hope of a visit up to the castle. More than anything I would have liked to have stood in the kitchens where Mary once worked. To have stood in her old bedroom where the event had played out.

I'm a great believer in places retaining the energies of the past. Residual imprints, former echoes, and that they remain in the very fabric of the building. Having grown up in a haunted three-story Victorian pile, I was more than familiar with this kind of peculiarity, and I so wanted to feel!

But everything would depend on Walter, of course, and oh boy, was he in for a shock!

As everyone settled down a man appeared from the vestry and for a moment, I wondered if he was lost. Dressed in a very casual manner, he seemed to be making checks as he busied about, a tall slight figure with a nervous air.

'Hello Walter,' the vicar said, as he made his way up towards the altar and I felt my eyes widen.

So, this was Walter de Winton!

I watched as he took his seat at the front. After a while, he stood up and gave a reading. I listened to his quiet tones, and he seemed a man who was deeply religious. I wondered how far his spiritual goodwill would extend once I identified myself.

As it happened, not as far as I'd hoped!

Once the service was over, Reverend Thomas made his way to the back of the church as the congregation then filed down to meet him. There may not have been many of them, but they all wanted a bit of the vicar, so I remained in my seat.

It was important that the introduction, when it was made, would be minus an audience. I was about to revisit an age-old scandal and privacy was key. I didn't want to embarrass the man in front of all and sundry, just talk to him.

As the subject of my attention made his way slowly down the aisle, I glanced back to see if the Reverend was free, but he was still under siege. I groaned inwardly.

How was this going to work?

It turned out I needn't have worried.

As I turned back it was to find Walter de Winton looking straight at me as he made his way down the aisle. His expression was benign and as I stood up, he gravitated towards me as though pulled along by an unseen force.

'Hello,' I stood up and extended my hand. I wanted my approach to be as normal as possible, and as he shook my hand briefly I could all but feel Mary glowering beside me.

That she was still with me, I had no doubt. Her presence may have been unseen, but it positively thrummed with tension and that underlying rage.

His eyes never left my face as I introduced myself and told him where I'd travelled from that morning and why. You'd think that 'Presteigne' would have rung a bell, but I'm not sure he caught all I was saying, as the organ continued to blast out at the front. But he remained smiling, an encouraging sign until the organ stopped and then he got it.

The change in his demeanour was immediate and I actually felt quite sorry for him. One minute he was welcoming a new member to his church, the next he was faced with a ghost from the past in the form of yours truly. I hastened to reassure him that I wasn't there on some mission of revenge. If anything, I wanted to make the peace. Compare notes. Have a chat. See if we couldn't get together and put old ghosts to rest.

Despite my best efforts however, he wasn't having any of it. The smile had become a grimace, his air between us increasingly strained. I gave him my card and asked him to think about it. It was the only course of action left, and as the saying goes, you cannot push the river, or in this instance, let go and let God - we were in His house, after all!

By this time, the organ-player, who turned out to be his wife, had now joined us. I'd heard she was fluent in Welsh, so I greeted her accordingly. She was very pleasant, and we chatted for some minutes before I switched back to English. To clarify why I was there I explained who I was and my reason for coming.

'Oh Mary Morgan,' she said, delightedly, 'Isn't she speaking at the Hay Festival?'

'Not that Mary Morgan!' Walter snapped.

I saw her face change as the penny dropped and with no small dismay, I must add, we'd been getting along so well.

The mood had changed, a most perceptible shift. Conversation was over.

Walter went back down to the front of the church and

disappeared from sight as his wife left via the main door. Extricating myself from the pew, it was to find the vicar eyeing me expectantly.

'How did you get on?' he asked.

'Okay I think,' said I, the eternal optimist! 'I've left him my card. The ball is in his court now, vicar.'

I thanked him and made my way out to my car.

A lone figure was walking up the long drive that led to Maesllwch.

Mrs de Winton.

The main entrance to Maesllwch castle.

I resisted the urge to call out and paused to watch as she took that well-trodden path up to the castle.

I could only imagine what must be going on in her head and thought it a shame we didn't have more time to talk. In that moment, I also had an image of Mary walking up that very same drive on a bright spring morning. Proud to be going to work up at the Big House. Young, spritely, and full of hope.

Then I felt Mary beside me, as she too, looked silently back into the past.

I turned away. It was time to go. Perhaps when the dust had settled, I might get a call. But deep in my heart, I doubted it.

As I was in the area, I thought I'd call on my former neighbours and scrounge a cup of coffee. The day was still glorious, so we sat out in their lovely garden accompanied by Pushkin the cat. Like a lot of people, Madeline and Tony are interested in the story and as we chatted, Madeline told me about a house in the village with links to Maesllwch. Apparently, a de Winton lady had purchased the property for the purpose of housing battered wives and single mothers.

Really?

'Wow, what an incredible gesture! When was this?'

Madeline didn't know, only that the house had been sold and was now privately owned. I found this information very interesting, if not telling, and made a mental note to follow it up.

In the meantime, it was time to go home. It had been a long and unusual morning that had given me much food for thought. But the only thing I wanted to do now, was get back and have some real nosh out in the garden.

As I made my way back towards Brilley Mountain something made me take a detour. I don't know why I did this; I just felt the need to pull in, and within minutes of doing so, the reason became clear.

I didn't so much as bump into this person as cross their path, and as we began talking, I happened to mention I'd just come from Sunday service at All Saints.

Had they heard of Mary Morgan? Did they know the story and how she was hung for murdering her baby?

Did they know!

Did they know?

It seems they did. But not the version we are all familiar with. The official version, the accepted version. And as I sat and listened in growing horror, it was like a big, dark cloud had suddenly covered the sky as a chill swept through me like a vengeful ghost.

My World had just been turned on its head and I had only one thought:

Oh, Mary!

I drove back over Brilley Mountain in a state of numbed shock. My brain was absolutely blown, my heart heavy as I struggled to make sense of this latest development.

That raw chill still coursed through me, and I didn't need to turn to feel Mary next to me in triumphant silence. Only this time she wasn't looking at the road ahead, she was studying me. An intense, penetrative stare as if to say: Now do you see?

Oh yeah, I was seeing alright, I was just having problems fathoming it. I had just been told, and with an unnerving and unwavering certainty, that "Mary had not murdered her baby. That someone from the House had done it and had drowned it in the river"!

'It'?

Dear God!

What an allegation to make. What a shocker! I didn't see this one coming. The words kept going round and round in my head.

Mary had not done it. NOT guilty! She was set up from start to finish. Poor girl didn't stand a chance . . .

Oh boy, if I thought the family connection had come as shock, it was but a drop in the ocean compared to this!

Totally!

When I got home, I called those close to me to share this bombshell out of the blue. I still couldn't believe what had just been divulged to me. What made it more difficult, was that the person concerned asked that I keep their identity a secret. Out of respect, I promised, of course, but it left me with a compelling allegation with no source with which to name. The fact that this information had come their way second hand, made the situation even more challenging. I could almost wish that nothing had been said at all. But then, it crossed my mind that perhaps I was meant to encounter this person, that this disclosure, whether it is true or false was meant to come to me?

Oh, what I wouldn't have done to be able to consult with Jenny Green on this! There was someone else, however. The author of the second book. Peter Ford, whose concise narrative of events had so impressed me. What would he make of this? I just had know.

I tracked him down and we arranged to meet at Hay Castle. Since extensive refurbishment this crumbling old pile has been given a new lease of life, so, if you haven't been yet, it's well worth a visit!

Over coffee and cake, we talked all things Mary, as I speculated, queried, and harried unanswered questions. Yet, despite being presented with this new development Peter remained firmly on the fence. I couldn't blame him. No one wants to make waves, and besides, my interest was vested on an emotional level, his was not. This was family business. Family honour, and as someone who comes from a boxing background, respect!

At the end of our meeting, I showed him the footage, but he retained a pragmatic attitude and that was okay. I wasn't there to convert him, and besides not all of us rock to the same vibe. It was good of him to meet with me, however, and I recommend you read his book.

Talking of which, this revelation changed the whole ball game as far as I was concerned.

I had embarked on this project on the basis she was guilty. Now, I wasn't so sure. I hadn't been thrown a seed of doubt as much as it had been thrown all over me.

Suffice to say, it wasn't going to be shaken off anytime soon.

I lost count of the times I rewatched the footage. The rise of the wind, the fury within. If these allegations were indeed true, little wonder she was up in arms. Who wouldn't be?

I now found myself in a really awkward spot. An unenviable position. Not to mention dodgy ground legally. What on earth was I supposed to do with this new twist? It changed everything.

I could try and ignore it, of course, but my integrity wouldn't allow that. I wanted to explore the possibilities while meeting it head-on.

As a self-published author who's dealt with hard men and 'colourful' pasts, this was a shade of a different kind and certainly no less controversial. Besides, where do you start with something that happened over two hundred years ago?

With the family, I reckoned. Who is who. What is the connection exactly. Time to get down and polish up that family tree!

After having received the call that night from my mother, one of the first things I did was to reactivate my account on Ancestry, an online genealogy site. I'd already compiled my family tree some years ago but hadn't visited in a long time.

The branch in question was on my mother's side and as yet unexplored. I knew that her mother, Nancy, had only one sibling, an older brother called William Gwyn Thomas. Uncle Gwyn, as we called him, married Agnes Alice Tanner, and their children are cousins, Mary, and her older sister, Hilary, who lives Down Under.

When Margaret Morgan was born in 1841 in Llanbadarn Fawr,   **Edit**
Radnorshire, her father, Francis, was 48, and her mother, Mary, was 40.
She had one daughter from one relationship. She then married David
Wilding and they had four children together. She died in April 1918 in
Pontypridd, Glamorgan, having lived a long life of 77 years.

I hadn't seen Cousin Mary in years, so a phone call was well overdue, as was a summary of how her line linked into that of Mary Morgan.

The story handed down, was that Cousin Mary's family had 'a skeleton in the cupboard'. A relative that had been hung for killing her baby. A piece of paper bearing the inscription from the main headstone had been sent to the family nearly a hundred years ago and is still in their possession.

The script is fairly faded but the date when it was sent in 1869 is just about legible.

This intriguing echo of family scandal had seen Cousin Mary and her family come to Presteigne on more than one occasion to learn more. Yet, despite their best efforts, they hit a stone wall whenever they made enquiries locally. The good people of Presteigne still guarded the ghost of Mary, and after Jenny Green's take on the story, memories were still fresh, and lips remained sealed.

Their interest remained strong, however, especially with her eldest son, Geraint.

Furnished with this information, I now turned my attention to building their family tree starting with Cousin Mary and a picture soon began to emerge. Her mother, who married my Great Uncle

Gwyn, was Agnes Alice, who was the daughter of Agnes Emily, who in turn was the daughter of Margaret, the youngest of eight born to Francis Morgan and wife, Mary.

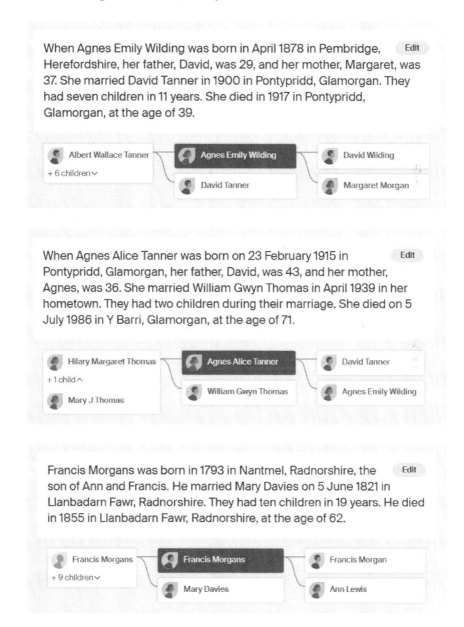

When Agnes Emily Wilding was born in April 1878 in Pembridge, Herefordshire, her father, David, was 29, and her mother, Margaret, was 37. She married David Tanner in 1900 in Pontypridd, Glamorgan. They had seven children in 11 years. She died in 1917 in Pontypridd, Glamorgan, at the age of 39.

Edit

Albert Wallace Tanner
+ 6 children

Agnes Emily Wilding

David Wilding

David Tanner

Margaret Morgan

When Agnes Alice Tanner was born on 23 February 1915 in Pontypridd, Glamorgan, her father, David, was 43, and her mother, Agnes, was 36. She married William Gwyn Thomas in April 1939 in her hometown. They had two children during their marriage. She died on 5 July 1986 in Y Barri, Glamorgan, at the age of 71.

Edit

Hilary Margaret Thomas
+ 1 child

Agnes Alice Tanner

David Tanner

Mary J Thomas

William Gwyn Thomas

Agnes Emily Wilding

Francis Morgans was born in 1793 in Nantmel, Radnorshire, the son of Ann and Francis. He married Mary Davies on 5 June 1821 in Llanbadarn Fawr, Radnorshire. They had ten children in 19 years. He died in 1855 in Llanbadarn Fawr, Radnorshire, at the age of 62.

Edit

Francis Morgans
+ 9 children

Francis Morgans

Francis Morgan

Mary Davies

Ann Lewis

I find them on the census of 1841, all living together in Llanbadarn Fawr.

1841 census showing Francis Morgan listed as an 'Ag Lab'
Agricultural Labourer

That part was easy. Dates, records, siblings, and marriages were duly found, and all slotted together perfectly. The great thing about Ancestry, is that it actively helps with hints to other family trees and possible relatives.

So, imagine my delight when I went looking and found Francis and Mary together on not just one tree, but three! Brother and sister! Same parents! Yowser, mystery solved! It would seem Francis was born ten years after Mary, in 1798, which would have made him just five years old when his sister died!

Oh, my goodness, the excitement was all but overwhelming. Enthused by this latest discovery, I got busy contacting the other tree-holders for more info.

Did they have anything more to suggest that these links were bonafide?

Were they aware that Mary had been hung for infanticide?

It was a mixed response that only served to somewhat muddy the waters, but I persevered. I had the parents, after all!

Rees Morgan, was born in Nantmel, Radnorshire. His wife, Elizabeth, who was a Watkins, was from Aberedw, near to Builth Wells. So, off I went one fine Sunday morning on one of the most scenic drives to this little gem tucked away in the Welsh hills.

The graveyard was my destination in the hope of finding some Watkins in eternal rest. The community-owned pub, The Severn Stars, was just before the church. In fact, it couldn't have been any closer, so I pulled in next to it before making my way towards the precincts of St. Cewydd's.

As I stepped into that sacred space, I cast about wondering where to start. Something drew me to the left, and off I went on what would be the first of many forays looking for names and family ties.

For such a little church it had a fair-sized graveyard, and as always, if the church door was unlocked, I would go inside afterwards and pay my respects. Besides, there was also something particularly poignant about this church. For local history says that it was here, that Llewellyn the Last Prince of Wales, prayed on the morning before betrayal led to his death. And as I approached the altar I pictured him, kneeling before it, his dark head bowed in quiet contemplation. A brave man, a tenacious man, who had fought so hard for the country he loved.

Legend has it he hid out in a local cave the night before he died, and that this bolthole, 'Llewellyn's Cave' is forever named after him. In the silence, I said a prayer for all lost souls before making a donation and signing the visitors' book.

Making my way back out towards the gate I couldn't help but feel disappointed. My gravestone reccy had turned up nothing and I wondered what to do next.

Next door a young man was sorting some recycling from the pub, and on a whim, I asked if he knew of any Watkins in the area.

I explained what I was doing and why and couldn't believe it when he said he had a list of all burials in the pub.

In the pub! Seriously?

'Yes,' he said, 'I did all the rubbings and made a file. We keep it in the pub.'

With lovely smells emanating from the kitchen, I needed no persuading to go and inspect this list personally and have Sunday lunch while I'm at it!

My mood lifted as I entered The Seven Stars, and a small table was found for me in the bar. The young man's name was Prys, and he soon set about trying to locate the file that had now become akin to the Holy Grail for me!

After some rummaging around, eventually it was found and no sooner did I delve in, than I found some Watkins. They had been laid to rest beneath the stone slabs to my left when I first entered the churchyard. Talk about being called from the other side!

I was thrilled to read the inscriptions and took photos before tucking into a lovely dinner as Prys brought me up to speed. He was a massive Welsh history fan, and very knowledgeable. But there were no Watkins still around that he was aware of.

It didn't matter, I was just so grateful for the information he had, and when I left The Seven Stars and its friendly staff, it was with a warm glow and a full belly. What an absolute quirk of fate that this young man should compile such a fortuitous file. I couldn't wait to get back and investigate my findings further.

Firstly, I had to drive down aways to turn around, and on the road, I passed an elderly man walking his Jack Russell. He had that air of being local, so I stopped, wound down the window and called him across.

I do this a lot. Accost complete strangers in the street for information, and to date, it's been most successful. This old boy had nothing on the Watkins', but he did tell me his father had done Jury Service in Presteigne, not once but twice, and that he himself knew something of the tale of Mary Morgan.

Just this little snippet made the risk of being told to sod off worth it. He also spotted I had a slow puncture, so all in all, it was an insightful interaction. I just wish I'd asked his name, but I do remember him calling his dog, Patch!

When I got home, I began a new tree gleaned from the info I had for Watkins, but I couldn't link it to Francis and Mary's mother, Elizabeth. That could only mean one thing, I needed to go after the father.

Nantmel, is just outside Rhayader, so, off I went in the hope of more joy with the Morgans, when on the road I spotted a sign for a small garden centre and café. I need to check that out on the way back, I told myself, before turning off at the signpost for Nantmel.

The lane took me up to St. Mary's church that sits on a hill overlooking the lush valley. I began my usual foray, murmuring apologies as I went. Unfortunately, searches often took me directly over final resting places, and I would acknowledge this intrusion with the greatest of respect. The ground is often overgrown, uneven, and in some parts will sink alarmingly beneath your feet. So, I would always proceed with caution scanning inscriptions as I went.

Many of the headstones were so weathered as to render them unreadable. As I mentioned previously, most burial records are now digital, and I could have saved myself a lot of trouble – and petrol! But I was a rank amateur who had spent the past few years immersed in the boxing world. All this historical stuff was a new one on me. So, as I stumbled about in between admiring the view, I finally found a Morgan or two, with the inscriptions reasonably legible.

Thrilled I took some pictures before heading off to a chapel I'd spotted earlier. This place was seriously overgrown with a sign on the door that warned you would be entering at your own risk!

I could soon see why. The ground was like the Wild West of graveyards, and despite a bloody big stick, the nettles saw me beat a hasty retreat, but not before I found more Morgans. I consoled myself with the thought of a nice cup of coffee and some cake in the little café down the road.

I didn't get either; the kitchen area was closed for a deep clean. But the shop was open, and after making some purchases I went into the restaurant area to pay.

Here I met Mercedes whose family owned the business, and a local lady who'd turned up for Knitting Club. I did my usual thing and said what I was up to and could they help.

Amazingly, the knitting lady remembered hearing the story of Mary Morgan as a child, and this gave me hope, because if her story was known about in these parts, there was a good chance her father's family may still be around.

Any Morgans in the area? I asked.

Yes, they told me, there were, before launching into a great debate of which farm was the Morgan one. Upper Cwm or Lower Cwm? I listened bemused as they talked names and neighbours, tracks, and directions. They finally reached agreement and off I went.

In no time I found myself high up amidst some of the most breath-taking scenery as the ground took me high up into the hills. Eventually I came to the turning for the farm, but it meant going through a gate and along a private track, to where buildings nestled in the distance. Suddenly, I found myself hesitating. As a rule, I'm usually very decisive, but as I paused, the engine idling, I had to ask myself why. Something was stopping me, and as a firm believer in my gut, I knew there had to be a reason.

Maybe my arrival would incite an unfriendly reaction. Turning up unannounced and asking questions as a complete stranger is one thing. But to throw in possible family connections is another. For the most part, farmers are inclined to be quite cagey if they don't know you. At best they could tell me to bugger off. At worst, threaten to set the dogs on me!

Would it be wise? Did I want to risk it? Besides the fact no one knew where I was, (except for the two women who'd sent me here), who really knew what I'd be walking into?

Something told me this was a no-no, so with no small reluctance

I turned off down the hill as something came hurtling towards me.

It was a man on a quadbike! Once again, I couldn't believe my luck! No one for miles around and then this!

I pulled up and waved for him to stop.

This he did with a rather bewildered look as I smiled widely.

'Did he know the farm up the top?'

'Yes.'

'Did he know the farmer?'

'Yes.'

'Was he a Morgan?'

'Yes.'

I felt like a hard-nosed cop, but I had to take the bull by the horns. I just had to know!

Considering this man had just been interrupted going about his business, he was very good-natured about it. Might have been a different story if it had been on his territory, mind!

I explained my story and that I had been sent by the garden centre ladies. He knew them, of course, and suggested I call up to the farm anyway.

I went with my gut and gave him a card instead.

Could he pass this on for me, please?

He stuffed it into his pocket and with a rev of the engine he went one way, and I went the other with the feeling, so close yet so far.

Back home I got busy with the info I'd collated from the headstones, but it was no good. I just couldn't link them in. The brick wall was back. I messaged the people again who had Mary and Francis on their family tree, but after explaining the situation, they were as clueless as me.

According to the records, Francis Morgan had married and settled in Llanbadarn Fawr. I looked at the map. It was just outside the coastal town of Aberystwyth, and the church I wanted was St. Padarn's. Aberystwyth is also home to the National Library of Wales, so I was well placed for extra research, should I need it.

It was Summer and it had been a while since I'd had a break, so

I booked a couple of nights in a nice place overlooking the sea. I was determined to crack this, if the mountain won't come to the Mohammed and all that. So off I went, a truly lovely drive through the Elan Valley before finding St. Padarn's and parking outside.

It was a hot day, but I made short work of the large area of graves on ground level. There was an elevated continuation of the site that was so steep I eyed it with no small concern. I had a couple of days; I could hit that part another time, I told myself. Fortunately for me, however, I was to be spared the risk of breaking my neck after an embarrassing moment in the Town Hall the very next day!

If there's one thing I've learnt throughout this process, it is that it pays to pay attention to detail. Literally! Despite being armed with all my family links, records, and information, I had made one very simple and costly mistake. I hadn't read the text properly.

I had the wrong county. The wrong Llanbadarn Fawr. There are two!

The one I wanted was in Radnorshire NOT Ceredigion where I found myself. As this was imparted to me in the Archives office, I found myself squirming on the spot. How embarrassing!

I had no option than to make the most of Aberystwyth's delights before heading back to Presteigne, my tail between my legs. I'd wasted time and money chasing the wrong ghosts and could all but feel Mary roll her eyes at me the next time I visited her grave. That I was out of my depth was not in doubt. If anything, I was seriously floundering and needed a miracle, never mind help!

Then the Universe sent me an archaeologist by the name of Rebecca Eversley, and the rest, as they say, was history!

I already knew Rebecca through our association as Trustees for the Heritage and Cultural Exchange, in Cardiff. Rebecca is also Head Honcho at the Historic Docks Project in Newport.

We'd crossed paths at a number of events but didn't know each other that well. This was about to change, however, when during a phone call about another project I happened to mention Mary.

Like me, Rebecca had never heard of her, but the story struck a chord and she wanted to know more. I explained how I just couldn't get past the parents of Francis, my Cousin Mary's ancestor. Something wasn't right. I'd searched until I was blue in the face and bursting with expletives.

Rebecca offered to have a look at what I'd collated so far and before you knew it, she too, was down the rabbit hole! It wasn't planned. Her involvement just seemed to happen, and in view of my tenuous grasp on things, it was good to have the company.

Her first task was to tackle the tree of Francis Morgan and start afresh with Mary. Now I had an expert at hand, I could begin making notes and continue to ask questions, and one conversation was particularly interesting!

Roger Millichamp, (related to Glenys by marriage), has lived in Presteigne all his life. At one time his family had a gun and clock factory in town, and there isn't much Roger doesn't know about local history. A chance meeting in the street one day saw him share an amazing snippet he had of the hanging tree as a boy. As far as his memory serves, he remembers seeing manacles melded into the bark of the tree. A chilling reminder of how loosely life was regarded when restraints such as this were just left to be claimed by nature.

Another extraordinary story is a childhood tale by a lady who wishes to remain anonymous. Growing up her family lived not far from the church, and when she was about nine years old, things started happening in her bedroom at night. This was also experienced by her sibling who shared the same room. They would be woken up by an extreme feeling of heat and pressure on the chest which, understandably, caused them no small distress. So much so, that their mother appealed to the vicar for help.

Two priests were sent to the house from Hereford Cathedral, and they blessed the room where the phenomena had been occurring. To the children's great relief there were no more visitations, but the speculation at the time, was that it was the ghost of Mary Morgan.

If it had been her, then she had certainly been getting about when another haunting was brought to my attention by Glenys Millichamp.

Her friend, Betty Creed, had had an extraordinary experience when she was newly married some sixty years ago. Without further ado a meeting was arranged at Glenys' house so I could hear the story first-hand, and I must say, it made for a fascinating tale!

At the time Betty and her husband had moved into a house on Hereford Street when one night they were woken by their son who ran screaming into their bedroom. Tim was just a toddler and absolutely distraught; there was a lady in his room with no head or feet!

Betty reassured him that the lady had gone to London and Tim never saw her again. Betty thought no more about it until she woke up one night to find a female figure leaning over the crib of baby Gill.

Terrified, she kicked her husband awake, never taking her eyes from what she knew to be a ghost and testified that her husband saw it too.

If it was Mary, and I feel in my heart that it was, her appearance and behaviour is of no small significance. To poor little Tim, she presented herself with no head or feet, yet he knew without doubt that this scary spectre was female. Why she would want to frighten a young child is open to speculation and sits at odds with her second appearance as she leans over the crib seemingly watching as the baby sleeps.

That Betty woke at that moment and witnessed the figure suggest to me that Mary was deliberately showing herself, and going by her behaviour, who else is it going to be?

Apparently the owner, Mrs Kinch sold the house some years later to a Reverend Gill, who was so against women in the church, he set up his own in the house next door and also witnessed 'the ghost'.

Wild horses wouldn't have stopped me as I hot-footed it down to the property in question. I just had to check it out for myself!

Once again, the Universe was looking after me as my knock at the door was answered by Bernadette who had recently arrived from France. Totally unflustered by the reason for my call, her response was like music to my ears.

'I've just taken cakes out of the oven and about to make coffee. Would you like to come in?'

I couldn't have timed it any better and spent the next hour bringing Bernadette up to speed as I enjoyed her hospitality – the cakes with homemade lemon curd were the biz!

No, she wasn't aware of any presence in the house but was interested in the story. As an artist who works the most beautiful wooden pieces, Bernadette was naturally open to things beyond our ken. As a gesture of appreciation, I played the footage to her of Mary's rage, and she acknowledged it with a shiver at the back of her neck.

Mary may not visit the house anymore, but she certainly passed by that day. On further investigation it transpires that the property had once been part of 'The Temperance Hotel' that encompassed the neighbouring houses. The rear of the building would have extended down towards the prison. The Judging's Lodgings may sit there now, but some echoes of the past still linger.

An example of this was a chat by with an elderly gentleman who recalled a friend in Primary school telling his grandmother's story of Mary's execution day. A tale passed down in the family, and how they had watched from the window as the death cortege went by on its way to Gallows Lane.

In contrast, there are also those who have no especial interest in Mary but memories of Jenny Green instead. Kay Hughes is one of the livelier locals, and probably the friendliest woman in Presteigne. Indeed, she made my acquaintance before I even moved up. She's good friends with Lynne Traylor and you'll often find her at her charity stall. Kay's grandfather left Bargoed, in the South Wales valleys, and set up a haulage business on the High Street. Just doors away from the Hughes old family home, Jenny had opened a café earning her the nickname, 'Jenny Green the

Coffee Pot Queen' from Kay, who got on with her very well.

I think it's fair to say, I've chewed the fat with many of Presteigne's finest, and their patience with my ponderings is to be highly commended! If it wasn't for the fact, I was Mary's family, my quest would not have been so well tolerated. Talking of family,

Cousin Mary and the rest of the clan had planned to come up for a visit. It had been years since they'd last seen the grave of their ancestor, and with all that had been happening, most keen to see the footage and where Mary had gasped her last breath.

My mother also came up, and it was akin to a council of war as we sat around the kitchen table bouncing theories.

To get a more personal feel of Mary's final days, I suggested a mini-tour that would take in the lay-out as it would have looked during her time. As a courtesy we began at her grave first to pay our respects. I then led my small party up Broad Street. I'd have liked to have taken them into the Judge's Lodgings, but unfortunately it was closed due to staff sickness. As we paused outside, I explained how the building was constructed after Mary's time, and that Presteigne Gaol has been a filthy, rat-infested hole so dilapidated, prisoners had been known to escape with ease.

Not so for Mary, however, although allegedly there had been a plan to break her out following her sentence of death. But whether this is true or not will be examined more fully in a later chapter.

'This is the site of the old Shire Hall where Mary stood trial,' I said, and stopped just before Lorna's Sandwich Shop. Admittedly, the building has changed greatly during the intervening years, and at one time was also the town Post Office. Indeed, the first dream I had of Mary involved this building just weeks after learning of the family link.

I dreamt a young girl was stood in the doorway holding a piece of paper before her. She was small in stature, no more than five feet, wearing an off-white shift, or some kind of smock, and had long fair hair. She was staring straight at me to where I was stood directly opposite outside the hospice shop. Nothing was said and no one else was about. We just regarded each other silently for some moments and then I woke up.

In the dream it was the post office I saw, not the old Shire Hall, which led me to believe that perhaps the paper she was holding was representative of 'communication'. That she was seeking to communicate with me. Or maybe, as the Madonna suggested, the piece of paper was to do with 'her verdict'. White is the colour usually associated with innocence. Either way, I strongly believe it was her, and I remember how petite she was. More girl than young woman. I'd have easily put her as looking more like thirteen or fourteen-year-old.

This other-worldly aspect of me was something my cousins had to come to terms with very quickly and was received with a mixture of bemusement and surprise. It didn't get in the way of why we had come together, however. And furthermore, they were as shocked as I had been at the possibility that maybe Mary hadn't killed her baby, after all.

As we stood just before the corner entrance, I pointed to a small, barred aperture in the wall where it meets the pavement. The building may have seen some major changes over the centuries, yet below ground a poignant part of its history remains.

Some months earlier, I'd popped into the shop for some of Lorna's fabulous fare, and while I was there, I asked if there had been any paranormal activity. Apparently, there had been instances of sweets being moved about in the night, but this soon stopped once cameras were installed. Down in the basement the old cells remain complete with iron rings in the walls! Here the prisoners would be held before going up before the judge. Could Mary have been held in such a cell before her trial? More than likely, and even more pressingly, could I take a quick look?

My request was granted but I was warned I wouldn't be able to see much on account of the stud partitioning that was in place. Here, Lorna keeps her stock, but I was still able to catch just a sliver of what lay beyond over the room divider. What wouldn't I have done to have been able to touch, never mind see, one of the iron rings that had held many a hapless captive!

Below the dazzling strip light, amidst the shelves of tins and dried foods, there was, just faintly, the residual energies of what those unfortunate captives must have felt. I'd have loved to have done an overnight vigil but knew better than to ask. I was just grateful to have been given the opportunity to have a glimpse of Presteigne's history, no matter how small.

Since this visit, Lorna's sister, Martha revealed an experience that rather disturbed her at Christmas last year. Upon opening the freezer, she suddenly found herself being pushed violently from behind. A ghost of Christmas past and definitely not a friendly one, it would seem! Martha responded with a firm telling off and it's never happened again (to date!). She described how she distinctly felt two hands on her back, and it goes without saying I believe her.

As I related this snippet to my family, we all gazed for some moments at the grated opening, each with our thoughts.

We could only imagine mournful eyes straining to look out as the town went about its business. The noises, the smells, or perhaps, friends and family shouting encouragement down to them as they waited to hear their fate. So, had Mary been held there before the Judge passed sentence, and what would have been going through her mind? This was something I was yet to experience, and in a way that would take me totally by surprise.

After this brief pause, we turned right and made our way up High Street before veering right into Scottleton Street, the route that would have taken Mary to the execution site. Despite Presteigne's bustling morning vibe, we tried to envisage her sat on her coffin as the horse and cart led her to her doom.

According to reports, no one could be found to provide the cart that would take Mary to her death. One was eventually found at Fold Farm and driven by a man called Vaughan. The farm, now called as 'Ted's Fold Farm', is still on Broad Street, but the original family long gone.

By the time we got to Gallows Lane, the mood had become subdued. As I led the small party through the gate and up to the clearing, it was, and I readily admit, all wrong. I'm talking about the actual execution site. At this point, I was still operating under the belief that the hanging tree was one of the two in the clearing. This, despite Jenny Green saying in her book, how she had sat on the stump. *The stump!*

For some reason, this most crucial part of the story had bypassed me completely. How on earth had I missed this! Indeed, it was Rebecca, who pointed this out to me some weeks later. And so, there I was like the blind leading the blind, yet once again, unwittingly captured more phenomena!

I have a theory for this that I'll go into later because it is most pertinent. But back to this day. Geraint, his wife, Becky, and I, have pulled ahead of the group and as we approached the stile before the clearing, I suggested that Geraint go first.

The reason for this is that he feels a particular connection to Mary and has done so since he was a child. Perhaps it's an ancestral thing, some kind of connection that has drawn him in so strongly he had the image of her gravestone tattooed on his wrist.

The second headstone, naturally, because 'He that is without sin among you. Let him first cast a stone at her' remember...

As Geraint takes in the tree and those horribly, gnarled roots, I ask if I can take a picture for the book. His wife, Becky, does the same from her position just feet away from me. I take a couple and upon checking the images, immediately see that something isn't right.

I ask to see the pictures Becky has taken at exactly the same time and I'm perplexed.

In my photos there is a strange kind of mist that covers Geraint's lower half. Yet, in Becky's pictures he is crystal clear.

How extraordinary! I've heard of supernatural mists, but I've never seen one before. Is there such a thing and if so, was this it? As this is the tree where it all began - no crazy wind this day, but perhaps a sign from Mary that she was very much with us?

We share this oddity with the others when they catch up but take no more pictures. The mood remained muted as everyone stood quietly, each with their thoughts.

As we make our way back to the road, I glanced at Cousin Mary to find her gentle face etched with sorrow.

'Are you okay, Mary?' I enquired and she gave a small shake of her head.

'It's just so sad,' she said.

I looked around to the rest of the family as we trudged across the field.

The mood was heavy as though the ghost of a girl, little more than a child, walked beside us.

Left: Geraint minus the strange mist. Photo courtesy of his wife, Becky.

And so how did she feel, Mary, having these long-lost family members come to visit?

Quietly joyful. Don't think she'd felt such love in over two hundred years. And did we love her? Oh yes!

All too soon it was time for everyone to return to South Wales, although Ed and Erin live overseas.

It had been a bonding and emotive visit, marked by their encouragement to keep digging in the hope that if this allegation was true, we could in some way, remove that stain of erosive guilt.

Indeed, my kin departed with a desire to uncover the truth on a par and as compelling as mine.

Do what you need to do, they told me. We were all agreed we wanted answers.

From left: Mary's husband Ken, my mother, Suzanne, Ed, Cousin Mary, Geraint, Ed's wife, Erin next to Becky, wife to Geraint and their son, Iestyn, with cousins (left) Malaika Gwenllian and Carwyn Llias.

Meanwhile, Rebecca had been going great guns and had blown a complete hole in the 'assumed' parentage of Francis Morgan. He wasn't, as thought, the younger brother of Mary, neither was his mother the Elizabeth Watkins from Aberedw. The father, however, did hail from Nantmel, but his name was not Rees. Here I learned the first lesson in the collation of accurate family research.

'You've been caught up in a mistake many people make when researching their family tree,' she told me. 'When the same hints come up in other peoples' trees, in the absence of anything else, it's the easiest route to take. It's when you get down to the nitty-gritty that major gaps begin to appear."

Besides feeling a complete fool and not a little disappointed, there was also a sense of relief. The uncertainty had been nagging at me, but it was nothing to the tangle that was vexing Rebecca!

The incorrect Elizabeth Watkins and Rees Morgan had been put to bed, but there remained the unknown parentage of Francis

Morgan. It was like he had just dropped out of the sky! Indeed, trying to unearth the missing links of both Mary and Francis was proving to be extremely elusive. In the first instance, we were concentrating on the latter because it was imperative that we find that all-important connection for the book.

Granted, documents can go missing. Between the attentions of mice and the forgetfulness of man, these things do happen and can lead to a brick wall. Only in our investigations, there were too many bricks and the walls kept coming!

It was time to go back to Llanbadarn Fawr – the correct one this time! Thanks to the Rector of Glasbury, I was put in touch with the Reverend Andrew Perrin, of the Holy Trinity,

Llandridnod Wells. It was a while before I was able to catch him in, but with a large number of parishes to cover, not surprisingly he's a very busy man!

He took the time to talk, however, and showed an interest in the case. After taking him through the reasons of my query, he in turn shared a snippet of his family history that, with his permission, I can share with you.

There had been a mystery surrounding the beginnings of his Great-Grandmother who had been in service to a 'well-to-do' family in Swansea. The word in Andrew's family was that she was the illegitimate child of the master of the house, but of course there was no way of proving this. Such liaisons, as we know, were not uncommon in those days, and such stories were often passed down. Thanks to the science of DNA, however, their speculation was validated. They are indeed related to the family in question, whose identity shall remain private.

Just the fact that the Reverend was willing to share this personal piece of information with me, gives a good indication of how the world is changing. At one time, such a disclosure would have been a thing of shame. Thankfully, not anymore. Such a pity everyone approached in this project wasn't so forthcoming. We can't change the past, but we can certainly put old ghosts to rest with the respect that they deserve, surely?

Happy to assist further, the good Reverend put me in touch with one of his curates, Lisa Morgan, who met with me one morning at the church in Llanbadarn Fawr. Unfortunately, there were no parish records in-house of any note, but we had a good chat afterwards about families, God, and spiritual matters. Before we parted ways, Lisa put me in touch with Emma, the clerical officer at Holy Trinity, who in turn said she had records there.

Fantastic! We arranged a time I could call by with the suggestion I might also like to check out Powys Archives while I was in the area. I got on to it immediately and duly booked an afternoon slot at the Archives later that week.

Finally, I felt I was beginning to make headway, but this was a whole new territory to me. I didn't trust myself to miss something or mess it up, so I put in a call to Rebecca.

Could she come up and help me with this latest development? Archives was her thing; I'd really appreciate it. Fortunately, for me, she wasn't too busy and took the train up the next morning. When I picked her up from the station, we were bubbling with excitement as we speculated and compared notes.

So, on Friday 23rd September 2022 we headed off to 'Llandod' and the Holy Trinity church full of expectation. Here we met with Andrew Perrin and Emma who were most welcoming, but the records they had were not what we wanted. It didn't matter, though, we had the Archives later, and it was nice to meet the Reverend in person. He explained that the church had actually been built by a de Winton, or Wilkins, as they were known at that time. Rebecca and I exchanged a glance; a de Winton built this church? Well, well . . .

We were taken to the vestry where a photo of the man himself hangs among other church worthies. A rather surreal moment, as Mary hovered on the side-lines, never far away, always watching. September 23rd was also the date on which Mary's baby came and departed the world so cruelly.

We were then invited to join the coffee morning the WI were

hosting in a room off the main body of the church. Why not? And here we met Brian Maund, who was once clerk of the Court at Presteigne. We couldn't believe it, and what an interesting man! Over coffee and Welsh cakes, he talked, we listened, and although he didn't venture an opinion on Mary, it was fascinating to hear him recount his time with such names as Major Dilwyn Jones, Sir Roy Margrave-Jones and Gwenllian Phillips. He was an absolute treasure trove of information who also happened to know the lady in charge at the Archives. Her name was Amanda, and that was our next call.

All I can say at this point, is thank goodness I had an expert with me, because after a few minutes at the screen I became nauseous. The wiggly movement and scrolling of the micro-fiche for me was akin to watching 'The Blair Witch Project', but without the thrills, so I pulled off and left Rebecca to it!

There was only one other person sat quietly doing research, so as I wandered browsing the bookshelves, I think Amanda finally took pity on me.

They had a manuscript in archive about Mary Morgan written some years ago by a lady called Patricia Parris. Such were the conditions of copyright no part could be copied or recorded in any way whatsoever, but I could have a read, if I was interested?

I felt my jaw drop. Unpublished work about Mary Morgan? Are you kidding me?

Yes, please!

Blown away by this unexpected gift from the Universe (and Amanda!), I pored over the bundle of pages, all neatly typed on A4 paper, and it soon became apparent this lady knew her stuff! Well written and brimming with previously unknown snippets of info that had me hooked. How did she know all this stuff? She also recorded crossing paths with Jenny Green during the time she was researching her book, yet for some reason, Patricia had never published hers!?

As soon as Rebecca finished scanning through the records, she came to join me at the table. Between us we studied the manuscript with observations and surprised comments. We couldn't understand why such a fine piece of work was allowed to sit gathering dust, and this was the topic of conversation all the way home. As was, Patricia Parris – who was she?

It soon transpired that our mystery lady had been a key member of 'The Radnorshire Society.' A further search showed she had also written a public piece about Mary's trial in 1983 under 'The Radnorshire Society Transactions'. We were quite blown away. We were also desperate to make contact because it seemed to us that Patricia Parris was a lady in the know!

I got back to the Reverend Andrew Perrin who put me in touch with the Very Reverend Geraint Hughes. Now retired but very knowledgeable about the area, he said the name Parris rang a bell before suggesting I contact The Radnorshire Society directly. This I did via email and despite enquiring very politely, was sent references for Patricia's articles and nothing else, which I found quite odd. I just wanted to know if Patricia was still with us, and if she was, could they put me in touch? It took another email before I received a very terse response saying they believed she had passed away. All rather vague and a little strange in my opinion. Maybe they weren't keen to engage with the kin of Mary Morgan? Perhaps my foray into what they may regard as their territory was not welcome? Who can say, but it did make me wonder what they knew?

But the trip out had not been in vain and had opened certain avenues in need of further investigation. There was still a problem with Francis, though. Despite searching, combing, and creating more trees than you could shake a stick at, we still couldn't connect my cousin's line to Mary's. This presented a huge problem. Not least because I'd publicly claimed this family connection, but also for the sake of authenticity. This is why I'd embarked upon this whole journey, remember? The all-important family connection!

So, it was back to the drawing board and the church records of St. Mary's in Nantmel. By hook and by crook, Rebecca managed to locate the parents of Francis, his forefathers, and his siblings, yet no record of birth could be found for him in Nantmel. It was all rather mysterious and frustrating, because despite there being parish records before and after his birth, the section that we wanted was missing!

Equally mysterious is how Francis came into FORTY acres of land in 1851 when just ten years before he had nothing? Forty acres! Where did the land come from? How did he come by it?

This was the first indication that there was more to the Mary Morgan story than infanticide and hanging. Bribery? Compensation? I was absolutely mystified and could find no answers. But at least his family had been found. Now all that was needed was to do was link it to Mary.

1851 Census showing Francis Morgan now listed as a farmer with 40 acres of land.

You'd think the early beginnings of such an infamous and prominent figure would be easy to find, but the brick walls just kept popping up. Beyond her baptism record and notes about the trial, there was absolutely nothing else to say that this girl existed. Data was limited, records sketchy, and the trail confusing at best. If anything, you'd be forgiven for suspecting that family details had been deliberately buried.

Her parents were Rees and Elizabeth Morgan, and according to the reports they lived in Glasbury. We found them, or rather Rebecca did, but nothing else, which then led her to spread the net even further afield. To our surprise another two couples turned up with the same names residing in Cusop and Clyro, respectively. These two villages, including Llowes and Glasbury, lie within a few miles of each other on the outskirts of Hay-on-Wye. We now had three couples who were the potentials parents, but which one? With so little to go on with any of them, the only hint of any note was that the Rees from Cusop originally came from Nantmel. Was this our man? Rebecca thought he was the most likely, but we couldn't know for sure.

We went round and round in circles, and with no real leads in place, I began to lose heart in the whole project. The puzzle would not be complete, the story could not be told, nothing could move forward without Mary. It was as simple as that.

It was 29th November 2022 and as we debated the possibilities for the umpteenth time, we finally fell into silence before Rebecca said, 'Come on, Mary!'

Her rally call to the other side bemused me, not least because I'm normally the hocus-pocus person. But someone must have been listening because that night I had a dream . . .

CHAPTER 4

Whatever your views on astral travel, know that I am fully signed-up, onboard, and have learned to listen when the subconscious speaks. Whether it's problem-solving, premonition, or even on the odd occasion, precognition, I'm in. All the way! As a rule, dreams are usually full of layered, cryptic messages that can take some working out. But in this case, it couldn't have been any clearer. I just had to convince, Rebecca!

You have to remember that we were still getting to know each other, and as an Archaeologist, she deals in hard cold facts, not messages from the other side. So, when I called the next morning to tell her about my dream, she was dubious, to say the least!

'It's Glasbury!' I told her excitedly, 'I dreamt I was stood on the road in Llowes. Clyro is to the left of me, Cusop is before me. A figure to my right is pointing towards Glasbury, and they said; They are the Rees and Elizabeth that you want. It's definitely them, I'm telling you!"

I could sense her reluctance and I didn't blame her. I joked it had been her who had put the call-out to Mary in the first place. I think she likes you; I said, either that or you have untapped abilities. I was cock-a-hoop, the Universe had come through and besides, we had nothing else to go on. The first glimmer of light was the marriage certificate of Mary's parents. Now we finally had a pinpoint for Rees's birthplace! He came from Llandefalle a small hamlet up in the hills just outside Brecon. Elizabeth was listed as from Glasbury, but firstly, I want to start with Rees Morgan, because the second revelation was his last will and testament!

And oh, What a find!

I couldn't believe it! My impression was that Rees and Elizabeth had always been depicted as little more than peasants. Too impoverished to pay for the services of a solicitor, surely? Much less have anything of means to leave behind in a will!

Seems that they did. And no small change, I'll have you know! A total of eight hundred pounds, my friends.

EIGHT HUNDRED QUID!

I was agog. In today's monetary value a considerable sum of money, as in eighty thousand pounds! EIGHTY THOUSAND!

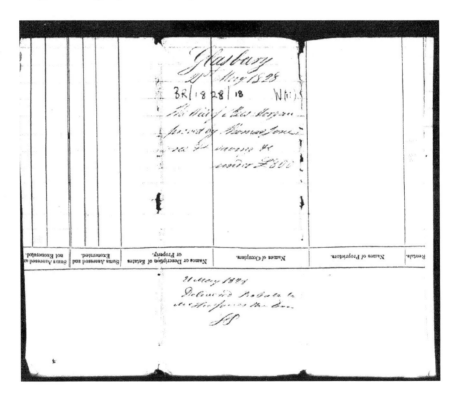

Just let that sink in a minute and then ask the question how a simple country man could amass such a fortune . . .

With echoes of Francis and his forty acres that had seemingly appeared out of the blue, just what was going on with the Morgans and all of this wealth?

And that wasn't the only surprise in the will, because there in black and white is none other than Walter Wilkins of Maesllwch! As in Walter Wilkins 'Junior'. Mary's contemporary, suspected lover, and father of the baby. Now Squire of the manor popping up in the will like some proverbial bad penny!

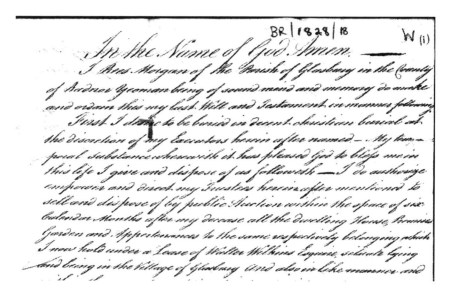

Well, well, I wasn't expecting that. Beyond intriguing, as was the fact Rees and Elizabeth had remained in the area after the death of their daughter. This really surprised me, because in the wake of such heartbreak you'd think they'd want to start afresh and leave the scandal behind.

Yet here they are, twenty-three years after the death of their daughter, not just residing in Glasbury, but dying there, and all beneath the weighty eye of the Wilkins family.

Why?

It didn't feel right, and my spidery senses did more than perk up at this point. There had to be a reason why they had stayed in the area. There were other options open to them, surely? Rees had siblings, after all. Yet they had stayed.

Further investigation went on to divulge some interesting links between the Morgans and Maesllwch yet let us first return to the will and a more pleasing revelation. For it was quite apparent that Mary had been part of a close and loving family. Aunts, Uncles, Cousins, and seeing their names written out moved me deeply.

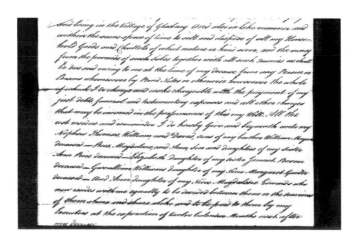

"...Thomas, William, David, sons of my brother, William Morgans, now deceased - Rees, Magdalene, Ann, son and daughters of my sister, Ann Price, now deceased - Elizabeth, daughter of my sister, Jennet Beavan, deceased - Gwenllian Williams, daughter of my niece, Margaret Gunter deceased – and Ann daughter of my niece Magdalene Edwards, who now resides with me ..."

Had Mary played with them before she went into service up at the castle? Grown up with their names upon her lips, played games in the fields of Llowes, the very air vibrant with their laughter? As I'm writing this, a wave of overwhelming grief comes over me. It is quite extraordinary. I have never felt anything like this since starting this book, but I know it is my answer. This unexpected surge of emotion saw me recall another dream I had had some months previously.

It was a golden summer's day and I watched as a man walked across the fields carrying a young girl on his shoulders. She was small and fair with a crown of daisies on her head, and I knew they were making their way to Hay. I felt her love for this quiet, gentle man, as I did his calloused hands warm upon her ankles. She felt loved, safe, and secure, and just behind them walked the mother. Fair and petite like the young girl, she was smiling, and I got a sense of great happiness in that moment.

It was only a short dream, but enough to give me what I believe was a glimpse of Mary's childhood. So, to have finally found her parents was extremely emotive as was the knowledge she had been much loved.

But back to the will. Rebecca had been busy. By now we also had the burial records for St. Peter's Church in Glasbury and these made for an interesting read! Not least for the discovery that far from being laid to rest in a pauper's grave, Mary's parents had their own plot and their own headstone! More money! More expense! An estate worth eight hundred quid, if you please, and the price of a solicitor to administer it. Wow, you'd be forgiven for thinking Mr and Mrs Morgan were quite the Rockefellers off their day, being simple country folk and all . . .

Suffice to say my instinct went into overdrive. Since finding the will, a whole new world had opened up and the Morgan clan were now in full clamour. Hints, clues, and outright facts that could be checked, cross referenced and recorded. Indeed, Rees had been so meticulous in his final will and testament, anyone would think he'd left a trail!

Maybe he did. So, what did we have so far?

Well, we knew that Rees was born in 1761 and died in 1828. We knew he began life in Llandefalle and that was my next call. So, imagine the dismay when upon further enquiry, the parish records are missing.

Missing?

Of all the church records these were the most important, not least for the hope it would link in to Francis. Most inconvenient and a major blow but apparently this is not uncommon.

Lost, destroyed, or eaten by local wildlife, perhaps? Take your pick.

Or did Rees like Francis just fall out of the sky!

I eyed up a trip to Llandefalle. In the absence of church records, a graveyard reccy was urgently needed so I thought I'd make a day of it. I arranged to meet the Madonna in Hay so we could travel up together and grab lunch afterwards. It's early November and a beautiful morning, and anticipation was running high. I'd sojourned so many churchyards over the past few months, would this one give up its secrets?

It was with great delight when we pulled up outside the church in Llandefalle. Pretty and unspoilt it really felt like we were stepping back in time. From the old lynch gate to a cluster of ramshackle buildings, there was a real sense of remoteness and history.

The church of St. Matthew didn't disappoint either. A beautiful lime-washed building that looks out over the most breath-taking views. We were both very taken with this haven of tranquillity off the beaten track. Before beginning the search, I nipped down to the lower part of the graveyard so I could take some photos of the church. I wasn't there a minute when I could hear the Madonna calling.

'What is it?' I called before taking another picture. She called again and this time I heard it. Something about the Morgans!

I hotfooted it as best I could over the uneven ground. Could this be it? Could this be them?

So much depended on finding Rees's family. His father, his

mother, sisters, brothers. Mary's grandparents, uncles, aunts!

I stumbled over to where the Madonna was studying some headstones with a big smile on her face. Small wonder, indeed, they were Morgans, and she had found them!

No faded, weathered slabs of stone with barely legible writing to transcribe, either. But well-defined unmistakable script! The names rolled before my eyes and my heart leaped.

William Morgan, Ann Morgan, David Morgan.

Finally! Mary's family had been here all along waiting quietly in their final sleep.

I couldn't have been any more thrilled if we'd found the Holy Grail!

Together we checked the remaining gravestones but found no more of interest. Now to go and pay our respects and give thanks for this fortuitous development.

Inside St. Matthews we were greeted by the most stunning poppy display that wreathed the simple and yet poignant interior. Once again, it was like stepping back in time.

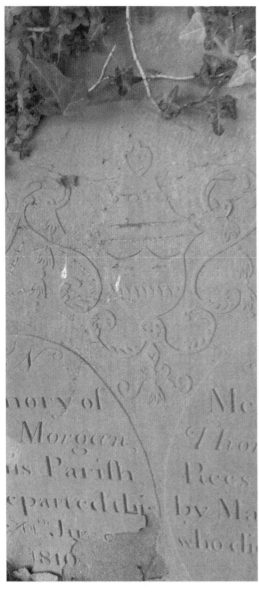

Of all the churches I visited throughout this project, this one, and St. Cewydd's of Aberedw, moved me the most. There is something about these old places of worship that retain the residual of past lives, and to think that Mary's father had been blessed in this very place.

Before we left, I went back to the Morgans grave to say goodbye. There was a warmth in my heart as I reached out and touched William Morgan's stone. And as I began to pull away something caught my attention. Something so subtle, yet strangely familiar and I leaned forward for a closer look. The warmth I'd been feeling receded as a sudden chill prickled the back of my neck.

Was that? Could it be?

As I pulled back the tendrils of ivy, I felt my eyes go wide. I could scarcely believe what I was seeing, yet there was no mistake.

I hadn't spent hours gazing at Mary's headstone without absorbing something of the detail, and the motif on William's stone was practically the same!

As my finger traced the fine design another part of the puzzle quietly fell into place.

The second headstone for Mary has been the subject of much speculation since it mysteriously appeared a dozen or so years after her death. No one knew for sure who had planted it. Some say the people of Presteigne, others, a member of the clergy guilt-ridden at her fate.

The most prevalent view, however, was that her folks had stolen into the churchyard one night, determined to leave a tribute of their own.

A message that was as accusatory as it was defiant; 'He that is without sin among you. Let him cast a stone at her . . . '

But Mary's family were supposed to be poor, remember? Unknown and obscure and yet here we are, Morgan headstones popping up here, there, and everywhere!

On the drive back to Hay I remained astounded. I don't know what excited me more, the gravestones or their engravings. But one thing I did know for sure, the dead were speaking loudly, and I was all ears!

Armed with this new information Rebecca found the artisan who had worked the stones. His name was Thomas Ravenhill and he lived in Glasbury, which means he would have been known to both Rees and Elizabeth. Besides, he'd also engraved the stone for Rees' father up in Llandefalle too, had he not?

Yes and no.

The elaborate engraving on the second of Mary's headstone bears an uncanny resemblance to that of the 'Morgan' gravestones in St. Matthew's, Llandefalle.

The work was Ravenhill's. But after a quick flurry of tree-building on Ancestry, it soon seemed likely that William Morgan was the uncle of Rees not the father!

They also had a son called Rees, as well as the one called David who lay next to them. Turned out Uncle William had also left a will and his land could be seen on the Tithe Maps. Indeed, William had quite a bit of land near Llanstephen (Llansteffan), south of the church, and some properties listed in the will were passed on to his sons.

Interestingly, most of the land later became Wilkins (de Winton) land after Mary's death. Interesting, indeed . . .

So where was Mary's grandfather? I searched high and low, different churches, various burial records, but thanks to the missing records the brick wall was firmly in place. So frustrating after the joy surmounting the last one.

Not to be outdone, however, we spread the net further, and a picture began to emerge. Far from being impoverished peasants, the Morgans were big into wool. So big, in fact, they were the largest wool producers in the whole of Wales! Since the search for Francis, Rebecca had always had an eye to the Drover's roads and with this latest development her nous had been vindicated. Below as taken from Welsh Drover's Road Walk*

"From the 1700s onwards, a man could only apply for a droving licence if he was over 30, married and a householder. Drovers were

well rewarded for their skill, typically being paid two or three times as much as a humble labourer. They appear to have had several roles beyond transporting animals.

Until the 19th century the few roads that existed in Wales were impassable for most of the year, so there was very little communication between the scattered hamlets, and the drovers were relied on as news carriers between the farms. Legend has it that it was from drovers returning from London that the Welsh learned of the victory at Waterloo in 1815."

Drovers often acted as bankers. Well-to-do families regularly asked the drovers to undertake financial commissions in London; and many a rich man's son, making his way to a career in law at the Temple or the Inns of Court, would rely on money brought by the cattle men to settle his lodgings account. Yet movement of cash is always a risky business in wild country. To avoid the risk of loss, the drovers started an effective banking system at the end of the 18th century. Anyone wanting a drover to deal with a financial transaction in London put the money into the drover's Welsh bank. The drover then paid the London bills in cash out of the sums he realised on the sale of the cattle.

The Morgans had plied their trade from the Nantmel Valley down to Brecon, Hay-on-Wye and beyond. Their propensity to move around saw them marry and settle all over Radnorshire. Rees' clan came from Llandefalle and Llanstephen and had been prosperous sheep farmers and landowners.

Now that we had Mary's father and what we could find of his family in the bag, small wonder he lived to a ripe old age. Sixty-seven years, no less! An exceptional age for those times. But if you think that's impressive, Elizabeth's tenure is even more remarkable!

I've deliberately left Elizabeth until last and with good reason, because this is where things start to get REALLY interesting!

According to Rees' will, his wife had passed away six months before he did in 1827. On her gravestone, her date of birth is given as 1742.

Now, I'm no mathematician, but it doesn't take a genius to spot the glaring anomaly here. Because if this date is correct, then not only was Elizabeth nineteen years older than Rees, but she would have been forty-six when she had Mary!

Forty-six!

Seriously?

Not impossible, but certainly more than debatable. Didn't women in those days usually die well before that age? Ill-health, disease, childbirth, poverty, all were contributors to an early grave. But if the figures are to be believed, then Mary's mother had lived to the AMAZING age of eighty-five!

Wow! I was suitably impressed but highly sceptical. Despite my initial misapprehension that Mary had a younger brother, (our Francis), it was quite clear from the will that there were no other surviving children from the marriage.

The fact Elizabeth had managed to conceive at that age at all was nothing short of a miracle! But hey-ho, things were about to get more interesting yet!

During **Elizabeth's** lifetime, people in **Wales** with the last name **Beavan** had an average of

6 children

Elizabeth was one of
5 children
born in **Glasbury** in **1734**

49
—YEARS OLD—

Elizabeth lived to be **93**, while the average lifespan of other people born in **1734** was **49**.

To illustrate further, below is a chart taken from: Graham Mooney. Johns Hopkins University | JHU · Institute of the History of Medicine Phd

1730s	18.2	1820s	34.4
1740s	17.6	1830s	36.9
1750s	20.1	1840s	36.7
1760s	20.5	1850s	36.1
1770s	21.6	1860s	36.4
1780s	25.5	1870s	39.1
1790s	27.5	1880s	41.4
1800s	28.0	1890s	42.6
1810s	32.4	1900s	49.0

Sources: Landers, 1993: 171, Table 5.4 (1730s to 1820s, reproduced by permission of Cambridge University Press); Woods, 2000: 369, Table 9.4 (1830s and 1840s, reproduced by permission of Cambridge University Press); remaining values calculated from the relevant Registrar-General's *Decennial Supplements*.

As you can see, women back then would be lucky to reach thirty-four never mind forty-four! Yet Elizabeth was still fertile when most women, if they'd been lucky enough to reach that age, would be going through the menopause. If I'd been told that the stork himself had delivered Mary, I couldn't have been more surprised. Or disbelieving.

So where did Elizabeth hail from? As Mary was baptised in Llowes naturally I turned my attention there. Like Morgan, Beavan is also a common surname, sometimes spelt as Bevan. And if I thought I had problems with Rees, trying to find Elizabeth would take me to a whole new level!

An exploration of St. Meiligs turned up a lot of Beavan's — but not the ones I wanted. Eventually Rebecca found them in Glasbury, but here the plot doth thicken!

In the parish records there was no entry for an Elizabeth Beavan born in 1742 – but there was for 1734!

What new devilry was this? Because if this was our Elizabeth, she'd have had twenty-seven years on Rees, delivered Mary at the grand age of fifty-four, and lived until she was NINETY-THREE!

That's not far off a century!

Rebecca checked and double-checked, but the only Beavan birth she could find for 1742 was a Sybil Beavan, who, it transpires comes up as Elizabeth's younger sister!

Just what on earth was going on?

Had the stonemason got the dates mixed up when he engraved the stone? Such instances were not unheard of, but the numbers are so far removed from each other, how could 34 be confused for 42? It all seemed very odd to me. So far nothing had been straightforward in the search for Mary's kin.

But we did find Elizabeth's brother, Laurence, who is buried in Llowes. Sybil, however, seemed to disappear off the face of the earth, which only served to intrigue me more.

Why did Elizabeth have her sister's birthdate on her headstone? I wasn't buying a slip of the ol' chisel of a careless craftsman. This, I believe, was a deliberate ploy to obfuscate, the whole history around Elizabeth - or should that be Sybil?

Confused? Join the club!

No one had written about Mary's parents before, and no wonder! Between missing records and dodgy birth dates, you'd be forgiven for balking at the first fence. Yet, the whole age, identity discrepancies aren't the only quirk in all of this. Mary, as we know, was born in March 1788 and in the parish book, her parents are recorded as Rees Morgan and 'Elisabeth', yet they didn't marry until seven years later in 1795!

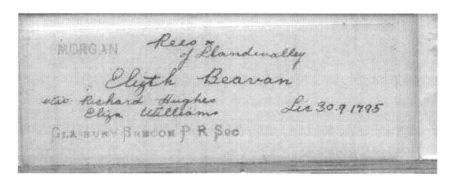

This wasn't unusual in those days, granted, but if they were a couple and he was Mary's father, what took them so long? Why a seven-year delay? Suffice to say, we could find no other children of the marriage.

I always thought it odd that Mary was baptised in Llowes when Rees and Elizabeth were always associated with Glasbury.

With St. Peter's church on the doorstep, you'd think they'd have christened Mary there, not in the neighbouring parish. So, what does all this tell us?

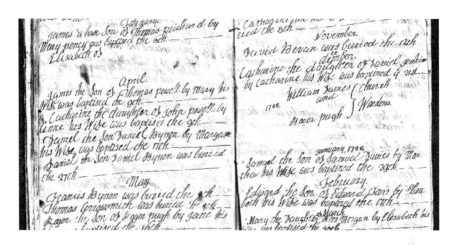

Above the record of Mary's baptism from St. Meilig's Church, Llowes

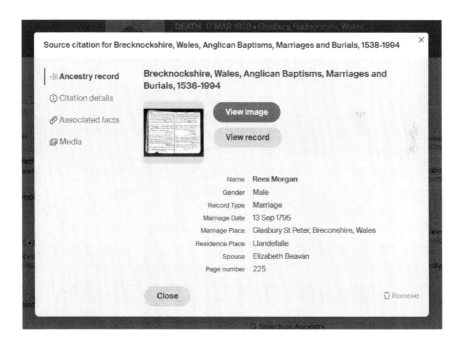

The age-gap, the date anomalies, the miraculous womb of Mary's mother all point to a different version of events that perhaps no one has wanted to address until now.

Could it be that Mary was not the natural daughter of Rees? His marriage to Elizabeth part of an arrangement so as to provide her bastard child with a father? But who would have had the means and the power to make such an association viable?

Can we assume Elizabeth had also worked up at the castle, and had, by chance, dallied with a fellow servant and got pregnant? Or had she been seduced by the Master of the House before being packed off to Rees with a nice lump sum?

These things happened, didn't they? This was not an unusual occurrence among the upper classes. Look back in history and you'll find examples by the dozen!

It doesn't take a genius to see that something is seriously awry with Mary's parentage here. Based on this an idea began to form. Or maybe it was more of a feeling. I mentioned it to Rebecca and Demelsa as far back as Summer 2022 because the thought kept returning like a whispering ghost. It was one hell of a hypothesis to make, yet it would explain why the baby was killed and why Mary had to die.

There are some things in the natural order that are not allowed to be, much less in the eyes of God. There are scandals and then there are scandals. Could an ill-fated liaison be at the heart of this? The coming-together of two young people borne of lust and ignorance, oblivious to shared blood until it was too late?

As I began this chapter with a dream, it seems pertinent I conclude it on the same other-worldly note. Of all the dreams and impressions I've had about Mary, this was the most extraordinary.

I am watching Mary's trial, and she is stood in the dock. The two servants who testified against her are returning to their seats when Mary suddenly begins shouting. She is furious and accuses them of bearing false witness against her. The older of the two women turns back, her face twisted in anger as she shouts: 'I warned you what would happen if you carried on, that you'd end up like Anne Boleyn!'

Dream then switches to Mary being taken to a small room that is all white, almost clinical. At one end sits a very large modern-looking bathtub. (It looks like the one I had in the ensuite when I stayed in The Exchange Hotel, Cardiff. The room is called the Roald Dahl and had a strange atmosphere). I watch as Mary slumps to the floor and begins a conversation with a red spider that appears in the corner where the wall meets the ceiling. Mary is still angry and is holding forth about the situation she finds herself in.

Make of that what you will, but besides being the colour of passion, red is also for danger. And as for the spider. Spiders are clever, they weave and entrap. The white room and the bathtub; a whitewash. But it is the reference to the second wife of King Henry VIII that resonates the most.

For those of you unfamiliar with the story of Anne Boleyn, it is indeed a tragic tale. Besides the charges of adultery stacked against her, she was also accused of incest with her brother. That there was another queen-in-waiting and she'd been a victim of trumped-up charges is for you to decide. But when the power of a King and his men move against you, there's only one way the verdict is going to go, and she was found guilty.

Anne lost her head by the sword. Mary ended up with hers through a rope that choked the very life out of her. The added irony in all of this, is that whilst Anne died for failing to provide an heir, Mary was executed for the very fact she had a child!

Which brings us on to the all-important question; did she kill the baby?

Let us take that walk with Mary.

Let us step 'back along that treacherous path' that led her to her doom, and where better than Maesllwch Castle, where it all began.

It was common for young girls to go into service from the age of twelve to their early teens. What wasn't so common, however, was to secure the position of Under-Cook by the age of sixteen. Yet Mary Morgan had somehow bypassed the years of drudge as a scullery, kitchen, or even under-dairy maid, to arrive at this prestigious position in record time! No mean feat for a mere slip of a girl unless she was singled out and favoured, of course!

Her employer, Walter Wilkins (Senior), MP for Radnorshire and vast estate owner, had made his fortune in the East India Company, before spreading his wealth throughout the land. Ironworks, South Wales canals, not to mention the family bank in Brecon, he made good on his investments and lived a comfortable life in the lofty heights of Maesllwch.

He married Catherine Augusta Haywood, and their marriage was fruitful producing three daughters and the all-important heir, Walter (Junior), as mentioned in Rees Morgan's will.

Such a large estate required numerous servants, and it was noted at the time that Walter Senior retained no less six male servants instead of the usual two. Make of that what you will, and so here Mary found herself in the kitchens and with her own bun in the oven at the tender age of fifteen.

The year is 1804 and any woman, or in this case, child, unfortunate to find themselves unmarried and in such a predicament, the future is bleak for there is no help at hand for single, expectant mothers. Trapped in this nightmare, and not always of their own making, desperate thoughts lead to desperate measures as tiny, innocent lives were snuffed out or left to the elements.

Those fortunate to have supportive families could expect succour for mother and child. But poverty was rife and adding an extra mouth to feed was not an option. Sadly, infanticide was common and the only way out, as many of these women saw it, was to take a life so that they could save theirs. A life for a life. That was the reality. Thus did Mary find herself in this position before committing the terrible deed.

They said.

I have to say, as someone who has worked extensively in hospitality (all captured in glorious detail in my memoir 'Custard 'n' Service'!), I find it impossible to believe that not one person who worked with Mary realised she was pregnant! Hot kitchen, under pressure, cooking to schedule, things going wrong, people around you – how on earth did her condition go unnoticed?

Can one assume there was no morning sickness, then? No penchant for certain foods and a sudden aversion to others? Did no one notice the frequent trips to the privy, as her bladder called the shots? Or what about fatigue and mood changes, not to mention a steadily growing belly. She is described as a slight little thing – must also have been one hell of a magician to have hidden that bump!

The work schedule in those days would have been gruelling and demanding. Besides preparing food for the rest of the staff, there would have been houseguests and entertainments, not to mention the family to take care of. Busy household. Busy girl! I don't know how she did it!

Actually, I do.

Having laboured in hectic hotel kitchens, (International golf tournament, Royal St. David's, Harlech. Five hundred crew members, The Rolling Stones, Cardiff), when you're grinding every day in close proximity with your work mates, any change in behaviour, no matter how small, is spotted straight away.

And let's not forget that Mary would have sat down daily and broke bread with these people. Talked with them, laughed with them. Yet, no one suspected a thing. Seriously?

Admittedly, the thick dress of the time would have afforded some cover to her growing midriff. But as she approached full term during the warmer months, with lighter clothing you'd think her condition would have been obvious. Besides, there are other signs when a woman is with child, the change in her complexion, the lustre of her hair. We're talking Mary Morgan here, not the Virgin Mary, and it is my belief that they knew.

They knew but they said nothing.

For someone so young and attractive to take up such a key role must have ruffled a feather or two. The hierarchy below stairs in all big houses would have meant that her elevation, not to mention her condition, was doubtless the subject of much gossip. Servants see and hear everything!

So, why didn't someone pipe up?

Perhaps the shift in the family dynamics might have had something to do with it. Walter Senior's wife had passed away in 1784 which meant the house was without a mistress and had been for some time. The children, as was the norm, would have been left to the care of nursemaids and nannies. Walter Junior would have been just seven years old when his mother died. His father didn't remarry, but one must wonder if a man of his calibre did not seek out female company. As Lord of the Manor, he could have his pick, and by the time Mary's storm hit the house, he'd been widowed for twenty years.

There's no doubt Walter Wilkins Senior was a busy man. With so many ventures on his plate, not to mention Parliamentary duties, seedy goings-on below stairs would have been well off his radar. That's what senior members of the household were for; to oversee the staff and deal with undesirable behaviours.

So, in the absence of the Lady of the House, and when Mary's condition became increasingly clear; who you gonna call? It's a delicate situation but not an unfamiliar one. Yet in this case, maybe no one was willing to lift their heads above the parapet. Perhaps the situation was more delicate than we think. And where is Mary's mother in all of this?

Born of Thomas and Mary Prothero, Elizabeth Bevan grew up just down the road and obviously hadn't gone far. Indeed, we found her parents as living in Ffordd Fawr, but with so many dwellings under the same name, we couldn't ascertain which one. As far as we could tell, however, Elizabeth's surviving siblings had remained local, although the only grave that could be found was of her brother, Laurence, in Llowes.

And then there was her father, Mary's grandfather, Thomas, who lived a long life and wasn't buried until 1809; four years after they hung his granddaughter. As for Mary Prothero, Elizabeth's mother, unfortunately there were too many of the same name to pinpoint with any accuracy. Maybe one day, eh?

On Rees' side, however, Mary had three uncles and one auntie, whose children are named in the will. So, it's not as though her family were scattered to the four winds. They were local, they were prosperous, and they were obviously close-knit.

Add to all of this, the fact that as a late (very!) child, and the only one; would it be unreasonable to assume that Mary had a close relationship with her mother? As the only fruit of her marriage, you'd think she'd have been precious and doted upon?

I believe she was.

Besides, Rees wasn't short of a bob or two, surely there would have been room to spare at the 'Morgan Inn'? There was certainly no shortage of family members who could have quietly taken her in. Yet, this young girl chose to risk everything by not telling the two people in the world who, in all likelihood, would have stuck by her.

It doesn't make sense, and in turn raises the next question: Did her parents know?

Had Mary taken them into her confidence? Or did they suspect but preferred to bury their heads in the sand.

I guess that depends on who the father was.

It all comes down to whose seed had been planted in that belly. And so, what promises were made?

You can well imagine the ones that were said as the seduction got underway. But what was said afterwards when it was clear there was going to be three lives in the pairing? What sweet words of assurance that could so fill a girl's head to believe she was safe? But then, if we refer to the fate of Anne Boleyn . . . She thought she was safe as well, didn't she?

What's more, have you ever had to try and reason with a sixteen-year-old girl in the throes of her first love? The stubbornness, the tantrums. Just because we've rewound two hundred years doesn't mean that behaviours and hormones have necessarily changed much – especially when it comes to self-assured young girls.

Ahhh Mary, was this you?

Would not listen to reason. Had faith in that age-old dream, the bane of many an innocent, gullible girl. How rosy the World looks when we see only the petals and not the thorns. But perhaps the thorns were much closer to the petals than they should have been. Maybe the guardians of this precious bloom tried to intervene, to distract and divert, but by then it was too late. A new rose was already growing and there was absolutely nothing they could do other than stand back and wait for the landslide that would bury them all . . .

Just a thought. A conjecture? Or maybe it was a dream.

Well, one thing's for certain, we can't change the past, but we can revisit that fateful day when Mary unleashed carnage on an innocent life. An act that put her on the map as one of history's most controversial baby-killers . . .

So, what happened?

According to the official version of events, on 23rd September, Mary became ill while at work in the kitchens. Unable to continue with her duties, she finally took herself up to the room she shared with under-dairy maid, Mary Meredith. It just so happened that her namesake had a free afternoon and went off to see her sister. But Mary wasn't completely forgotten. She was visited by the housekeeper, Mrs Simpson, who brought her a cup of warm wine. A bit later on, the Cook, Mrs Evelyn, also popped in with some tea, accompanied by another servant, Margaret Havard.

Sometime later, Mary's roommate returned but couldn't gain access because Mary had locked the door saying she wanted to rest and told the dairy maid to go downstairs. This Mary Meredith did, only to return with the Cook and Margaret Havard, both of whom accused Mary of delivering herself of a baby.

Apparently, Mary denied their claims vigorously for some time before finally confessing. She then showed them the baby she had stuffed inside the mattress with its head practically severed from its body.

Shocking, isn't it?

And absolutely heart-breaking.

That poor little one. The brutality of it. The violence. Could Mary not have found a more bloodless, less dramatic way of killing her baby? Was it necessary to have used such force when she could have simply smothered it in a blanket? This was an accomplished member of staff, remember. A young woman who could work under pressure and deliver in her role. That is in itself suggests more than a modicum of intelligence.

Therefore, riddle me this; why, after going through great pains to conceal her condition for so long, would she behave so recklessly in the final hour?

It doesn't make sense. Nine months of carefully planned subterfuge ruined in a few moments.

I have to say, though, prior to the dastardly deed, the staff members who check in on her are most solicitous, don't you think? A cup of wine, a dish of tea, I wonder if they also plumped her pillows while they were there . . .

Mrs Evelyn, Margaret Havard, Mary Meredith; it is these three fellow servants whose word against Mary would send her to her doom. Suffice to say, I will be looking at their statements in more detail. But in the meantime, what happened next?

Well, as you can well imagine, all hell broke loose and if this had been modern-day, I can see the headlines now: Murder in Maesllwch! Infanticide in the Castle! Servant Girl Slaughters Illegitimate Baby! Feel the shock, reel with horror, such a scandal!

But what if there was another scenario?

What if the version of events saw Mary taken to another part of the castle as she went into labour? What if the breaking of her waters as she stood in the kitchen saw no other course of action than to take just that. *Action.*

Picture it now, the scurrying about, the panic. The cuckoo in the nest that everyone had been ignoring is about to make an appearance. It is a secret that can be kept no longer. The master of the house must be told. The other members of staff must be told. The undercook is about to have a baby and it's going to be as welcome as the Devil himself.

Someone has to let the cat out the bag, but who is it going to be? Who's willing to walk into the lion's den and divulge the drama of this dirty little secret?

Your first thought might be the Cook, she was Mary's immediate superior, after all. But then, as the overall head of female staff shouldn't it be Mrs Simpson, the Housekeeper? This situation had happened under her watch, of course, and yet somehow this mere stripling of a girl had managed to fool them all!

The truth must come out, but who will be the messenger?

There can only be one man. The right-hand man. The ultimate servant who sits at the top of the tree and whose loyalty binds him to no other than his master.

So, as Mary brings forth her baby there's no time to bond as the squalling child is swiftly wrapped up and taken away. Taken away as Mary is soothed and the spinning of the web truly begins . . .

But back to the facts and the official version, because 'they said', remember?

According to the records Mary remained at Maesllwch for a fortnight so she could recover. The trauma of having given birth alone and then wielding the knife at that tender throat would have obviously taken its toll. And for that, no doubt she would have been moved to somewhere more quiet, somewhere away from the rest of the household so she could . . . recuperate and reflect . . .

To be fair, such attentiveness to her plight is to be commended. She was a callous, scheming, creature after all. Such compassion, and to one who had shown not an ounce towards that poor beleaguered child. Her own flesh and blood. You'd think they'd want to ship her out of the house at the earliest opportunity!

Yet there she languished for a whole two weeks, as the inquest was held, testimonies taken, and preparations got underway.

Indeed, no doubt the household of Maesllwch became a hive of activity. Within hours of the terrible event Walter Senior had sent word to the Coroner of Radnorshire, Hector Appleby Cooksey. This gentleman appears to be something of an enigma with, it was said, a keen interest in medieval mysteries, including alchemy. He obviously liked to put himself around a bit. Besides his role of Surgeon at Presteigne Gaol, at one time he'd also kept tap at the Radnorshire Arms. This fine old building once occupied by Christopher Hatton, a favourite of Elizabeth I (these Tudor connections just keep coming!) remains a hostelry to this day. Seems strange to think I have dined and discoursed in the very rooms Cooksey would have frequented. What little we could uncover about this man suggested an erudite individual who seemed to take his duties earnestly.

How earnest was he, however in the examination of Mary's baby?

I think it's fair to say he didn't bust a gut once Walter Senior put the call out. He took all of two days to get to Maesllwch where he would have seen the infant's body and determined the cause of death. Next it was his turn to put a call out. A Grand Jury was needed to sit for the all-important inquest. Their job was to reach a majority vote on whether there was a case to answer. But then with the poor baby's head all but hanging off, I don't suppose there was much opposition.

So, on the 25th September, two days after Mary committed her most heinous crime, twelve men who lived locally were sworn in by Thomas Beavan, a solicitor from Hay-on-Wye. Despite an extensive search to learn more about this learned man, with as many Bevans about as there were Morgans, we couldn't make a firm connection to Elizabeth. Another disappointment was met with the trusty twelve, for there are no names recorded that we are aware of, at least not publicly. I'd have given much to have known who they were, and how affiliated they were to Maesllwch. By this time the three witnesses, who were illiterate, had signed their statements with an X and these had been submitted to the hearing. After examining the evidence, including the baby's body, all that was left was for the Grand but nameless Jury to reach a decision and the die is cast.

"Coroners of Radnor on view of the body of a new-born female child upon the oath of Thomas Beavan, Esq, and with twelve other lawful men duly sworn and charged to inquire for our sovereign, and by what means the child came to her death, do upon their oath say that Mary Morgan late of the parish of Glazebury, a single woman, did on the 23rd day of September being big with child, afterward alone and secretly from her body did bring forth alive a female child, which by the laws and customs of this Kingdom was a bastard.

Mary Morgan, not having the fear of God before her eyes, but moved and seduced by the instigation of the Devil afterwards on the same day with force and arms on the child born alive, feloniously, wilfully and of her malice aforethought did make an assault with a certain penknife made of iron and steel of the value of sixpence which she, Mary Morgan, there had, and held in her right hand, the throat or neck of the child did strike and cut and gave the child one mortal wound of the length of three inches and the depth of one inch.

The child instantly dies so the Foreman of the Jury and fellows do say the child came to her death and not otherwise. In witness thereof the Coroner, as the Foreman of the Jurors on behalf of himself and the rest of his fellows in their presence have to this inquisition set their hands and seals this day, year and place mentioned.
Hector A. Cooksey, Coroner."

All seems pretty conclusive, the back of this document signed by Hugh Bold, the bailiff of Brecon – the only other individual named in these proceedings.

It is interesting to note the use of strong language used to infer the wicked nature of this girl. "... having no fear of God before her eyes..." Ignorant and godless. "... moved by the instigation of the Devil ..." weak, easily influenced.

Doubtless in such cases it was the language of the day, but it certainly paints Mary in the worst light possible. "... feloniously, wilfully, and of malice aforethought ..."

What a bad girl! Bad to the bone! All but damns her before she's even come to trial, don't you think!

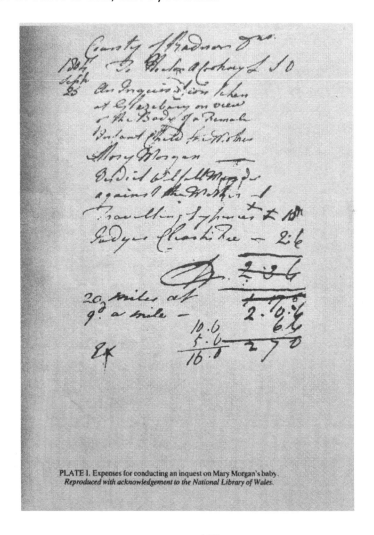

PLATE I. Expenses for conducting an inquest on Mary Morgan's baby. *Reproduced with acknowledgement to the National Library of Wales.*

On the 6th of October Mary was considered sufficiently recovered to move onto the next stage. This would be Presteigne Gaol, some twenty miles away and the seat of the County Assizes. There she would await her fate until the next sessions in the Spring of 1805. It would be a long haul. It would also be her last few months of life.

She didn't know that, of course. She had faith in the judicial system, as we all do, right? And besides, they'd stopped hanging woman for Infanticide quite some years ago. No doubt there had been reassurances. She would be punished, yes, but not with a death sentence. It's alright, Mary, it's a terrible thing that you did, but no need to worry, you won't hang . . . You can all but hear the echoes of those age-old voices as she was ushered into the horse-drawn wagon that would take her to prison.

It would have been a chilly, bone-rattling ride across the rugged roads through Painscastle and Gladestry as the fields of Llowes were left far behind. I've often wondered about that journey, and on one of my many graveside vigils I asked her.

After closing my eyes and waiting, I saw her huddled on a seat wrapped up in a blanket, her meagre belongings wrapped in a bundle. She wasn't in irons, but she wasn't alone. A big burly man who gave her a portion of his bread and cheese sat opposite her. There was no talking. No other impression other than she feels as though she's in a dream and is well and truly cowed.

After what must have seemed like an interminable journey, they finally reached Presteigne where a dank, rat-infested cell awaited her and a fellow prisoner by the name of Margaret Bird. I've often wondered about Mary's cell mate and what conversations they had during the long, dark hours. Did Mary break confidence and tell all? Or did she hold her peace?

Margaret was up on a charge of larceny in a dwelling place and was one of the three other prisoners that stood trial with Mary. Margaret pleaded not guilty and was duly acquitted.

Interestingly there are 'Birds' still amongst us in Presteigne. Lorna of the Sandwich Shop, site of the old Shire Hall married one. I've tried to link the connection in but in this case, the Jury remains out.

Poor Mary, the conditions she now found herself was a far cry from the comforts of the warm kitchens at Maesllwch. It must have been a rude awakening, but her basic needs were catered for, and she was fed and watered.

This is one of the two doors that is all that remains of the old Presteigne Gaol. The current cells of the Judge's Lodgings were built well after Mary's incarceration, but the doors are from her time.

So, as she sat in the dubious fastness of Presteigne Gaol, friendless and alone, where were her parents? There is no reference to them visiting her at all, except for the night before her execution when Rees was allegedly plotting to spring her out.

Quiet, mild-mannered Rees Morgan?

Hmmm . . . Wouldn't have been too difficult, mind. The gaol was so dilapidated some inhabitants had made good their escape on more than one occasion!

What must've been going through Mary's mind as she huddled in her cell and dreamed of freedom.

Did she think about the baby?

The trauma of its birth, the anger of the household? Or was she comforted by the knowledge that all was in hand; she just had to be a good girl, take a hit for the family and all would be well, as the Angel of Death kept company.

With the inquest now out of the way, things are in motion. By the time the Great Sessions came to town, Presteigne is more than ready. This was a massive event, and the Judge and his entourage make nothing less than a flamboyant entry with pikeman, officials, and coin to be spent.

For the locals, this is party-time and a welcome distraction from the daily toil. So, as events got underway, Presteigne echoed with sounds as bears and cockerels fought for their lives, as folk made merry and ripped up the town.

For Mary the time had finally come. As it was for the other three prisoners who would be tried alongside her. Tension must have been palpable as they waited in the dark confines of their cells. They would have heard the sounds of celebration going on and a quickening in the step of their jailor, as the day of reckoning drew nearer. Fine, death or deportation? No one knew for certain until they were brought up before the Judge, and what a character he was! George Hardinge, man of many and flowery words, whose background and education couldn't have been any far more removed from a simple sheep dealer's daughter.

As an MP and senior JP, he liked to keep his finger on the pulse and could boast powerful connections from the political to royalty. He was, for want of a better expression, a mover and shaker of his day and quite a hit with the ladies.

The Petty Jury that were no less blessed each in their own way.

Image courtesy of The National Library of Wales.

Apparently, it was not uncommon for some members of the Petty Jury to have also sat on the Grand Jury. This was the initial hearing that the Coroner had put together two days after the incident, as we know, and at no small speed! There was just one small stipulation, however; all members had to be landowners and notwithstanding, would have been empowered by their position and filthy rich!

A list of the illustrious gentlemen can be found in more detail in Peter Ford's excellent book; Mary Morgan of Presteigne: Victim or Villain of Infanticide. Suffice to say, all parties would have been known to each other.

Third name on the list is Walter Wilkins (Junior), with a small cross next to his name. There has always been uncertainty as to whether he was actually there or not. But if he had been present, what torture that would have been for that young girl seeing him sat in judgement. Eyes cast down or hard with hate. Lips that had once kissed and whispered words of honey now tightly set. Can you even begin to imagine it? Hell hath no fury like a woman scorned? Hell hath no torment than a woman loved and abandoned unto death!

So, on that note, let us go back to the morning of April 9th, 1805, when Mary and her fellow prisoners were escorted from their cells and taken to those below the Shire Hall in readiness for trial. Now it all would have felt very real as the court began to fill up and the street noise reached a crescendo. Nerve-wracking to say the least, yet by the time Mary was pulled up before the Judge she was, by all accounts, remarkably calm - even when the death sentence was imposed.

Now why would this be?

After months of having to endure deprivation, not to mention her own thoughts, you'd expect some level of anxiety to be present in her demeanour. Yet, despite standing before the bench, with Walter Wilkins Senior himself sat right next to the Judge, she was as cool as they come. Almost to the point of inertia. Just the fact her former employer was directly in her sights, you'd think, would give some cause for concern. She had spilt blood in this man's house, after all. Brought scandal and speculation to the family name. Took the life of an innocent baby . . .

Murderer.

With no shame.

She did have the foresight, however, to look to her defence, and apparently asked Walter Junior for a guinea to pay for it. How was she able to make this request if he wasn't there? Or did she ask him when she was confined at Maesllwch? Neither are plausible scenarios, and I can't imagine any contact being allowed once the key turned in that lock. Besides, the request was turned down, and if it wasn't by Walter Junior, then maybe it was his father. Did she ask Walter Senior? Embarrass him by tendering her request before the whole court? Or was the appeal made privately in a last-ditch effort for help?

I guess we'll never know the full truth, but given Walter Senior was there in the court, it wouldn't be unfeasible.

Fortunately, chivalry wasn't completely dead, as a knight in shining armour by the name of Charles Rogers, offered up the guinea for her defence. An interesting anecdote in view of the fact he was such an important personage - the High Sheriff, no less! This gesture of kindness touched me deeply. Or was it a less than subtle offer of support?

My mojo said there may have been more to this. I'm sure not all members of the nobility rub along, and I wondered if there had been bad blood between the Wilkins and himself.

With this in mind, I did try to contact his descendent who still resides at the family seat in Knighton. I was advised the best way to get his attention was to write him a 'quirky' letter. Unfortunately, due to time constraints and postal strikes, I couldn't leave it to chance.

The other option was to just arrive at the front door, and so I set out one day to find Stanage Park only to get lost up in the hills. I did bump into a Morgan though, when I stopped to ask directions.

A very nice chap who welds and digs graves for a living! After a family briefing it seemed he wasn't related to Mary, but he did give me directions to the estate, and his parting shot was that Mary had the last laugh when her grave became a part of consecrated ground.

To touch further on this, after Mary's execution her body was taken and buried in a quiet unconsecrated corner of the rector's garden. Sometime later, no one seems to know the exact date, the garden became part of the graveyard and so we find Mary as she lies there today.

After my chat with Mr Morgan, I understood that turning up unannounced would not be to open arms, so if you ever get to read this, Mr Coltman-Rogers, thank you on behalf of the family and we still owe you a quid!

And so back to the courtroom and what happened next?

Mary had the means for her defence, yet we see nothing of it. Not a jot. Not an iota. Absolutely nada. Yet, a solicitor called Richard Beavan from Hay (another one), took the coin, and did . . . what exactly?

What else? What was said? Where are his words, that is, if he even pleaded for her case! And was he in some way related? These Beavan's just keep popping up, yet we are unable to link them into Mary's mother's family. More frustrating is to know that despite Mary having the means for a defence, we can find no record of it.

Plenty about her, though, eh? No shortage of statements, hearsay and most compelling of all, the admission from her own lips as to why she took the knife to that baby.

So, let's move on to then, shall we? Let's look at this plethora of information starting with the testimonies of the three women who knew Mary well; had worked with her, ate with her, conversed, instructed and, as per the under-dairymaid, slept in the same room as her.

All servants. All paid hands. The hired help, whose livelihoods depended on the whim of the master and which way the wind blew. This was the norm back in the day, and there's no reason to expect things were any different at Maesllwch.

The first to give evidence was Margaret Havard, who had been brought in to cover Mary's shift that night. This information seems to suggest that she lived locally and had helped in a similar capacity before. What I find interesting is that it is Margaret, not the Cook, who is the first to give evidence. Mrs Evelyn is an established senior member of staff, yet she is superseded by one who is not.

Why would this be?

Perhaps Patricia Parris, formerly of The Radnorshire Society of Transactions, can help us with that. She had much to say about Margaret Havard in her unpublished manuscript. Indeed, she even went as far as to suggest jealousy on Margaret's part towards Mary, due to the younger woman's position.

How Ms Parris came to this conclusion, we can only hazard a guess; but she pulls no punches in her rendition, and you have to ask yourself why?

What did she know that we didn't?

The fact Mary was favoured would no doubt have been of umbrage to an older woman who perhaps had coveted the role for herself. Job security up at the big castle would have been paramount at a time of great poverty, especially for an unmarried woman.

As the saying goes; there's no smoke without fire, and for my part, I'm with Patricia. Just wish we could have met to have chewed the fat on that one.

As statements go, Margaret's is a bit haphazard, to say the least, with much emphasis on Mary's fury, referring to it not once, but twice. Talk about putting the boot in. Just another tick against the nasty, ill-tempered girl well-versed in deceit.

Poor Mary, I guess she didn't have any redeeming qualities for her work colleague to speak about her thus, and so on that note, over to Ms Havard: -

"Margaret Havard came to Walter Wilkins, Esq. to assist the cook in place of Mary Morgan who was taken ill on Sunday 23rd September 1804. Saw her about four o'clock in the afternoon being then very ill, returned to her quarters at seven of the clock then charged her with being very like a woman in labour which she strongly denied, and was very angry at being asked the question. She desired the cook not to suffer any person to go upstairs to her for an hour... fastened by the under-dairymaid, the witness returned with the cook and then charged the said Mary with having delivered herself of a child. She strongly denied it with bitter oaths for some time, when she owned that she had delivered herself of a child which was in the underbed, cut open, deep sunk in the mattress, with the child's head nearly divided from the body, supposed by a penknife which was found by the cook bloody under the pillow of the same bed. The morning following being Monday the 24th
of September 1804.
Witness the mark of Margaret Havard."

Next up is the Cook, and I have to say, I'm very impressed with Mrs Evelyn. If I thought Judge Hardinge had a finger on the pulse, his was nothing compared to that of this woman! Seemed she would play a key role in the uncovering of Mary's villainy. How commendable, quite the Miss Marple.

Yet despite working in close proximity with her undercook, she didn't notice she was pregnant.

Her statement is as follows: -

"Elizth. Evelyn cook to Walter Wilkins Esq. of Maeslugh in the County of Radnor desposeth that opn Sunday morning the 23rd September, 1804, her fellow servant, Mary Morgan, under-cook to the above Walter Wilkins Esq. was taken ill about two o'clock of the morning and continued her work till near one o'clock when she went to bed and about three o'clock in the afternoon. Mrs Simpson, the housekeeper gave her some warm wine. Between

six and seven she had some tea when witness left her. About half an hour later returned and found said Mary Morgan in bed (who lay upon two beds) and then charged her with having delivered herself of a child from some particular circumstance which she saw, when she strongly denied it for half an hour or thereabouts and then owned she had delivered herself of a child which was in the underbed cut open, amongst the feathers, with the head nearly divided from the body supposed by a penknife which was found by the witness under the pillows of the same bed the day following being Monday the 24th September 1804.
Witness the mark of Elizth. Evelyn."

The first thing that struck me about this statement is that the two principal witnesses seem to have a lot of time on their hands. When you'd think they'd be hard at it in the kitchens, they're popping back and forth keeping tabs on the undercook. I'm assuming the servants' quarters would have been right at the top of the castle. Quite a trek for such a senior member of staff when she could have sent a maid instead. Added to which, interestingly, it is Margaret Harvard who is the first one up those stairs. The fact she had been specifically brought in to help the Cook would suggest they were busy. Yet, there she is at four o'clock checking in on Mary who hadn't been in her room an hour. Why the interest?

Next up the stairs is Cook.

Mrs Evelyn, with the afore-mentioned cup of tea, visits Mary between six and seven in the evening. I'm just amazed she and Margaret Havard could spare the time, but hey-ho.

Cook's recollections of time are also vague to say the least, '...between six and seven...'. As someone whose working life is dependent on the clock, wouldn't she have known?

She is slightly more specific, however, when she returned to check on Mary, 'About half an hour later...' All a bit disjointed, yet it seems to suggest they knew something.

And let us not forget Mrs Simpson, who for some strange reason was not required to make a statement. According to Mrs Evelyn, the Housekeeper had given Mary some warm wine.

What time was this?

Before Mary retired to her room '...around three o'clock...' or did Mrs Simpson take it up to her afterwards?

Again, precision is found wanting. Either way, I like to think it was a gesture borne of a kindly disposition. Shame we never get to hear any more about this lady, and you have to ask why not...?

As the most senior member of female staff, even over the Cook, one would naturally assume she'd have been in the thick of it. Ensuring the welfare of all the female staff was fundamental to her job. The undercook is ill and has taken to her bed. Such is her condition; Cook and her replacement are chary enough to keep an eye on her despite the call of duty.

I thought they were busy!

So where was Mrs Simpson in all of this? Why wasn't she at the helm of the unfolding crisis, supporting her staff, but more importantly attending to Mary?

Yet, her only role is the passing of a cup of wine before she exits the stage, never to be heard of again.

Odd! Bizarre! And, in my opinion, downright suspicious . . .

But back to the Cook and her damming indictment because the timings bother me. A lot.

According to her statement, on Sunday 23rd September, Mary became ill at two o'clock in the morning. Seems a strange time to toiling away in the kitchen when one would assume the entire household would be asleep – including the servants. But without more information, one can only guess there might have been something going on at Maesllwch that required all hands-on deck. The Harvest, a shooting party, a celebration of some kind, perhaps? But what was so pressing that Mary wasn't abed?

And what devotion to duty that this young girl could stay awake and work until one o'clock the following afternoon! I know servants worked long hours in those days, but was she allowed any sleep the Saturday night? Or maybe she'd had a late start or even an afternoon nap before such a gruelling shift? Suffice to say I'll stop at breakfast in bed, but it does make you wonder.

So, if we are to take the timings at face value, Mary would have still been at her duties right through until the end of day – that being the Sunday night – that's practically 48 hours on your feet! Or rather hers.

Hmmm . . .

I make much of the timings for a very good reason, because in the next statement by Mary's roommate there is no mention of any. At all. This strikes me as rather odd in view of the fact it is with Mary Meredith that things really kick off.

As under-dairymaid, you get the impression she is of no importance whatsoever. Indeed, any reference to her is almost as brief as it is with Mrs Simpson. Remember this paragraph, will you? Make a note, but in the meantime, her testimony is as follows: -

"Desposeth that she was under-dairymaid with Walter Wilkins, Esq. at Maeslugh in the County of Radnor that returning home from a visit to her sisters on Sunday evening the 23rd September 1804 she went upstairs to change her clothing to the room with the said Mary Morgan, but not in the same bed, when she found the door fastened, and called to Mary Morgan to open the door, which she refused, and desired the said witness to go down as she thought she could have some sleep.

Witness the mark of Mary Meredith."

A couple of things stand out here. Firstly, what time did Ms Meredith return exactly because I don't see it in her statement. Are we to deduce her time of arrival from the testimony of Mrs Evelyn, as being sometime after seven o'clock? Which meant Mary must have locked the door straight after the Cook had brought up the tea. Why was this not logged or even considered important enough to be included in Mary's Meredith's statement?

Secondly, and most importantly of all; why would Mary risk her roommate, and other staff uncovering her situation by taking to her bed? Rather defeats the object when you think she'd managed to conceal her condition for nine months, only to then pop a sprog in her own nest.

This is the undercook, the smart cookie, who'd wrangled pots and pans to feed the hungry masses of Maesllwch. Why would she have been so stupid?

Could she not have said she needed some air, gone for a walk, fled to her parents, found a quiet spot in the woods and given birth there? But no, this young girl with the invisible bulge in her belly, goes to her room leaving herself wide open to the prying eyes of the likes of Margaret Havard.

Ok, so let's go with this scenario. She would have been frightened, in agony, and keen to get it over with before Mary Meredith gets back. As they shared such intimate space, I assume they didn't do so in silence. They would have chattered, shared secrets, Mary would have known of Meredith's free afternoon, as indeed she would've had a close approximation of when she'd be back. Free time, never mind half days were a rare occasion in those days. Mary Meredith would have been over the moon at the prospect of seeing her sister.

How opportune that this free time should coincide the exact time Mary goes into labour. How odd that the dairy maid, despite sharing this intimate space, should have previously noticed nothing untoward.

Take toileting habits, for instance. In those days they used chamber pots, usually stashed under, or near the bed for when nature came a-calling. One of the first signs of pregnancy is a marked increase in the need to urinate. Mary would have been on and off that chamber pot like the proverbial blue-assed fly.

Are we saying that such shenanigans would not have been picked up on? That Ms Meredith slept undisturbed through these night-time releases? Or perhaps our Mary was blessed with a cast-iron bladder, and was able to keep it in.

Which again brings us onto the question of morning sickness, but I'm guessing Mary Morgan didn't have that either. Maybe she'd inherited some kind of physiological trait from her mother, Elizabeth, she of the 'wonder womb'. It has to be said, they'd both make a fascinating case study in today's modern medicine, don't you think . . .

Meanwhile, back to Mary who has locked herself away like a sitting duck as pain wracks her body and murder is on her mind. She's managed to fob off Cook and Havard, and the Housekeeper is nowhere to be seen. So, as the baby comes forth, with a knife already in her possession, she slashes the tiny throat, and the baby dies instantly.

A brutal, uncompromising act borne of fear and desperation. Keen to hide the evidence, she then stuffs the lifeless body into the underbed. But she reckoned without Mary Meredith. Her roommate has returned and wants to change her clothes. But the door is locked as Mary tells her to go downstairs and let her sleep.

Doubtless confused, the disgruntled dairymaid does exactly that and hotfoots it down to the kitchens to tell Cook.

Instead of informing Mrs Simpson, Mrs Evelyn takes it on herself to make a third trip upstairs with Ms Havard in tow. After the interest they'd shown in her welfare, you'd think Mary would have known her actions would further fuel their suspicions.

There then ensues a most extraordinary situation, as fresh after giving birth and despatching the very fruit of her loins, Mary is still robust enough to argue, swear, and vehemently deny all accusations the two women throw at her. Indeed, according to Ms Havard, this exchange went on '... for some time ...' Mrs Evelyn, '... she strongly denied it for half an hour or thereabouts ...'

'... thereabouts ...'?

Poor Cook, talk about vagueness personified – did she even know what day it was? And as for Mary, such stoicism before a rabid inquisition that went on for nearly thirty minutes, clearly demonstrating, once again, the almost superhuman qualities of this girl!

It has to be said, the emphasis on Mary's heated response suggests an unpleasant temperament mired in deceit, not averse to using bad language. But then, if this panned out as both women said it did, poor Mary would have been fighting for her life. Alternatively, if you're looking to besmirch someone's character, then you'd be hard-pressed to find a better hatchet-job!

Interestingly, Mary Meredith is absent from the scene. No doubt she was instructed to remain downstairs as Cook and Margaret Havard hauled her roommate over the coals.

Once Mary capitulated and drew the dead body from out of the mattress, it was game over. Caught red-handed – literally! Yet, nothing is said about any blood. You'd think after severing a main artery, there would have been quite some spillage. Which brings us onto the underbed and the aforementioned feathers therein.

Question: Did all Maesllwch staff have feather beds in the servant's quarters, or just Mary?

Correct me if I'm wrong, but I was always under the impression that straw mattresses would have been the norm for the folk below stairs – unless you held a senior position like a Housekeeper or a Butler, of course. I raise this question because it seems strange, yet you have to admit, it certainly paints a picture: Tiny, abused little body covered in blood and feathers pulled out of hiding like some worthless gobbet of meat!

Was that the aim, then? Another cleverly constructed strike against the morals of this cruel and wanton creature? Listen carefully and you can all but hear that hatchet doing the business.

And what about the afterbirth? Was that stashed amidst the feathers, too? Or had Mary the forethought to take care of that on top of everything? Maybe there were complications with that which was that why she needed two weeks to recover. And if that was the case, who attended to her? The family physician, or experienced hands of the house, I wonder.

But just to establish that Mary's act had been one of 'premeditation', it was Mrs Evelyn, who retrieved the murder weapon. Yep, that's right, good ol' Cook! Talk about hot on it! Instead of doing what she was paid for, she'd gone full Ms Marple! Had returned to the scene of the crime, rummaged around Mary's bed before finding the knife stashed under the pillow!

How fortuitous! Sterling work, I'd say, for someone seemingly caught up in a permanent time-warp!

It's also worth noting that as one of the most senior members of staff, her integrity would have been deemed unimpeachable. In every household, great or small, Cook was a position of great trust. For in their hands was the power to poison family, guests, and staff alike, if they were of the mind. So, I think we can safely say that her word on this would have been unquestionable. Although whether anyone actually got fed during all the hoo-ha, however, is seriously open to debate!

All rather extraordinary and quite incredible, don't you think?

So many thoughts, and too many to count. Not that the lack of detail made any difference, however. The testimonies of these three individuals was more than enough to place Mary Morgan firmly on the hook. And what a great big hook it was! Caught, trapped, bang to rights! Didn't matter that she pleaded 'not guilty'. Was of no consequence that she might have been innocent. Her voice and what may well have happened had no place in the proceedings. She was as good as sentenced as soon as she stepped up into that dock.

Guilty as charged, m'lud!

GUILTY!

Bye, bye, Mary . . .

But before we move on any further, I'd just like to share this little snippet that Mary gave to me on 28th July 2022.

It was a Saturday evening, and I was lolling about in my sweats watching TV when I got 'the call' about half past eight. It was absolutely chucking it down and after a couple of glasses of wine, the last thing I wanted to do was venture out.

Grumbling, I duly got changed and with my rain mac and brolly made my way up to the churchyard before squelching across to her grave.

'Hello Mary.' I murmured, 'what's so important you need to drag me out on such a night, my love. What is it?'

As I leaned back against what I call the 'sanctimonious stone' and faced the smaller and more apt one, I quieted my mind and waited. I knew she wouldn't have drawn me up here for nothing.

As the rain pattered down all around me, I closed my eyes as her energy began to feed through.

Once again, I felt the frustration, her voice rising with indignation at her enforced silence all these years. How she had been shackled, her hands, her tongue, her entire being, in every way. As she held forth, I absorbed her pain until she was spent. This wasn't the first time I'd borne witness to her inherent rage, and once it was over there was a stillness before I heard (felt) one word:

Belvoir.

Belvoir?

Mystified, I mulled it over. What did she mean, Belvoir?

I waited for more but there was nothing.

'Ok, Mary, I said, 'I don't know what you mean, but when I go home, I'll look into it.'

Back at the house, once I'd divested myself of my wet gear I got onto the computer and typed it in.

I don't know what I was expecting, but I certainly wasn't expecting Belvoir Castle to pop up. As a castle enthusiast I've seen several in my time; Berkeley, Caldicot, Harlech, Llansteffan, Ludlow, Oystermouth, Pembroke, Raglan, Sherbourne, St. Briavels, Stokesay, Weobly, Windsor, to name but a few. Belvoir, pronounced as 'Beaver', however was a new one on me!

Intrigued I clicked on the link. Belvoir Castle is described as 'A Historic Gem in the Heart of England', I wasn't inclined to disagree, but what was the connection?

As I scrolled through the site, all the while I'm thinking, what on earth has this got to do with Presteigne and Mary Morgan?

Nothing, it seemed, so I exited the page and went down to the next and then BINGO!

It was an article from the *BBC website dated 31st October 2013* with the headlines that all but jumped out at me.

'Witches of Belvior 'may have been framed'.

What the. . ?

Well, I hadn't been expecting this!

As I pored over the article, sufficed to say, it made for a riveting read . . .

"... Now, fresh research suggests three so-called witches blamed for cursing a nobleman's sons may have been framed.

The year is 1619 and sisters Margaret and Philippa Flower are hanged.

The two sons of the Earl of Rutland have died - believed cursed - and the prime suspects are the Flower sisters.

They had recently been sacked from their jobs at the earl's home, Belvoir Castle in Leicestershire, and revenge was believed to be their motive.

Their mother is also accused of witchcraft but dies before the women's "trial".

The sisters were two of about 100,000 people sentenced to death for being witches in Britain between the 15th and 18th Centuries.

Many were victims of nothing more than a neighbourhood dispute or a community vendetta....

And, she says, the case of the "Witches of Belvoir" highlights how those accused stood little chance of survival.

According to historian Tracey Borman witches were accused of making "pacts with the devil", poisoning cattle and causing famine.

The Flower sisters had been employed by the earl as servants in preparation for a visit by King James I.

But they proved unpopular with the rest of the staff and were accused of stealing and other misdemeanours, said Ms Borman.

The sisters, who were known to be herbal healers, swore their revenge, the story goes.

They got hold of a glove belonging to one of the earl's young sons and buried it, chanting "as the glove does rot, so will the lord".

The Flower family had fallen on hard times but still "tried to lord it over their neighbours", said Ms Borman

"Their case is typical of the witch hunts," the historian added.

"It involved fairly obscure women, with little evidence to support any of the accusations against them.

... "Most trials involved pretty much local squabbles - it was a way of getting rid of a neighbour you didn't like - or getting a bit of revenge if they were doing better than you."

She said the Flower women were known for "being obnoxious and welcoming the men of Bottesford to their home in the middle of the night" and were generally regarded as "a thoroughly bad lot".

However, she said new evidence she had uncovered in documents pointed to a possibility the woman might have actually been framed by a member of the aristocracy.

The rumours were James I's favourite, the Duke of Buckingham, had wanted to marry the Earl of Rutland's daughter.

Ms Borman claims that with the sons out of the way, the Duke of Buckingham stood to inherit all of the earl's wealth.

"There is evidence to suggest he put those boys to death - he had them poisoned - then framed Joan Flower and her two daughters as witches to create a smokescreen to cover up his own guilt," she says.

However, Belvoir Castle guide Rhi Clark says local people at the time were convinced of the curse and believed the Flower family were witches.

"People were terrified of these women - and witches in general - because once a witch pointed a finger at you that was you cursed forever," she said.

She said that for years people had believed the curse.

... "But our present duchess, who is a very enlightened lady, decided to blow the curse," said Mrs Clark.

"And about 12 years ago we started doing re-enactments here at the castle."

But whoever was responsible for the death of the boys, if anyone - the fact remains the Flower sisters stood "no chance" at the trial.

"They were uneducated and had to defend themselves - the average witch trial lasted just 20 minutes," says Ms Borman.

"[The authorities] conducted them at lightning speed - then sent the guilty for execution."

The sisters were hanged at Lincoln Castle, while the Earl and Countess of Rutland remained convinced their sons had been killed by witchcraft.

So much so, it is inscribed on the family monument at Bottesford Church, and reads, "Two sons - both died in infancy by wicked practice and sorcery".

As for Joan Flower - she is buried on the crossroads at Ancaster.

"It's very important to bury a witch at crossroads - so when they come back, they don't know which way to go," said Mrs Clark.

"And, if you can possibly put a tree on them, all the better."

Well, if this wasn't inferring something, I don't know what is. Not that Mary had ever had the charge of witchcraft laid at her door, but Anne Boleyn did, and after that reference to her in the dream, I couldn't help but make the comparison. Ambition borne on the wings of love has seen many a woman – and man! – punch above their weight, only for it all to come crashing down around them.

Had Mary got ideas above her station? Set her cap at the son of the house? Saw herself as queen of the castle?

In all big houses jostling for position and petty jealousies would have been the norm below stairs. The Flower sisters and their mother were certainly the worst-case scenario of what could happen if you rocked the boat, and Mary's pregnancy had rocked the boat, alright!

If there's one thing I've learned about the Universe, or God, if you prefer, is that the message is never one-dimensional and is usually steeped with hidden meanings. These are not always clear straight away until something pivotal triggers them off.

At the time, I read the Belvoir Witches story as Mary simply flagging up confirmation she'd been set up. And whatever your beliefs, it has to be said, the concept certainly resonates . . .

But that's not all.

Turns out that there was a bit more to this, but before I share this little snippet of significance, let us turn our attention to the other poor little soul caught up in all of this.

The baby.

CHAPTER 5

Mary's baby.

Baban bach.

A tiny scrap of hope-filled life, created in love, born into chaos, her tragic demise the cause and the catalyst. The unwanted guest, the penultimate victim.

Having always been referred to as 'the baby' or 'the child', let us do away with the anonymity of her brief presence in the world.

Let us show some respect to her ill-used soul and bless her with a name.

May she be known for ever after as Mari bach; little Mary.

It is the least we can do for this precious being who came forth only to be despatched into darkness, never knowing a mother's love or, the softness of her breast.

Oh, Mari bach, how hearts have ached and questioned the cruelty of your fate. And do you sleep in eternal rest? Or are you waiting still for the comfort of those arms who sought only to hold you and would hurt you, never . . .

Never.

And so, we look to the coroner's report that says the wound that sliced your tiny throat was three inches wide and one inch deep. Oh, Mari bach, how I hope you didn't suffer, that your final moment was no more than that last unknowing breath. That you knew the anguish of your mother when they took you away. And away they did. Unto death.

But do you know what else, little one?

There is another report that states the wound was even bigger than the accepted three inches and one inch depth. Indeed, the wound is described as six inches long and four inches wide. A notable difference, as I'm sure you'll agree.

Such a careless stroke of the pen can be found in the case files at The National Library of Wales. And whoever made that meaningful mistake left only an 'S' to show that they were there.

That's how much they thought of you, Mari bach . . .

But they made much of the knife that took your life. They made much of that, the pitiless blade wielded against your tiny neck. Taken from the kitchens, they said, your mother a thief as well as a murderess. Oh, little, little, baban bach, could she have been mired any deeper?

So, when they took their words to court, and spoke their truth before the Judge, in their eagerness to seal her fate, they neglected to include one thing.

To be fair to the Judge, he picked up on this, and referred to it during his summing up.

". . . There is a familiar experiment in these cases upon the lungs of the child when detached from the other subjects of the dissection. I have no judicial knowledge whether it has been made in the case before us or has been omitted. It should always be made and for this reason, the result as evidence against the culprit is equivocal and I should never deem it improper to be received, but, if the lungs had sunk, it would have been decisive to show that it was a child still born, for which reason the poor creature in your hands had a just claim to the benefit of the experiment in her favour. I, for one, am so confident upon that subject that upon the fact of such an experiment and result, I would at any time encourage to direct an acquittal . . ."

So, what does this mean, little one?

Well, first of all, it means that a very key part of your autopsy was missing from the Coroner's report. Maybe Cooksey lost the paperwork, or perhaps he simply forgot to submit it. Either way, this is very significant - and to no one more than those that know - and notwithstanding, to me.

Because when I was informed of your demise by different hands, the cause of death, I was told, was by drowning!

Which means, if this is true, then your little lungs would have told their own story, just like all the babies whose souls leave their bodies before they are born.

So you see, Mari bach, when I read that section of the speech, I felt what I call a 'whoosh'. It's probably not unlike what you felt when you left your body. They're very powerful, don't happen often, but when they do, it's the mother of all spiritual cues to pay attention.

Well, I've been doing just that ever since the day that disclosure set me off on a different path to learn the truth. And when I saw the words of the Judge, they made me angry. Very angry.

In fact, they made me so mad it was on a par to the fury I felt in the wind when I first met your mother. This rendition gave substance to the rumour, indeed, it lent more than speculation. This was, and should have been, key evidence in your mother's conviction, for heaven's sake! Where was it? What was there to hide? The only person who really would have known was the Coroner, Cooksey, and he wasn't talking.

Mother Bear was well and truly in the house!

What enraged me particularly was the idea of your poor little body being mutilated after death. Did this happen? Was this diabolical deed inflicted as your heart stopped beating and your skin cooled so as to devise a case to lay at your mother's door?

Did the Judge suspect, which was why he flagged it up?

For my part, I believe Judge Hardinge knew much more, but not as much as we thought. His hands were tied, his choices limited by the constraints of a ruling class. Because let's be honest; he isn't going to risk the wrath of the established boat by throwing a lifeline to Mary, is he?

He is the Captain. But a Captain is nothing without his crew.

How can we forget Nordhoff's classic, 'Mutiny on the Bounty' and the message therein?

Better to let your mother sink, methinks.

She was just a serving girl, after all . . .

So, with all the evidence presented – primarily the three witness statements and, can we assume, the initial Coroner's report? Mary now finds herself at the mercy of the Petty Jury and the constitution of the Judge. The echoes of her hearing resound with all of the trappings of an archaic process designed to uphold the law - no matter what.

Not that it made any difference to Mary's situation. The fact Judge Hardinge had tried a similar case just weeks before was seemingly irrelevant. A young woman from Hay had killed her baby with a pair of scissors. Her name was Mary Morris, and she was a few years older than your mammy. That Mary stood trial at the Brecon Assizes and was sentenced to two years hard labour. Just two years and the rest of her life.

No murder charge for Ms Morris in this instance. Her 'Confessing the Birth of her Bastard Child' was deemed good enough, courtesy of Lord Ellenborough's Act of 1803. Aunt Rebecca said this new law allowed for more lenient punishment; that if a woman concealed the birth of any child born out of wedlock, she should be acquitted, or else jailed for no longer than two years.

Yet, for some reason, your mother was accorded the rope!?

Judge Hardinge, in his wisdom, obviously felt she warranted no such mercy. Neither did the Jury who returned a vote of 'Guilty' to a man. No mutiny there. But lots of words from the Judge.

He liked his speeches, did the Judge. Would send them out to the newspapers afterwards so everyone could reap the benefits of his lyrical delights. To say that he liked the sound of his own voice would be an understatement. And he certainly didn't hold back with your mother!

I wish I could spare you the long-winded spiel, Mari bach, but needs must. This man liked to play to the crowd, but he did flag up the autopsy anomaly. So, I guess we can give him his five minutes, but not without interruption . . .

"Gentlemen of the Jury, in addressing you I call upon humane and public-spirited men for their help in painful trust which is apportioned between us. You are interposed by the constituence of this merciful Government, as friends and guardians of liberty and of innocence, and you have made a compact, though by tacit agreement with the prisoner accused before you who is unheard in her defence and personated only by the evidence against her and the voice of her defender."

Defender? So, who might that have been, then? We know that your mother was not allowed to speak, once she had uttered her plea; so, does this mean that someone did speak for her? Was it the Beavan fellow, and if that was the case, then where are his words . . .

"You have also made a covenant of a more elevated kind with a God of truth, whose Ministers, gentlemen of the Jury, you are and in whose presence we have a very solemn oath. What is that covenant? It is to be merciful if we can, to be firm if compassion is perjury and a violation of your trust.
I am to address men so described upon a subject of a most lawful and melancholy nature, it is upon the guilt of murder, the culprit, and one's heart bleeds at the recital..."

'Heart bleeds!?' Here we go! Already, this dude is making it about himself, and he's not even warmed up yet . . .

"...is a girl whose age of seventeen is annexed and the victim, as alleged a new born child, her own illegitimate offspring, born as well as conceived in shame, but therefore making with its

infant cries a more eloquent appeal to the mercy of that female parent, as well as to the fond impulse of maternal attachment which cannot be separated from the essence of her office, and implanted by the parent of us all in her bosom."

He's speaking for her, here, and all expectant mothers. The arrogance of it. The audacity! How times have changed, eh, Mari bach?

"Whatever shades of mitigation the God of infinite mercy, in the counsels of his unfathomable wisdom should have destined for this class of murder, which bears not the least analogy to other homicide, the laws of the realm have made no distinction of mercy in its favour.
They were, and for near two centuries more severe upon women accused of this crime than for men accused of homicide whatsoever. It was the enacted provision of the law that concealment of the birth on the part of the female parent should operate as proof that she was guilty of the murder imputed, if she could not prove that the child was born dead."

He's talking about Lord Ellenborough's Act here, baban bach. And even if it was the case, she had no chance of that with the missing autopsy report!

"This enacted law was recently done away with, but I, who will yield in principles of mercy to none, am not yet right for the conclusion that, arraigned as it has often been for its cruelty, but administered as it was by the judges in that spirit of mercy, which is vital to their branch of office, it was not salutary in the terror of it. I am not ready also for the conclusion that, as the law is now understood, sufficient care has been taken of the helpless child, who as the offspring of incontinence of seduction is brought secretly into the world."

Seems at this point to me, he has already made his mind up. He's as much as admitting the fact he can be a heartless b*stard, Mari bach, (excuse Auntie Mandy's language!).

"Cases occur to me, but I will not point them out, in which murder would escape. Distinctions, however, still prevail which are powerful barriers against this painful crime. The concealment of a birth is material evidence against the mother, because it indicates the wish to guard against the shame of the illegitimate birth."

Ignore that bit, lovely, your mammy wanted you!

"It is, however, though competent and material as far as it extends, presumptive grounds of inference. This can be counteracted by another presumption which is that nature would prompt the mother to save her infant's life though desirous to conceal its birth. If it stood upon these two presumptions alone, the merciful one is the safest and perhaps in philosophy is the most correct of the two.
In truth, however, these contending presumptions on both sides depend chiefly for their weight upon a due and sound comparison to the other leading facts in the evidence before us."

Just so we're clear, the primary evidence against your mother was the testimonies of those three women. And just how 'sound' were they, I wonder . . .

"Your province, in general, is to enquire if the culprit was the mother of a living child and robbed that infant of its life either by her own hand with a desire to kill it, or by an act both wilful and criminal which has killed it in effect."

Never . . . Just remember what I told you, baban bach.

"I take this opportunity of stating the latter example in mercy to other young women who may have been seduced into the delivery of an illegitimate offspring in secret. These young women are to know, that if they expose their child when living and it suffers death or if they deprive it wilfully of sustenance in their power to bestow upon it and it perishes, they commit as palatable a murder of the child as if their own personal hand had inflicted the death wound. But in so dreadful a penal case you must be thoroughly convinced that life that previously existed was destroyed by a wilful act of the parent, either as the act of killing it, or as the act of killing it, or as an act which must in its nature have been calculated for that end result, whether intended for it or no. This inference may be collected from the circumstances without ocular evidence to the living child or by the mother's crime of killing it."

Well, as nobody actually saw your mammy commit the crime, the evidence rests solely on those three testimonies, as I said. And - lest we forget - the knife retrieved from the scene by none other than the trusty kitchen mechanic Ms Marple herself! Think we can safely disregard the Coroner's report, as there doesn't appear to have been one, and so . . .
Are you with me hence far, little one?
Stay focused 'cos he ain't finished yet!

"I put one case for the illustration; if the child is found in the necessary with no marks of external violence, and where no evidence appears against the mother, except her concealment of birth, it has often happened that she has been acquitted because women are liable to the accident of a delivery there, which has perfectly unabled them to save the infant."

Again, I feel the need to intercede here. Because what he's saying is that had you been found unmarked instead of with your throat cut, there would have been no murder charge. There would have been no circus. There would have been no noose at the end of all this. Mammy would have been found guilty of nothing more than 'the crime' of trying to hide you!

And so, I also want to say this; Hay-on-Wye is not so far from Glasbury. Are we to suppose that the case of Mary Morris had not reached the ears of the staff at Maesllwch? That the constant traffic of tradespeople and folk passing between places would not have heard about it, gossiped about it, and passed it on? Mary Morris was a local girl, after all, and her employer, a certain James Watkins, would also probably have been familiar to many. Especially, as word had it, he was the local saddler!

With infanticide so widely common, there must have been some awareness with the change in the law. They had stopped hanging women for this crime. The death sentence was no longer bandied about and so, I ask the question again; why would your mother so recklessly endanger her life − and her position − when a simple smothering would have sufficed?

No fuss, no blood, no case to answer other than 'concealment of the birth'.

Go figure, little one. It is enough to make all our 'hearts bleed'.

"It is certainly no legal excuse that fear of the consequences, remorse of the illegitimate birth or a sense of delicacy and of shame were the motives so desparate an extremity, if stings of this kind can be called frenzy of the moment, they cannot escape unless they have obliterated all traces of moral distinction between right and wrong. If any such case appears, you will act upon it, but it would be dangerous and false mercy to infer it as a course and presume it."

Well, there certainly was a frenzied moment, Mari bach, when your head was practically taken from your body!

But the only presumption in all this, was that your mammy did it . . .

"Confessions of the parties accused are too often received in these cases, when they have been most unduly obtained by menace or by the artificial tampering with hope. I conjure you to repel all confessions thus obtained..."

Did this also apply to the witnesses involved? Elizabeth Evelyn, Margaret Havard, Mary Meredith – were their testimonies *'obtained by menace'*?

Had their integrity been *'tampered with'*? Because 'hope' can go both ways, can it not? Hope of reward and hope that things don't go against you if you don't 'play the game'. I'm guessing both options cannot be discounted, because he who pays the fiddler, calls the tune, right?

The Judge goes on to say . . .

"Many are the cases where the influence cannot in strictness be called external, but results from the situation itself. I should be happier for one, if no party accused could be heard before this time. I must however add that confessions however obtained, if they terminate in discoveries of the fact, are competent as leading to such discoveries, and are no bars to the weight of the facts so discovered."

Did he know, or suspect something amiss with the *'discoveries'* surrounding your mother, I wonder? He certainly seems to labour the point. Talking of which, the next section is where he mentions the autopsy report that should have been presented but was not. How remiss. I could go on, baban bach, but the Judge hasn't finished . . .

"I am not afraid of telling that, offences like this are of late becoming prevalent, and that a culprit has recently escaped from her doom, whose crime was in local vicinity and near to the scene of this. It will on one hand induce you to be firm, if the exigency is imperative but it will guard you against all prejudice resulting

from the policy of example. We must not redress the unjust opportunity of yesterday by the overstrained convictions of a similar offence today."

Think he's talking about Mary Morris from Hay, here, little one. Hold hard, he's nearly done.

"I consign this life into your hands without fear, convinced we shall hear of her no more as a criminal, if you are not sure of her guilt and I am convinced to less, that if you are thoroughly possessed of her guilt, no effeminate and vitious mercy, will shake the public spirit and courage of your trust. Go now and consider your verdict."

Well, they certainly did that, and post-haste, apparently! Yet, despite all the verbal fluff, there was only really going to be one verdict, was there not? The odds were so stacked against poor mammy, it would have taken more than a miracle to have changed the outcome at this point.

The three other felons who stood trial with her were more fortunate. Margaret Bird, John Owen, both up on charges of burgling and William Burgwynne for sheep-rustling. Duly acquitted and free to go.

How Mary's heart must have been beating before the Judge passed sentence upon her. How hope, that had sustained her all these months must have kept company in that dock.

And pass sentence the Judge did, in his usual verbose 'hear me now' style. A bewildering experience for any proverbial lamb to the slaughter, and this is where it gets tough.

So, brace yourself, my darling. Cwtch up close now, and we'll read this bit together . . .

"Mary Morgan upon evidence which leaves not a shade of doubt upon the mind, you are convicted of murdering your child, a new born infant of your own sex, the offspring of your secret and vicious love. You are convicted of murdering this child with a knife, deliberately selected as the implement of a purpose deliberately formed and before your infant came into this world.

You could not hate the victim of this murder; it never offended you. It is true, if it had lived it would have proved your crime in its birth and your shame would have been the consequence of that proof.

Was this a reason to kill it, if its first cries to you for sustenance and care made it by force a living accuser of your guilt and infamy?

Had it lived you might have lost your place, you might have lost other places, you might have lived in poverty as well as shame, but was this reason to kill it?

Was it a reason to acquire a false character and flourish in the world with a guilty conscience upon your pillow and cries of a murdered infant in your ear?

When did this fear of shame and poverty begin? Was it an obstacle in the way of your criminal intercourse with your lover?

No!

When you had criminal passions to indulge, you had no fear of risk. When those passions were satiated and the mischief had been done, you became a coward and sacrificed your infant offspring's life, as well as the interest of your soul thereafter, to that new born fear..."

Oh, Mari bach, you grow restless at the telling, so here, let us pause for a moment. His words are ferocious, I agree. Powerful in condemnation, merciless in their delivery. That an act of love can be deemed as 'criminal' is hard to countenance, I know, as is the charge that your mother slew you in order to save herself.

So, cariad bach, hear me now; you were never regarded as an obstacle or a sacrifice waiting to happen by your mammy. Not once. Not ever. She had family enough who would have taken care of you. Of both of you. A loving family. A prosperous family. A family that had love and money to spare, so, don't you take those words to heart. The Judge was playing his part. As did all those caught up in the cause célèbre of your mother.

"Alas, how dreadful are the landing places of the guilt when it ascends in its progress. You began with incontinence, criminal in itself, but full of complicated perils in its tendency to worsen crimes. Your next guilt was a mask to the world in the concealment of your pregnancy, which, besides, the sin of the imposture, was dangerous to the infant you had conceived, and your last crime was the murder of your child inflicted by yourself.
You have killed the human creature, whom of all others had the most affecting right as well as claim to your mercy and love."

Ahhh, baban bach, how I wish I could cover your ears. It is hard, I know. Stay with me . . .

"You have murdered the offspring of your own guilt entailed by the shame of its wild descent upon her innocent life. At your wild and youthful age, undisciplined by fear as well as unenlightened and with such early habits of depraved self indulgence, it is not probable that a religion, which breathes in every page of it the love to infants, could have been impressed upon your mind, but the God of Nature has written a book that he that runs may read. You have read that book and the letters of it were stamped upon your feelings at your birth. It was a written law upon the living tablets of the heart, which told you how unjust it was to punish the offspring of your own guilt for no offence but the wretched life you had forced upon it, by that guilt alone."

As a quick aside to this part of his speech, I wonder what 'His Holier Than Thou' would make of this book? Because mammy's heart has stamped and breathed on every page of this book, so hold that thought, hold it, and know that she loved you. She loved you . . .

"You should have exerted every moment of your own life in atoning, by redoubles affection to daughter so born, for the calamity of such an existence. Instead of projecting this atonement, you were deaf to her infant cries, and stifled her breath with a murdering hand, but in this choice of difficulties, in this conflict of chance and risk, what is it you have done?

You have taken a leap in the dark, you have encountered the peril of detection and of punishment by death, as the murderer of your child.

You took the chance of dying impenitent – which God avert – or with a conscience ill-prepared for so dreadful a change as from this life, at once into eternity and its judgements.

You took the chance and had you escaped from human detection, had you imposed upon the world ever so well, of living self-accused, and self-accused upon a bed of lingering torments.

Thus is it that one guilt produces another especially in your sex when seduced into its criminal intercourse with ours."

I know. This is tough. We're nearly there, my love . . .

"The natural delicacy of the female character entangles all its progressive guilts and a succession of crimes take their birth from the master key to them all, your dread of shame.

At last the mind is buried in the confusion of shifted expedients to escape from the importunate eye of the world, but there is an eye about the path and about the bed, from which darkness can escape and from which nothing is hidden.

That eye is never closed, and it brings guilt like yours into light, in a manner for which human conjecture despairs to account.

Guilt is always a coward, guilt like yours often prompts the sinner to accuse himself and prove his crime by other evidence to the fact in a fit of despair, surprise or fear.

Madness like this comes too late. It is the effect and the doom of guilt, but it is no shelter from it. You had no pleas of sudden impulse to this act, not that any such plea could avail you if it existed. **Yours was a deliberate murder, the deadly implement was procured and set apart for that purpose."**

Ahhh the knife. All 6d of it. Too much coin to have come out of your mother's wages, apparently. But then, why buy when you can swipe one from the kitchen adding thievery to the charge sheet! All just seems so . . . opportune. But hold tighter still, because he's about to pull a few knives out of his own now . . .

"Had you escaped, many other girls, as thoughtless and light as you have been, would have been encouraged by that escape to commit your crime in hope of your impunity. The merciful terror of your example will save them. Desperate acts like these often escape from punishment. Merciful juries, merciful rulers of law and merciful judges give occasion to that impunity. If it is a defect, I hope it will never be repaired but the same juries, the same law and the same judges are firm in their trust in cases like yours.
The life that you destroyed, lost its mother when you were its executioner for guilt of your own. But it found a parent in heaven. There is not a more sacred object than that parent's love, whose children we all are, than a new born child. Its blood is like that of Abel; it cries from the earth and that cry is heard upon His Throne in whose image your murdered child was created."

Good grief, this man could have pontificated until his tongue fell out of his head!

"What your inducement was to sacrifice this pledge of your love with your crime, we have no power to ascertain, your conscience knows it, but we are able to know that it must have been unjust and cruel."

It was unjust and cruel. He got that right!

"I have talked with you hitherto as a Judge, going to pass a

sentence of death upon this convicted prisoner before him. But look up to me and I can give you comfort, for I can tell you without impairing the weight of punishment in this world, that you can turn away your eyes to the Judge of us all, whose mercy has no limits and whom no sinner can implore in vain, appealing to Him with tears of penitence and remorse, if they are deep and sincere.

You must have expected your fate and I hope in God you have prepared yourself by a new made heart for a better world, having made all the human atonement in your power upon earth."

Let us take a pause here a moment, so we can fully absorb the sanctimonious tone of this vainglorious man. To be bombarded from the bench by this paragon of virtue would have been quite something for anyone, never mind a seventeen-year-old girl!

And it gets worse . . .

"To cut off a young creature like you in the morning of her day, for it is a little more than a day to the oldest of us all, is an affliction thrown upon me which I have no power to describe, or to bear so well as perhaps I should."

I want to pause here again because the latter part of what he's saying is of interest. What is he talking about exactly when he refers to *'an affliction thrown upon me I have no power to describe, or bear as well as I should'*?

Is he talking about his role as Judge, or the fact he's about to send your mammy to her death? What an extraordinary statement to make. This from an unbending, self-assured man who, by his own admission declared, "I, who will yield in principles of mercy to none" appears to be having a wobble . . .

Could this be some kind of indication that his stance had been compromised in the matter? An admission of helplessness in the face of a situation greater than himself? Judging the Judge, now there's a thing, little one, but he isn't finished yet, and his next words are a blinder!

"You must not think we are cruel; it is to save other infants like yours and many other girls like you, from the pit into which you are fallen.

Your sentence is a mercy to them. If you have repented your crime, it is a mercy to yourself. Had you escaped, your mind perhaps would have been so depraved that mercy could not have reached it in time.

You have the tears and prayers of us all; in the abhorrence of your crime we have not lost compassion for your personal fate, nor our hope that you will find mercy at the Judgement seat of a redeeming intercessor who dies, that penitent sinners through him should be rescued from the doom they had incurred and should expiate their pollutions in the atonement of his blood."

According to reports he became quite emotional at this point, and I should bloody well think so! He is sending her to her death and is all but seeking her approval to do so. Unbelievable! As is his reasoning that your mother, Mary Morgan, be sacrificed on the altar of 'the greater good', so all fallen women may look upon her fate and be warned.

Oh, Mari bach!

And now we come to the final deposition of this weighty man of law, as he slips effortlessly into his role of renown as 'The Hanging Judge'.

So, draw nearer, cariad, as he places the black square of silk upon his head and remember, these words are but an echo of the past, for Mammy is past all suffering now.

Mammy is at peace.

"I am now to pass upon you, the awful sentence of your legal and inevitable fate in this world. It is, that you be taken from hence to the place from whence you came and from thence to the place of execution the day after tomorrow.

You are there to hang by the neck until you are dead; your

body is then to be dissected and anatomised. But your soul is not reached by these inflictions. It is in the hand of your God! May that fountain of love show mercy to it when it shall appear before him at the day of judgement."

There . . .

Now let us take a moment, Mari bach. Because after that elaborate, torturously drawn-out homily finally we have it. The end of the road, the *coup de grâce*. The complete annihilation of Mary Morgan and anything that may remain of her beleaguered state by the time the rope has finished with her.

A harsh and horrible finale to a young woman's life.

Your mother's life.

I'm so sorry.

Apparently, there were tears in the court when sentence was passed, including from the Judge himself. Your mother, however, remained dry-eyed throughout, exemplary in her composure.

'They said' she seemed immune to the gravity of the charges against her. That she had an air of indifference throughout the whole proceedings. Exceptional and questionable behaviour, admittedly, considering her life was on the line.

The only sign of animation was when it was said she wore **'gay apparel'** in court. *Gay apparel?* This, from the young girl who didn't have the money to buy her own bread! How could this be? And why?

Indeed, to have been decked out in such a manner would suggest two things: anticipation of acquittal, and a sure-fire way of antagonising the Judge.

Who would stand to gain by her alienating 'His High and Mighty' with such inappropriate attire? More tellingly, who had the means to have provided such dress in the first place?

The questions are as tiring as they are never-ending. So much just doesn't add up, which brings us back to your mother and her strange demeanour.

What was she thinking? Why was she so detached?

To be honest, baban bach, I don't think she quite knew what was going on around her. Indeed, it is my belief that she had been induced into a state of complete obedience and disassociation. How I reached this conclusion, I will go into later, but first I want to share something very special with you. Because I saw your mammy that day in court. It was a dream, of course, and the only time I saw your mother close up. Just a few moments as the Judge was summing up. But her image and her beauty will stay with me forever.

She was stood in profile facing the Judge. Her brow was as clear and as calm as her almond-shaped eyes, that were blue. I did not see the **'gay apparel'**, only her face, as she gazed forward.

Her hair, that was fair and straight, had been drawn back into a kind of bun. She looked delicate and demure, her skin pale but smooth, her nose, small and neat, her lips gently pursed as though in concentration. And young. So very young.

In those moments as Judge Hardinge thundered forth, I sensed her unconcern, She was like an island by itself as the storm raged all around her. Unmoved to the point of surreal. She was in a different place. Completely.

'They' hadn't been wrong about that.

There is a saying, What's normal to the spider, is chaos to the fly. But in this case, I think I can honestly say that she was oblivious to the danger.

Like prey caught up in a web of false silk, I believe she no idea how tightly she was bound; not until it was too late.

Poor Mary.

Poor mammy.

Your mammy.

And poor you, Mari, bach.

It is time to part ways now, little one. There's no need for us to journey back any further on this hard and harrowing road. We have revisited and reminisced, rewrought and reflected. All that needed to be said, has been said. But before you go, baban bach, I will leave you with this . . .

On my numerous visits to mammy's grave, I often asked her about you. Before I went to sleep at night, I would ask if you were together, if you were in her arms, safe and sound, bound forever by eternal love.

It was quite some time before I had my answer and in a way I least expected. But the message could not have been any clearer and came through my usual medium of dreams.

I saw you on the platform of a station, swaddled in white and lying in a cradle all alone. Alongside was a long, dark train, festooned with cobweb, decrepit with age.

On the other side of the train was another platform, and there on a bench sat the lonely figure of your mother. The mood was sombre, brooding, recumbent with quiet despair. The darkness so tangible I could almost feel it.

I knew from the dream you were waiting for mammy to board that train. But the tragedy that had befallen you both, continued to separate you in death as it had in life.

Well, it has been a long, old wait, my darling, but we are nearly there.

For when mammy steps up and onto that train, the engine, that has stood silent for all of these years will finally fire up, and the wheels, that have been frozen for so long, will finally begin to turn, as the guard, who has found their place, can finally blow the whistle.

I am that whistle.

I am the whistle-blower and the messenger for both mammy and yourself.

With these words, with this book, with my commitment to telling your story, and this I have done with only love in my heart. But, before you embark on the next part of your journey, little one; you need only know two things . . .

Firstly, that the long wait is over, and you will finally be reunited with mammy. And secondly, before you disappear together into the light, know that you were loved, little one. Know that you were always loved, and that we, your family, whether by blood or marriage or none - will always love you, as we claim you, and this we do with all our heart . . .

. . . our most precious Mari bach x

CHAPTER 6

It has to be said, I've felt some emotions during the writing of this book, but never more so than in the closing of the last chapter and another experience I will share with you now.

Mary's trial lasted two days, and for the duration, she was moved from the Gaol to one of the cells beneath the court.

As I mentioned previously, the cells of the old Shire Hall remain in the basement of Lorna's Sandwich Shop. What I didn't know, was that there were other cells in the vicinity, and Mary's had been identified!

Well, you can imagine my excitement! As I hadn't been able to access the place where she'd lived and worked, this to my mind, would be the next best thing. It was quite a moment, and I wasted no time in knocking on the door. Fortunately, there was someone in, but they were not the owner. I explained my interest and they let me in for a quick look.

The door in the picture leads down to the cell. I did open it and looked to where steps ended before a very low opening. Beyond was the cell itself and complete darkness. I wanted to go down – desperately - yet something repelled me.

At first, I thought it was the builder's debris, that would have made any descent quite dangerous. But it wasn't just that.

What I needed was a torch, and with just my phone to light the

way, it came down to taking a picture in pitch darkness or having a quick look.

I dithered and that isn't me. I was torn between wanting to go down and 'feel' where she'd been, coupled with a sense of foreboding I just couldn't shake off.

So, I withdrew and left my card in the hope that the owner would allow me to visit another day. I so wanted to see this space, but not just see it. I was avid to pick up on what residual energy may still remain. So, after a couple of weeks when I'd heard nothing back, I decided to return and, for want of a better description, beat on the door!

My compulsion to get down into that cell swayed between strong desire and an intense repulsion.

It was quite extraordinary and a strange place to be in my head. It took me back to my childhood when I'd explore dark, derelict Victorian piles with a mixture of exhilaration and fear. But as I set off that morning, I wasn't prepared for just how deeply the prospect of going into that space would affect me.

The first sign was a slight uneasiness before I even left the house. This grew steadily into a sense of anxiety as I made my way up the street. And by the time I came to the building in question, I was all but in full panic.

Just what on earth was going on?

As I tried to still my beating heart, I knocked on the door and seeing it ajar, pushed it open. The owners were home but were tied up and busy. I could come back another time, they told me, when the area was made safe.

I thanked them and took my leave, with a deep feeling of gratitude on two counts. Firstly, that they were willing to accommodate my request, and secondly, the fact I'd been blocked off from going down there.

Down into that darkness.

Down into that cell.

As I walked away, I realised that if the thought of going into that space was making me feel this bad; then full immersion would be worse. Much worse.

This knowledge took me aback quite a bit. This is the woman who wanders around woods and graveyards at night. Who doesn't scare easy and certainly has no fear of the dead.

So just what was going on here?

Despite trying to distract myself, the intensity of the feelings persisted which meant there could be only one explanation.

Mary.

I made my way down to her grave; my whole being still resonating with this terrible fear. That she was giving me a flashback, a memory, I had no doubt. But of all the times I'd felt her anguish, it had never been this strong before, not even up in Gallows Lane when she first showed herself to me.

As I took up my familiar position she let rip, and I can't begin to tell you how frightened she was.

So, with this in mind, I'll let her tell you herself. This needed no three-week analogy of deep contemplation like the opening chapter did. When I say she let rip, she let rip and upon my return back home I chronicled her response immediately . . .

'As they took me back down into that cold dark place a great fear overcame me. My heart was like a wild bird beating its wings against a cage. I gasped and fought for every breath as the gaoler called for the rector.

I knew this man, of course. He had attended on me almost constantly in the time leading up to my trial, and as he hurried down to my cell, Mr Browne was also with him.

In the fervour of my distraught state, they sought to soothe me, concern in their voices and etched upon their faces. These men, who knew well my fortune, had always been kindly disposed towards me. But now, in those moments, as the walls closed in, I was beset with the knowledge that my fate had always been decreed, and that they, who had held my hopes aloft, had always known it.

'As my fears gave way to impassioned sobbing, I had never felt so abandoned, so alone. And despite their whispered words of solace, I heard only the sounds of my own anguish as I realised, with profound horror, that I was going to die.

There would be no succour. All the words, all the platitudes, all the promises were like leaves in the wind. No longer dancing, they lay dead unmoving upon the ground, as I would be soon beneath it. For with them I would return to the earth. Buried and bedeviled for ever, may God have mercy on my soul.

Never again would I walk the fields of Llowes and gaze at my beloved mountains. No more would I sit and break bread with my family, see another sunset, and dream my dreams. For there would be no reprieve for me. No new dawn for Mary Morgan. Only death.

As the storm inside me began to abate I drew back from all counsel and held my peace. In my growing awareness, I realised that there were no friends here. No comfort to be drawn from soft persuasions, only what they could give me. And this they did, and this I took, before that familiar heaviness assailed me, and I slipped into merciful darkness . . .'

With such words ringing in my ears, and her terror still thrumming through me, I then asked that she 'take it off'. I'd been dealing with these conditions for best part of an hour, and if you've ever had a panic attack then you'll know how debilitating they can be.

I have yet to gain access to this cell below the ground, and to be honest, I'm more than happy to remain above ground! I sure got the message and so much more that I didn't comprehend at this time. Then some months later a chance encounter saw some pictures come into my possession.

Just one look at the images filled me with that familiar foreboding and overwhelming sense of despair.

What a truly horrible space.

Friends of the owner told me as kids how they'd frighten each other with stories of the haunted cellar, and the ghost? Don't think I need to spell that one out. Mary making her presence felt and mock her at your peril . . .

Less distressing was revisiting the day of her execution. The date was 13th April 2022 – two hundred and seventeen years after Mary was carted up to Gallows Lane where death waited at the end of a rope.

Her final night was spent in the 'condemned cell' on the first floor of Presteigne Gaol, away from curious eyes. Isolated, but not alone.

Allegedly, there was a plan to break her out – they said. That Rees, her father, was willing to risk his neck by saving hers, although quite how he would have managed that, stretches the realms of possibility – never mind incredulity!

Reference to the 'Great Escape' as from an article from the Newspaper Archives.

At the Radnorshire Great Sessions held at Presteign, last week, there was not a single cause. Four prisoners were tried for capital offences, but three of them being acquitted, the only one that excited particular attention was Mary Morgan, aged not more than 16 years, arraigned for the murder of her illegitimate child, of which she was found guilty, condemned, and executed near Presteign on Saturday last. Previously to her trial and conviction, she exhibited no impression of guilt, or apprehension of her fate; but from the time of her condemnation, on Thursday, till the next morning she was much agitated. After, however, an interview that morning with her father, she again appeared unconcerned, and listened not at all to the advice given her to prepare for the near approaching hour of her dissolution. This was afterwards found to be owing to a plan which had been formed for, and her certain hope of, escaping the following night. Such intention being discovered, she was removed from her former room of confinement in the gaol to one of greater security; and from that time, all hopes of escape being gone, she became more alarmed, and employed herself as one becoming her situation, and died truly penitent. The Rev. Mr. Scott (brother to the Countess of Oxford), Mr. Davies, the Under Sheriff, and John Brown, Esq. of Presteign humanely visited her almost continually from the time of sentence to that of execution, endeavouring, with all their abilities, to prepare and bring this poor young creature to die in the resigned and submissive manner which she did. We are also happy to add, that before her dissolution, she made a full confession of her guilt, and, without the least embarrassment or hesitation, declared the father of the child to be a man in the service of her master as a waggoner, which has completely refuted a wicked and idle report that was before prevalent.

Was this intended course of action a fabrication? A ploy to further besmirch Mary and her immediate family by implying an inherent contempt for the law? Up to this point, it has to be said, it's a struggle to find any redeeming features pertaining to this young serving girl. So, let's just keep making the shoe fit, methinks.

Apparently, Rees went to see her and laid bare his daring plan. But nothing came of it, of course. Her goose was well and truly cooked! Which leads on to the question of the sauce – for Mary's goose, I mean.

And the reason for this speculation lies with the two gentlemen who also came by to visit. Not just the night before in her condemned cell - but also, in the days leading up.

So, who were they, I hear you cry!

Why, none other than the Reverend Smith and a certain Mr Browne. As Rector of Presteigne and Chaplin of the Gaol, one can understand the presence of the former.

But what business does this Mr John Browne have with our Mary? Why, as a member of the Jury who had passed judgement on her, was he visiting her before and after the trial?

There was something about this Mr Browne that had always bothered me much like a thorn beneath the skin.

He was akin to Mrs Simpson, the Housekeeper - now you see me, now you don't!

Just what was going on?

On the anniversary of Mary's last day on this earth it as fitting I pay her a visit.

It was a beautiful Spring morning when I made my way down to her grave and closing my eyes, I assumed my usual position. According to reports there had been a fierce thunderstorm the night before she died, and for those who had cause for superstition, such a display of 'bad' weather would doubtless have been noted. But on this fine morning of April 13th, 2022, all is calm and so I wait, as the clock ticks towards midday the time of her appointed demise.

It was said that as they transported her from the Gaol up through Presteigne and towards the execution site she was all but paralysed with fear. Sat (supported) on the coffin that would receive her broken remains, she was wrapped in a winding sheet, her hair loose, her eyes half-closed, but her spirit was aware. Oh so, aware . . .

Here, in her own words are the final moments:

"As we drew near to the place of death, my fear sought freedom from all restraint, but the heaviness that assailed my limbs, held firm, and bound me to my lips.

As those around me prepared me for death, a bee passed close to my face, and suddenly I realised I would never hear that sound again. Nor would I the joy of birdsong as it filled my ears, and grief for all that could not be cried out in the darkness from deep within.

The crowd had fallen silent, but I could feel their eyes upon me as a gentle breeze paused in passing and kissed my brow.

It was nearly time.

Inside I became still.

I felt the noose embrace me and draw tight.

I closed my eyes.

May God have . . .

Then, in the final moment, I felt something else. A warmth like a caress, that filled my being, and as the rope pulled, I knew it to be Love, and it was the last thing I felt as I left this world and passed into the next."

Not long after this revelation of Mary's final moments, I had a dream of what happened in the aftermath, and did she suffer? Yes, is the answer, although, thanks to merciful intervention, it wasn't for too long. There was a report of some young man being paid a shilling to hasten death by pulling on her legs, but it wouldn't be until some months later that she would elaborate on this. At this point of communication, I sensed that she did not want to dwell on that moment. If anything, the feeling was that her spirit left the body quite quickly once the death throes had begun. Small comfort, perhaps, but for Mary, it was blessed release.

My dream, once again in Mary's words . . .

"Suddenly I was floating. I was free. The warmth was all around me, and I was rising, rising, borne on the wings of love that lifted me higher and higher, an array of spinning colours all around me. It was so peaceful. I felt safe. I reached out to the baby. My baby. But as yet she was hidden from me. Her little spirit wrapped softly into folds of love, a special place where new-borns go.

Then after what seemed like an interminable time, and yet of no time at all, I watched as they cut my body down. I looked so small, like a cloth doll my mammy once made for me. And as they lowered my body down to the ground, I felt the cold dispassion of the men who tended me. As I did the heaviness of those who had stayed, their troubled eyes and sorrowed hearts testimony to the tragic demise of I, once known as Mary Morgan.

Since that cruel and unjust day, I have remained between Worlds. Waiting and watching and wiser for it.

I am still here.

I have always been here.

I never left."

Talk to local people and they will tell you the same. Not all are sensitive to it, but there are many who are. She has always been here. Read on, and you'll know the reasons why.

If I heard Rebecca say, 'There's something not right here' once – I heard her say it a dozen times! For those familiar with the case, we all know there are gaps in Mary's story, but nothing prepared us for the sheer level of obfuscation once we got started!

Obfuscation. It's great word, isn't it? Means to baffle and bewilder people, obscure their understanding of something; lead them up the garden path! Well, it would seem 'They' had been assiduous in taking care of business.

First port of call, as I mentioned, was the mysterious Mr Browne, 'Esquire'. He was also affiliated to The East India Company, so was obviously a man of means. Despite his attempts to disappear into the mists of time, however, I refused to let him off the hook and Rebecca had been busy!

Turned out he was a resident of Presteigne and in 1801 had been living in Hereford Street, no less! He was a lodger at a property listed as belonging to a certain Mr Hugh Pyefinch. Upon further investigation it transpired that Mr Pyefinch had passed away in 1752. So, I think it's fair to assume his widow, Elizabeth, remained in the property or another family member. Nothing special there, you're thinking, until we learn that Mr Pyefinch had been an Apothecary and Surgeon! Well, well . . .

There was something about this chap and the family name that drew me. There is a very prominent grave in the churchyard bearing the name Henry Pateshall Pyefinch; could Henry be Hugh's brother? Further investigation showed that the name 'Pyefinch' was quite common to Presteigne and there were three branches, all related. Linking them together was no mean task, and once again, there is a figure in the shadows.

Hugh also had a brother called Henry (not the Pateshall chappie), and there's lots out there about him, as there is on Hugh's wife, Elizabeth Goodere of Puddleston.

Hugh, however, remains something of a mystery, and he passed away after just five years of marriage. So, what is the link between the Pyefinch's, Mr Browne and Mary in all this?

Some of the pieces began to fall into place after a great find by Rebecca.

She had this to say:

"When looking for the graves in Presteigne Graveyard I happened to notice one for Vincent Cooksey, Surgeon. It really can't be a coincidence that two Cooksey's are surgeons but when looking into Vincent, a journal in the Radnorshire society transactions discussing the Poor law Union, mentioned how Vincent and 2 others were practicing Surgeons. But under The stricter Poor Law Union Standards they were not qualified.

An old man was also mentioned as practicing and the only experience he had was in the army. There is dismay mentioned about his injuries which prevent him from carrying out his duties fully and the investigation into standards, successfully identified the gentleman as Mr Henry Ince of Presteigne.

This is interesting.

Mr Ince had a wife, Charlotte, who we know had a liaison with Henry Pateshall Pyefinch. It doesn't look like they were married, however she had children by him who were born in Presteigne. The baptism record for the children records him as a courtesan. (records show he is also a surgeon and is a mason with the Grand Lodge).

So, we have two Cooksey men who were surgeons and two Pyefinch's who are surgeons...

A journal article on medicine and law mentions Hector Cooksey and discusses how it seems that he acted as both providing medical evidence and did the inquest as well, which isn't great practice.

I also found that he died bankrupt and that a Charles Cooksey (who lived on High street at number 16 was dealing with the Radnorshire Arms after his death. Charles is the brother of Henry Cooksey so I'm suspecting he is Hectors brother. Charles is listed as Esq.

It also intrigues me that Mr Pyefinch is a courtesan and also a surgeon. I'm hoping to find more on him being a courtesan, but it could be that this is where the story of the reprieve comes from. No documents show that anyone wrote asking for Mary's pardon..."

What makes these findings significant, is that whilst under the Pyefinch roof, did Mr Browne have access to herbs and powders that would have been used to treat conditions and disorders?

Admittedly, medical attentions were quite brutal back in the day, bleeding, leeches, and Dutch Fumigation, the latter, I suggest you Google! But there was one treatment that was widely used for all manner of nervous and medical complaints. Indeed, this magical drug was so effective, it was also used widely as a painkiller and sedative.

Laudanum, taken from Latin 'Laudare' which means 'to praise' is a derivative of the poppy seed, more commonly known as Opium. Widely available, potently powerful, highly-addictive, and it did the job.

So was this tincture given to Mary as she awaited the fate. Its bitter properties disguised in a nice, sweet drink by the nice, sweet Mr Browne?

Was it as result of these administrations the reason why she was so unperturbed in the dock? Why she went to her death drugged up to her eyeballs so as to keep her calm in the final moments? Because God forbid, she be allowed a few words before the rope choked the life out of her!

Banish the thought she might call out and cast aspersions after so much effort to ensure her conviction!

And let's not forget the Coroner here. The esteemed Mr Cooksey of the missing autopsy report, who among his varied interests, is recorded as being a druggist!

Yep, read that again and go figure!

The Coroner and the man called Mr Browne have links to the blessed 'Laudare' and what better way to keep a prisoner quiet!

All the times I visited Mary's grave and she'd rant about her 'lips being bound', her 'lips being sealed'. I referenced this several times to Rebecca because I didn't understand what she meant. Now, however, it all made sense . . .

What better way to ensure compliance and composure as your young victim endures the horrors of a rat-infested hole! How many whispered words of reassurance were dispensed with a few drops of Laudanum?

'Here you go, Mary. Have a sip of this. I know it doesn't taste very nice, but it'll make you feel better and will help you sleep. There's a good girl, come on now, drink up!'

I can all but hear the words . . . Can you?

Once again, I felt anger as the impetus sank in, but it was nothing compared to Mary's. No wonder she'd been raging; they had shut her down in every way possible and had had the means to do so.

Think about it; what person in their right mind stays calm when a sentence of death is thrown at them as everybody about them falls apart, including the Judge!

Why wasn't she affected?

Was it only when she was back in the cell that the enormity of the situation finally superseded the reverie of a drug-induced state?

I'll never forget her terror in the starkness of that moment when she realised, she was going to die.

So, who led her to believe that she would be acquitted? Because words can be just as potent as drugs when dispensed from those in power. Indeed, to a frightened young girl it would have been a concoction hard to resist. As would have been the opportunity to escape the rigours of prison with a poppy-tinted drink courtesy of Mr Browne.

Was this why he'd been visiting? According to the reports, he'd been in attendance right up until the cart came to transport her to the noose. And let's not forget that he did not come alone.

Besides the attentions of Gaol Chaplin, the Reverend Smith, Mary also had another man of note come a-calling.

A certain Reverend Scott, who also happened to be the brother of Jane Elizabeth Harley, Countess of Oxford, and Mortimer, respectively. The daughter of a Reverend herself, despite making a good marriage, Ms Harley had succumbed to the charms of Lord Byron, among others. In fact, her offspring were known as the 'Harleian Miscellany' because nobody knew who had actually fathered them. A most telling snippet that clearly denotes one rule for the ruling class and another for the likes of Mary Morgan!

But returning to the two Reverends and their obvious interest in the eternal soul of this devious, murderous, slip of a girl. Reverend Smith, as the Rector of Presteigne, perfectly understandable. The Reverend Scott, not so.

Like Mr Browne, his presence is questionable at best. So, why was he there? Why was he concerning himself and were he and Mr Brown already acquainted?

Well, as his sister, the Duchess of Oxford, had an estate just outside of Presteigne, I think we can safely assume so.

Also in attendance was the Undersheriff, Mr Davies – again, a tad confusing, but in his role, permissible, although what pearls of wisdom he had to offer I can only imagine!

But back to the Reverends, to both of whom, according to reports, Mary made a confession. Why it took two of them, one can only speculate, but it's certainly odd and so what did she say?

To Reverend Smith of the Parish, she repented of her sin and then embraced the ministry of the church; apparently. To the Reverend Scott, she also, allegedly, admitted that the father of Mari bach was a waggoner.

A waggoner?

How extraordinarily banal . . . and predictive!

A humble waggoner, a fellow-servant, who also happened, according to the Judge, to offer Mary a way out.

Now, this is where it gets interesting – and confusing.

So, let's start with this chap, whose knowledge of poisonous flora, to my mind, is as convenient as it is far-fetched.

Presented with Mary's pregnancy, this fount of herbal wisdom suggested certain plants that would ease her pregnancy. Or was this just a ploy to see off Mari bach? If so, a rather a brutal offer of support when he could have just married her – or was he already wed?

And why haven't we got a name? Surely, if he was the father, they could have done better than just 'a waggoner'?!

But let's just go with this theory for the moment. Mary is with child and the father, (the waggoner) has a cunning plan. Take the plants, abort the baby, no dramas, problem solved.

So why didn't she?

Why did she go full-term only to take the life of the baby

anyway?

It doesn't make sense. Seems to be something of a feeble attempt to accord some honour to a girl whose reputation had already been trashed. Which brings us on to Walter Wilkins . . .

Walter, 'Junior', son of the house. Betrothed to a rich heiress as the Mary Morgan scandal kicks off, and despite conflicting reports, his involvement is key, and yes, without doubt, I believe he was the father. Yet surprisingly I have no beef with him. Not since I woke up one night to find him stood in my bedroom. Whether this was a genuine sighting or the tail-end of a dream, I'm not sure, but it was real enough for me to sit up with the demand, 'What do you think you're doing here!'

Vivid enough for me to get a good look at him. A small, slight man, with thinning mousey hair, more on the sides than on top. Some kind of moustache with sideburns and pale blue eyes that regarded me with sad reproach. I'd love to see a portrait of him, and there must be a picture somewhere, so I could make the comparison.

But as someone who doesn't' get unearthly guests in their bedroom on a regular basis, I know in my heart it was him. And as he duly left as instructed, in that moment, I felt as though I 'got' him.

He wasn't a bad man. If anything, he was soft and kind-hearted and sorry, so sorry for all that had befallen Mary. He was young, he was smitten, and throughout the course of events, powerless to do anything other than he was told, and he dared do nothing else.

So, did he love Mary?

Yes, I believe he did.

Did he know about the pregnancy?

Yes, of course. But the matter was taken out of his hands. I feel he was in fear of his father's wrath and what Walter Senior said, went. It was as simple as that.

My sudden-found sympathy for this weak-willed young man came as something of a surprise. Because the Walter I saw in my bedroom was not the young 'Mary's gallant', as the Judge described him. But Walter in his later years, and in that otherworldly moment, solemn, reflective, and repentant.

It was the last that solicited my attention. His knowing and acceptance of the part he played - and that he'd showed himself in order to communicate this, resonated on a level I hadn't expected.

So, what's the story behind this rather grey figure? Look for him and in comparison, to his father and son, you'll find scant information. Unlike them, he didn't go into politics. He wasn't 'out there' in any particular way. Just lived the life of a country squire and a very nice one at that.

So why would I take a kindlier look at this man who stood back as his lover and the mother of his child took the fall?

My reasoning is this: He lost his mother at a young age. Growing up with a feisty father ruled by ambition would have been difficult, and with no maternal presence in the house must surely have left him emotionally wanting.

So, what did he do?

What do many of us do in the search to feel loved and wanted? He sought companionship and for Walter, the opportunity to do so was on his doorstep and over it, within the house, on the estate, females, servants, everywhere, and willing or not, readily available, and there for the picking!

And pick, he did.

There is a family not far from Glasbury where the 'love-children' live. That's what I call them and with the maximum of respect.

I have met with them, talked with them, and had the privilege of seeing the details of their family tree all laid out in a beautiful book. They also informed me of their red hair, courtesy of the Wilkins gene-pool, which may be of significance, as you'll see. For they are the descendants of Walter Junior and an unknown mother. A discovery of extreme importance, thanks to Margaret Morris of Llowes, who gave me the connection.

Marriage certificate of Liz Smith's ancestor, Henry Anthony, whose father is named as Walter Wilkins (Junior)

Hilary Marchant

Ivan Monckton thank you for that - a very interesting read. When I used to work in the Judge's Lodging, a lot of our visitors would ask about Mary Morgan. On one occasion someone said they thought that the young man of the house (Walter Wilkins) probably had a lot to answer for. Another visitor who happened to be in the building at the time said that she was descended from another of Wilkins's illegitimate children and that he set them all up with money and a trade, so she wouldn't hear a word against him!

2 y   Like   Reply   3 👀🫠

Apparently, there were other 'love-children' whose descendants are still with us. Walter had certainly been busy!

This excerpt, as taken from the 'Presteigne History' page on Facebook, is with the permission of Hilary Marchant, who remembers the conversation well.

So, what does this tell us? Well, clearly not only was Walter a bit of a boy, but that he was more than willing to step up to the plate and provide a future for his children. And in all fairness, you have to give him some credence for that.

It also adds weight of him fathering Mary's child – and you have to consider that, even if you choose to discount it. Furthermore, I was informed by one of the love-children, that she herself had been contacted by up to half a dozen descendants of Walter when she made their family tree public. Perhaps some of these will see this book and come forward.

There is no shame in what happened two hundred years ago, and if this allegation is true, then it only serves to further my argument.

Not that I need convincing. I would also assert that if Walter Junior had had his way, then I'm sure Mary would have been allowed to live. As would Mari bach.

I find it hard to believe that the imminent birth of a love-child was deemed such a threat to the forthcoming nuptials of young Walter and his bride. There were ways and means – and money, lots of money! – that could have guided the situation quietly and with compassion.

This wasn't the first time the master, or sons of the house, had begotten children on their serving staff. Indeed, if the trail of love-children is to be believed, then Walter certainly had no qualms once he'd tied the knot and even installed his mistress inhouse, allegedly!

What I'm saying is that in the scheme of things, was it really necessary for such a brutal end of both mother and child?

Again, the Judge had a few things to say about young Walter and described the Wilkins as 'profligate.' But on a more personal level, in a letter he described how Mary had spoken of Walter with affection. That she had spurned his offer of marrying her if she declared the child as his.

Did she?

Did he?

And when did these conversations happen? More keenly yet, why didn't Mary take up the offer? Why didn't she grab the helping hand that would have saved her?

Once again, these scenarios just don't make sense and besides, does one really believe that young Walter would have had any say in the matter? Defy his father and shrug off a match with a banker's daughter for the love of a humble undercook? Besides the scandal, he'd have been the laughing stock and his father wasn't having that.

So, forgive me for not getting caught up in the whole Cinderella romanticism. But I do believe that Mary was given assurances, and that promises were made in moments of bravado, even good faith and that she had lapped it up like an eager young puppy!

There are few things more reckless or foolish than young love, and Walter, according to Judge Hardinge, was more than a little taken with her. So, why do we need to look any further?

Still unsure?

Ok, then let us return to the mysterious Mr Browne, because we're not done with him yet. Neither are we with the three women who testified against Mary.

We'd been trying for months to find out more about this trio, but it was like banging your head against a brick wall. Something told us that they were key to all this and their role of 'shocked servants stumble upon the scene' synopsis wasn't washing.

At all.

Remember the under dairy maid, Mary Meredith? Roomie and runner of tales, humble servant, key witness? Well, we'd been hot on the trail of young Mary, but the surname is as common as Morgan or Beavan.

So, after scanning every and any Meredith within miles of Maesllwch, this particular young lady was nowhere to be found.

There was also a need to pin down her family – she'd been visiting her sister on the day of the murder, remember? But like the other two witnesses in Mary's case, she just seemed to disappear into thin air . . .

Cue Rebecca in what was probably her finest hour, as she

painstakingly scrolled and scried before coming across the smallest glimmer of light. Drawn by what seemed to be an impossible possibility, she probed and pushed and probed some more until persistence paid off and she hit upon the biggest development in our quest yet!

To use the word 'shocked' at this juncture, would not do justice to our sense of incredulity; we could scarcely believe our eyes!

Yet there it was, all recorded, all in glorious black and white! From Presteigne Parish Records the *marriage of Mary-Ann Meredith and John Browne dated 20th June 1815!!*

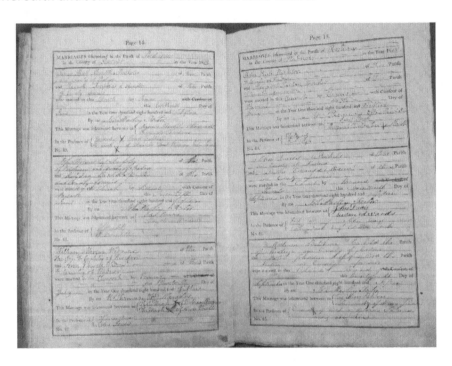

You know what they say, you can run but you can't hide, and young Miss Meredith was certainly no runaway bride!

For there, in the Presteigne parish register dated 1815, we find our elusive under dairy maid getting wed to the equally elusive Mr Browne!

By license.

No banns.

No pre-announcement.

No fuss.

And all deftly undertaken by a certain Reverend John Harley! You couldn't make it up!

But just to jog your memory, this man of God is the brother of the Duchess of Oxford, remember? The other Reverend who visited Mary in prison and to whom she made confession.

Oh, but there's more. Much more . . .

Old romantic that he was, Mr Browne, then whisked his bride over to the Emerald Isle to start a new life. But for what possible reason, I hear you cry!

Well, on this we can only speculate. Perhaps they preferred the Irish weather. Or maybe, Mary wanted to meet the faeries, because at the time of her marriage, she would have been no more than twenty, and Mr Browne? Older . . . much older. Possibly twenty years her senior, if not more.

And so, what is an Esquire, a gentleman, doing shacking up with a former dairy maid whose place in the pecking order would have been less than consequential?

What was her appeal?

Her ability to make cheese?

Or was it something more sinister, something more . . . orchestrated?

Maybe because John Browne had links to the Browne family with a huge estate in Sligo, whose holdings also saw ownership of sugar plantations in Jamaica.

We checked, but the link is tenuous at best, courtesy of the fire that destroyed so many records in Dublin, 1922.

Yet the connection is there, nevertheless. Why else would Mr Browne be visiting Ireland if there wasn't already some kind of association.

Furthermore, with the Brownes' of Sligo having interests in

slavery and the East India Company, it would not be unfeasible to assume a family link with Mary's dashing groom!

Is it her?

Rebecca has no doubts and neither have I and suffice to say her sojourn in service had been short and sweet, to say the least!

Now we have her – and him – firmly in our sights, next up was the census of 1851 and another revelation.

For here we find the former 'under dairy maid' visiting with none other than a Mrs Simpson in a very nice house in Great Marlowe, Buckinghamshire!!

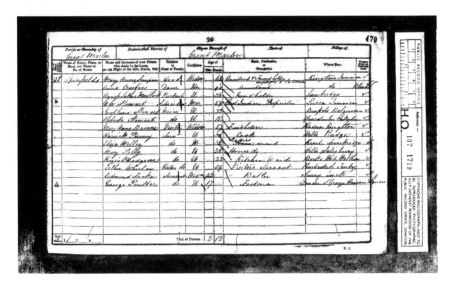

The 1851 census

I think it's fair to say that at this point I nearly went up into the stratosphere!

Mrs Simpson! AT LAST!

The Housekeeper, the wine-giver, that slippery almost mythical member of staff and residing in a very nice property called the Spinhouse, no less!

Picture courtesy of The Francis Firth Collection

Well, seeing the name Mrs Simpson sure got us in a spin, alright, especially when her place of birth was given as Jamaica!

Jamaica?

This was the most surreal of moments, I can tell you. The former Housekeeper of Maesllwch, born in the Caribbean?

But was it her?

Like Mary Meredith, we weren't expecting to find either of these two ladies living the life of just that: Ladies! And living comfortably without a duster or a quart of cream in sight!

But we had to be sure.

From the census Mrs Mary-Ann Simpson had formerly been married to a Mr Crosbie, so this was her second marriage. Disappointing – very! This Mary-Ann had also been born a Stewart, so could not be the ambiguous housekeeper.

What's interesting, however, is that both husbands are linked by the East India Company. Indeed, Mr Simpson, and his father before him, had sugar plantations in Jamaica and of no small size!

The Stewart family also had holdings in Jamaica, and further digging revealed quite a network, as described in Rebecca's own words.

"In Summary, the families all have links to the Law and large wealthy companies. They are all linked to the East India Company and in some cases to each other by marriage.

They have strong connections to Presteigne as well as Radnorshire and many have learned their trade in London or have links to Hanover square in London. They are part of the 'Great and the Good' and not humble servants.

I can't directly link them to Walter, but each person involved is linked to money and power with most having considerable knowledge of the law...

Basically, the old boys club have roots deep within East India Company in India and then gain positions in Jamaica as attorneys and Merchants."

Wow, quite the matrix! But the only real link was the name and Ms Meredith, now Mrs Browne of course!

So, what was going on? And what's more, what were the chances of finding these two together?

Sheer fluke? Or more than just a coincidence.

Was there an affiliation with the Simpsons that helped engineer 'a Mrs Simpson'.

A malleable member of the family who could be relied upon to give evidence if called?

Could this be why there was no testimony from this senior member of staff, who, it was recorded, had encountered Mary in her afflicted state and had kindly given her wine?

Once again, I'll ask the question; why wasn't she in court that day to give evidence?

And for that matter, why wasn't the wily waggoner!?

So, let us return to the census where we find Mary Meredith aka Mrs Browne listed as a widow.

Poor old John has obviously popped his clogs, probably worn out from all the globe-trotting. Left his widow well provided for, however. Her occupation is listed as a 'Freeholder', which translates as an independent woman of means!

So, what happened to Mr Browne?

Despite an extensive search, the only evidence of his passing was that his will had been indexed in Ireland. From that we can deduce that he died there, and, despite his one-time residency in Presteigne – had been born there.

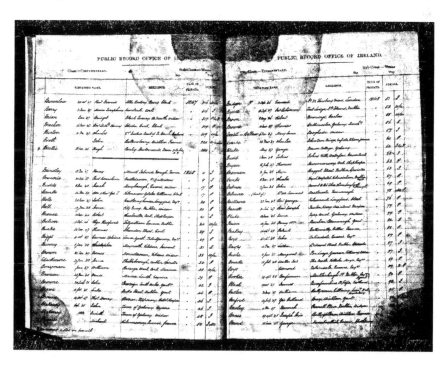

John Browne's name is listed six up, bottom left.

Unfortunately, due to the records destroyed by fire during the Irish Civil War, there was nothing more to go on. But can we surmise Mr John Browne was related to the Marquess of Sligo, John Denis Browne of County Mayo?

Who knows, but it makes you wonder. Interestingly, one of his ancestors was a servant of Christopher Hatton. Courtier and favourite of Elizabeth 1st, (that Anne Boleyn connection again!) who, it is said, once owned the Radnorshire Arms!

The idiosyncrasies of the Universe as it just keeps giving. If only those walls could talk, eh?

So, with John Browne seemingly having dropped off the face of the earth, thankfully we still have his wife, now a very rich widow, and sitting pretty in the census of 1861 with none other than her son and his family!

The Reverend Henry Browne, if you please, and rector of (oh, the irony!) St. Mary's Church in Eastham, the Wirral. And guess where the Reverend Henry Browne first made his appearance into the World?

Jamaica!

1861 Census

I think if he'd been born on planet Mars, I couldn't have been more surprised. Or intrigued.

Just what were Mr and Mrs Browne doing in Jamaica – calling on the Simpsons?

Did this mean that the Browne's also had holdings in the 'Land of the Hummingbird'? Soaking up the honey, no doubt, as did all those who had made their fortune on the back of slavery!

Indeed, we found a great number of those on the 'Ancient Briton' list as having links to Jamaica and the slave trade.

In fact, wasn't that how Walter Wilkins made this fortune in the first place - through the offices of the East India Company?

Was that why the family changed the name from Wilkins to de Winter - so as to disassociate themselves from the misery of the slave trade?

Or perhaps the Mary Morgan case.

Remember, you are the Judge and Jury, dear reader, I'll let you decide!

Meanwhile, back to Ms Meredith. Let's take a closer look at Mary, or Mary-Ann, as we see her named on both the marriage record and census.

Yet in the court transcripts she is known only as plain Mary Meredith.

But then, I suppose most servants didn't have more than one name, did they? Maybe some did, which leads me to believe that her middle name was deliberately omitted.

Was this so that if anyone went looking, they would be . . . obfuscated in the quest to learn the truth?

Could it be because Mary Meredith was no more an under-dairy maid as mine own good self, and had been cultivated to play a part? Had her name been used as a witness?

Her identity?

Again, I will let you be the Judge.

But for clarity, here is her family tree.

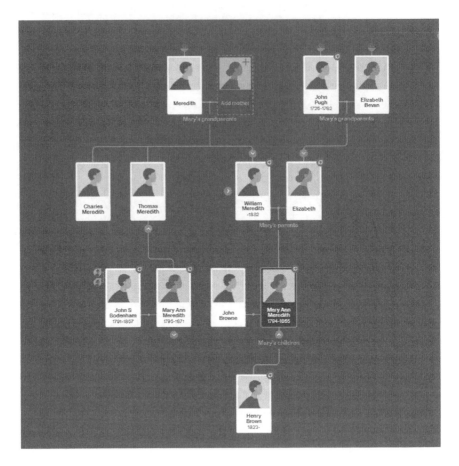

Mary was the daughter of a William Meredith, who along with his two brothers, Charles, and Thomas, were solicitors in Knighton. For those not familiar with the area, this historic little town sits just down the road from Presteigne.

So, why would the daughter of an attorney at law be doing milking cows and lugging buckets? Unless she was illegitimate, of course . . .

Was that why she was shacked up with our Mary; two little bastards cooped up together at the top of the house? I considered the possibility, but it just didn't seem feasible.

The Meredith's of Knighton were well-to-do, and the records are all there, including Mary's cousin with the same name who came to live in Presteigne.

So, just what on earth is going on? Was Walter Senior known to the Meredith brothers? As fellow men of law, you'd think so. Paths would cross, connections made. Isn't that how these things work? Take a look at the names in the list below. Recognise any?

This was printed three years after Mary's death. Besides William Meredith, Mary-Ann's father? We have John Harley, Henry Pyefinch and of course, good old John Browne!

PRESTEIGN, RADNORSHIRE.

NEW MAY FAIR.

WE the undersigned, the Magistrates and principal Landholders in and near the town of Presteign, taking into consideration its central situation, and the great advantage of having good accommodation, (there being no less than Ten reputable Public Inns,) have resolved upon bringing Stock of the different kinds, viz. Cattle, Sheep, Horses, and Pigs, in order to sell them on the Ninth day of May in each year, the first Fair to commence on Monday, the Ninth day of May next ensuing the date hereof. There is a very pleasant eminence near the town called Warden, which will be a very suitable place for Servants to attend in order to be hired, and there can be no doubt of their experiencing very flattering encouragement, as there is every prospect of its being numerously attended both by Servants and Hirers.

Oxford,	Thomas Bodenham,
John Harley,	John Bodenham,
Edward Jenkins,	William Powell,
H. J. Hague,	John Powell,
John Grub,	James Davies,
John Brown,	Peter Stephens,
John Fencott,	John Edwards,
William Meredith,	William Phillips,
Henry Pyefinch,	Edward Morgan,
Thomas Galliers,	John Galliers.

April 9, 1808.

But back to Mary Meredith, the under-dairy maid, and the girl of the same (almost!) name and age who would have been eleven years old at the time of Mary's trial. Ten, when she made her statement.

It was a strange turnaround, because in my head I'd always imagined the youngest witness as being vulnerable, malleable, and probably half-frightened to death. If indeed she was the dairy maid!

You can see my struggle because we have only the word of Maesllwch that she worked at the castle. The Coroner's report that put her forward as a witness. Records of the trial that this eleven-year-old girl testified against her friend and former room-mate. Yet, here we find her, not just marrying Jury member and prison visitor John Browne Esq. ten years later. But leaving the country with him, living in Ireland with him, going to Jamaica where their child is born, before coming back to Ireland, (we assume), where he gives up the ghost leaving his widow and son to return to this country.

But not to Wales. Or even to Knighton, as you'd expect.

In the census of 1851, Mary turns up in Buckinghamshire, visiting a Mrs Simpson.

Then in 1861, we find her living in Merseyside with her son.

On both, she is listed as being born in Knighton which brings me neatly back to Belvoir and one of those weird anomalies that have so marked this case.

There must be something about the women from Knighton, for the current Duchess of Rutland also began life in 'Tref y Clawdd' (the town on the Dyke) as a farmer's daughter, no less! So, not only were both ladies born there; each had married into a lifestyle and position we can only dream of. Each, also, by association, are linked to Mary Morgan. More than a little intriguing, don't you think?

As a footnote to this section, sadly we didn't find Mrs Simpson, but I did have a dream about her. After the case and the scandal had died down, I dreamt she went to live in Llandudno with another woman, (Mrs Evelyn aka Miss Marple, the Cook, perhaps? Because we couldn't find her either), where they opened a boarding house together. It would be interesting to know more about this if it resonates with anyone – because you know what they say, if it's meant to be, the Universe will find a way.

Always.

So, as we step back from the saga of Mary, Mary-Ann, Browne née Meredith, let's now turn our attention to Margaret Havard. And of all the witnesses involved in this case, I believe she was possibly the only genuine servant involved.

Interestingly, I also had a glimpse of Ms Havard during one of my nightly sojourns. A thin, middle-aged woman with short greying hair and an anxious air. In the dream she came across as extremely unstable who did not kindly to the next influx of servants who came over the border after the Mary Morgan saga. Not because she had any particular dislike for our English cousins, but because this was a woman who feared for her position and viewed any new incomer as a threat.

So what happened to her? Did she remain at Maesllwch? I believe she did, for a short time at least, before seemingly dropping off the face of the earth. And she was the first one I went after before Rebecca came on to the scene.

Like Mrs Simpson and Mr Browne, she bugged me a lot. I was hoping there may be Havard's still in the area, and after an internet search found some high up in the hills not far from Maesllwch.

It was like finding gold and with great anticipation I called them up.

What would I say? How best to tailor my approach? It's possible one of your ancestors was responsible for stringing up one of mine on a rope – can we have a chat about that, please?

Nope, definitely not, but I would need to play it straight. No fanciful fluffing around, just the honest truth of what I was about.

If there's been one thing that's marked this project, it is the utter ease with which people have received my random phone calls, the knock on the door, the questions in the street, and in this case, it was no exception.

My enquiry was met with a gentle curiosity, an invitation to visit and directions how to find the farm.

As someone who refuses to have a sat-nav, on this occasion I'd have given my eye's teeth as I got hopelessly lost! But it was worth it for the lovely countryside and the hospitality when I reached the other end. Over coffee and biscuits, I was treated to a full rendition of their family history and documentation of their family tree. An incredible gesture of open- heartedness and respect.

It was soon apparent that no Margaret Havard was to be found in their family, but the farm had once belonged to the Wilkins Family. There was another branch in Glasbury, they told me, although the last of the line had died some years before. Her name was Roma Havard. Could her line have been the link to Margaret? I vowed to get searching on Ancestry as soon as I got back!

In the meantime, Mr Havard told me a story about a painting that once hung over the main hearth. It was a large picture of Maesllwch Castle with deer in the foreground. He wasn't sure where it went to, but he remembered it distinctly as a child. This was an interesting snippet of information that struck me as quite significant.

At the time this painting was given to the Havard's they were tenants of the Maesllwch Estate, and one can't help but wonder the reasoning behind such a generous gift. A thank you gift, perhaps? Or maybe as a reminder of who was in charge . . .

Who knows. But I don't expect many humble farming folks would have received such a gift from their Lord and Master, unless perhaps, they had provided an exceptional service, of course!

With no direct links that I could see to Margaret, the farmer then told me the remarkable story of when he was born, that with his kind permission I will share.

Having come into this world in this very same house, his appearance was marked with great sorrow as it was soon apparent that he was not meant to stay. The midwife took the tiny body into the next room and placed a piece of muslin over him in the drawer of a chest.

You can only imagine how heartrending this must have been for all concerned, especially his mother. But a miracle was about to happen . . .

After some time, the grandmother went to the room to fetch some candles as the day turned to dusk. She happened to glance across to the tiny, covered figure in the drawer and saw the material move for just a moment.

Hardly daring to believe her own eyes, she went across and tentatively lifted the covering and . . . the baby was breathing!

She rushed back to the mother the babe in her arms, and you can only imagine the joy that greeted this incredible moment! What a story and what a wonderful tale to pass down to future generations. Their very own 'Lazarus' and still very much alive and kicking and named after the doctor!

Before I left, I was given a quick tour of the farmyard and their lovely listed old barn. Despite learning no more about Margaret, I was genuinely moved by their candid manner and willingness to help.

So, it was back to the drawing board as the ghost of Margaret Havard continued to elude all efforts until a foray into "The registers of Glasbury, Breconshire: 1660-1836; Transcribed by Thomas Wood" offered some credible leads.

Here were listed no less than four 'Margaret Havards', but it was one who had previously been a Beavan before her marriage to a William who caught my eye. Could that be her? But with little else to go on, it's more than a little tricky.

Patricia Parris thought she might have found her. In her manuscript she refers to a Margaret Havard, the daughter of William and Margaret, who was baptised in Llowes January 1766. Again, this could be her?

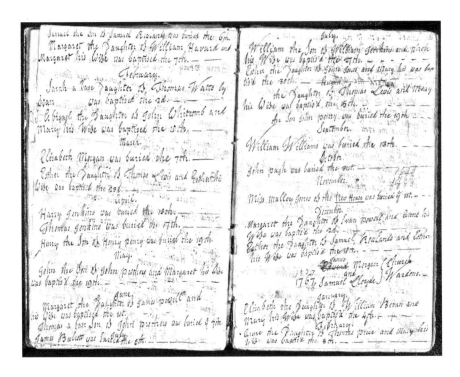

Baptism record for Margaret Havard, St Meilig's, Llowes. Same church where Mary was baptised.

Then there was the Margaret Havard of 'Peny-wain' (Pen-y-Waun Farm) who passed away in 1814 aged fifty-six. After a fire in 1995 what's left of the property is a listed building, and it sits not far from Maesllwch itself.

Can we assume it once would have once been a part of Wilkins land? Was this where Margaret was living when she got the call to come in and cover the shift for Mary?

With no other records available we can only speculate; maybe one day Ms Havard will emerge from the shadows and give up her secrets . . .

1816.

11 Jan.	Elizabeth Evans, Boughrood, 73.
13 ,,	Andrew Prosser, Colebrook, 78.
17 ,,	Eliz^th Powel, Commonbachan, 85.
18 ,,	Alice Jones, Village, 61.
11 Feb.	John Michael, Penwern, 34.
17 Mar.	Elinour Allen, Cwmbach, 81.
2 Ap.	Margaret Havard, Peny-wain, 56.

Thanks to the Powys Family History Society, there is a list of all burials for St. Peter's church, Glasbury, and it was through this Rees and Elizabeth's grave was finally found.

I was over the moon and couldn't help thinking I'd have saved myself a nettle-strewn stomp had I known of its existence before! But this was pre-Rebecca when I still had a lot to learn.

Armed with a rough idea of where their grave was situated, I made a return visit this Spring - not just to find them and pay my respects – but also in search of another.

But before we address this hugely significant find, let us just swing by Mary's parents for a moment and how the visit panned out. Because despite knowing the rough location and having a map before me, do you think I could find it?

After stumbling around apologising profusely I literally gave up the ghost and called Rebecca.

If we went on to video-chat, could she direct me?

Yes.

Thank goodness!

With my phone filming outwards and the sound up, I must have presented an unnerving sight as I weaved up and down, back, and forth with a mad glint in my eye.

The ground was wet, I'd pulled a muscle, and was struggling to find the grave. A couple passing through nodded at me with the kind of look that hopes a nod will suffice and that I don't come any closer. And of course, seeing this I felt the need to try and explain. They hurried on.

The graveyard at St. Peters, Glasbury.

I got back to the business of grave-hunting and into a patch where a stone stood half-buried in the brambles. Nope, that wasn't it. Out of the brambles, back onto the path, up on to the bank, this way, that way, it has to be nearby, surely!

'It's next to Roma Havard.' Rebecca told me.

Next to Roma? You couldn't make it up!

I retraced my steps and found our lady, her place marked with a simple wooden cross, and then . . . Just beyond and set back was a dark weathered slab sat as though waiting quietly.

I made my way across and hunkered down in front of it. The stone face was weathered so badly much of the wording had crumbled away, then suddenly I spotted something.

It was a date and part of a name. I leaned in closer tracing the outlines with my finger.

Yes, it was them. It was definitely them.

At last!

The final resting place of Rees and Elizabeth Morgan

Huge relief! A sublime moment of happiness that also felt weird; stood on the resting place of the couple alleged to have been Mary's parents. I wondered if they were watching, but I didn't feel a thing.

They were long gone.

The grave of Rees and Elizabeth Morgan

I'd brought daffodils, some water, and a jar to put at the grave. After a few words and a moment's silence, I then took some pictures, before calling Rebecca back.

'Ok, where's the next one? Am I close by?'

I was, as it happened, and as I made my way to an older part of the graveyard I groaned at the sight of the tumbled headstones and uneven ground.

'It's around here somewhere.' Rebecca informed me cheerfully.

As I began scanning the nearest crumbling tomb, I could feel myself begin to lose heart. I needed to be somewhere else, and the clock was ticking. There was also the fact I was torn to pieces, aching, and gagging for a coffee.

'I'll come back another time. There's too much damage and too much ivy, it'll take too long.' I said and scanned the camera so Rebecca could see what I was up against.

Then I spotted a headstone sitting by itself beneath the branches of a tree. It struck me as odd as it seemed to be isolated. It was accessible and seemed to draw me.

I panned the camera so that Rebecca could see.

'I'll just have a quick look at this one before I go.' The coffee was all but shouting my name. Next port of call was the Railway Garden Centre, in Three Cocks to check out a link, then a catch-up lunch with a friend.

My stomach rumbled as I clambered over to the gravestone, and as I swept the branches back to read the script, I saw . . .

In front of me.

The name.

His name!

My eyes nearly popped out my head. I couldn't believe it! I may even have gasped at this point. After such onerous attempts to locate the Morgan grave, the other is found with practically no effort at all!!

I think there might have also been a bit of swearing at this point. Wow! We had found him, or rather Rebecca had after weeks of painstaking searching.

Who? Who? I hear you cry!

Why, a rare thing – a rare thing indeed. A servant of Maesllwch and one who was about during Mary's time and so, on that note; let me introduce you to John Wood.

Or rather, let the wording on his headstone, as commissioned by Walter Wilkins, Senior, of Maesllwch Castle! As follows: -

Sacred

To the memory of Mr. JOHN WOOD for thirty five years the faithful

head domestic of WALTER WILKINS Esq. M.P. for the county

The honesty of his character and his unshakeable fidelity rendered him highly

respected he died at Maeslough much regretted the 24th of November 1808

You can see why this had roused our interest. What an elaborately-worded tribute, almost ostentatious, or to use a more common term – gushing!

For a servant?

But no mere servant, it would seem, for John Browne had been the butler!

The head of male staff. The main man. The chief banana! And with such an 'appreciative' accolade on his headstone, obviously the right-hand man, 'the fixer'.

A loyal retainer whose services were so valued in life, his final resting place is recorded as 'Sacred' in a quiet corner, almost hidden because...?

Unlike my usual moments of 'knowing', the significance of finding this long-lost servant didn't trigger me immediately. It kind of crept up on me, bit by bit, as I made my way back down to the car.

Experience had shown us that to pursue the servants of Maesllwch was elusive at best, yet there was something about this John Wood and his fancy headstone.

So, what's the story here? Who is this guy?

Where does he come from and what did he do to warrant such slavish recognition?

My interest grew enough to set Rebecca on the hunt.

'Find out what you can,' I said, 'because something tells me . . .'

The thought began to form as I waited on Rebecca to dig up his secrets.

And she found them.

Or rather his last will and testament.

Once again, I'm going to have to ask you, the reader, to step into the realms of 'impossibility' and tell me, how a servant, no matter how mighty or favoured, could shake off their mortal coil and leave a veritable fortune in their wake?

I'm talking one thousand, two hundred pounds!

One thousand two hundred pounds!!

Four hundred smackeroonies more than Rees Morgan, which in today's money, adds up to a staggering one hundred and twenty thousand and eighty thousand, respectively!

£120k to the butler.

£80k to Mary's father.

WOW . . . For what?

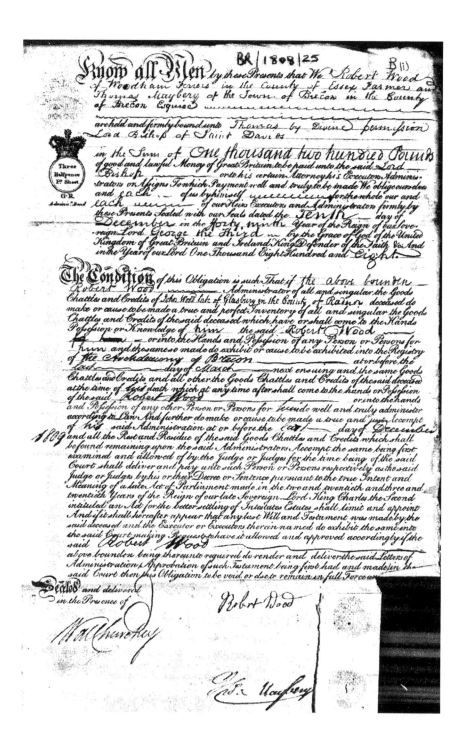

And then I felt it.

Oh yeah, I felt it alright.

It came at me with all the power of a hurricane and once again the World flipped on its head.

Was it him?

Did this man kill the baby?

Senior servant. Man of fortune. Good, old, dependable, John Wood, whose undying loyalty reaped the rewards of his master's trust unto death . . .

I felt a rising tide that threatened to overwhelm me like some angry, ravenous sea monster surging up from the depths.

A scene from the 'Lord of the Rings' flashed through my mind when Sméagol battles at the pool side with the monster he has become.

Golum! Golum! Murderer . . .

I will never be able to watch that scene again without thinking of John Wood.

So was he our man?

Read on and draw your own conclusions, because it is as much as inconceivable the sum of money left - as to whom he left it to!

The Archdeacon of Brecon, if you please! A mighty, influential man of God, who, it's quite obvious he believes, can save his sorry ass. More than two thirds of his fortune to the head honcho of his Diocese over a hundred miles away.

Go figure!

For this is the gesture of a man who fears for his soul. Who has looked to right a wrong in the hope this generous gift will smooth the path to heaven.

Well, whatever your beliefs, I don't think God can be bought. Do you?

With the main whack going to the church, the remaining portion had been left to his brother, Robert. There were no other family members listed. No wife or children – at least none that we could find.

John Wood had seemingly lived his life as a single man, devoted to his job – and Walter Wilkins, Senior, who, in turn, not only paid for the burial of his trusty manservant, but also felt the need to honour his loyalty on a slab of stone for all the world to see.

Now why would that be?

What great services, or service, must have been rendered to deserve such praise, and in my heart, I knew.

My mind flashed back to the inscription on the smaller of Mary's gravestone that decries the unfairness of her fate: "In Memory of MARY MORGAN who Suffer'd April 13th, 1805. Aged 17 years. He that is without sin among you Let him first cast a stone at her. The 8th Chapr. of John.."

John.

Is this a coincidence? Or a definitive nod to the killer should anyone get close enough to the truth? Because if it is the latter, then it strongly suggests that there were those 'in the know'. Namely, Mary's 'parents', and quite possibly the stone mason himself because, I don't know about you, but the pattern of that engraving looks familiar.

All sworn to secrecy, all bound to silence upon fear of death.

Or did they just suspect?

John Wood would've had been a force to be reckoned with back in the day, as was his Lord and Master. You upset one, there was a good chance you'd draw the eye of the other. Not an attractive, or a particularly safe bet in either instance.

Think 'Mafia' – and would that be so far from the truth?

In relation to the timeline of working on this project, this veritable bombshell landed near to fruition. But it was a rotten fruit we couldn't ignore. This age-old, shrivelled core of information that had sat undetected for over two hundred years. A shadow of a man whose grave sits aloof from the great and the good beneath the banner of 'Sacred'.

Sacred?

Well, if I'd been fired up before, I was really mad now as my mind went back to what I was told all those months ago by someone who just happened to cross my path.

Not by accident. Not by coincidence. Not via some chance encounter.

That meeting was the catalyst that brought me into the eye of the storm that is Mary Morgan and has never gone away.

The questions, the ponderings, the strange gaps, and the legal posturing of the day that all but scream 'miscarriage of justice'.

But Mary couldn't scream, could she?

Mary wasn't allowed to say anything other than 'not guilty', and even then 'they' didn't listen. They closed their ears and set their course, for God forbid, she could be innocent!

God forbid, indeed . . .

Then I had an encounter with John. Or rather, he came to me in a dream, and it was, how shall we say – not the friendliest of meetings because when I called him out, he sneered at me.

He sneered!

The audacity!

I woke up in a fury with his image fresh in my mind and scrambled out of bed to commit him to paper.

It's been years since I've sketched a living person and a first trying to capture someone who's been dead for over two centuries!

A big, burly bear of a man, with a thick head of hair, low brow, dark eyes of which the picture does no justice. Cruel mouth. A man who knew secrets. A man who had done things. King of the understairs and a person to be feared.

Suffice to say I wanted words with him. I had some serious beef for the fact he showed up in my dream so supremely self-assured he pressed buttons.

It was also time to pay a call on Walter de Winton. He had never got back to me and if ever we needed to have a conversation, it was now. But first, John.

Around the same time all this was happening I'd become quite close to Demelsa. We had visited Gallows Lane a couple of times together and walked the site and surrounding land in the hope of capturing more phenomena.

It soon became clear to me that Demelsa is extremely gifted. As a local girl, born in Dolley Green just down the road, she also knows her history. Indeed, her knowledge of Presteigne and the surrounding area is enhanced with a sixth sense that delighted and astonished me in turn. She's very modest about this gift of 'sensitivity'. Is hesitant about it and lacks confidence, but this was all about to change!

We'd come a long way since that morning in the shop when she'd sent me up to Gallows Lane. Seemed an age since I'd conferred with her and her partner about my ghostly activity. So, it seemed apt that she rode shot-gun with me over to Glasbury, where I wanted a word with two individuals connected by over two hundred years of history. The fact one of them had been dead for this period was irrelevant, as had been the silence from the other, who was living. Time to chew some serious fat and I wouldn't be taking any prisoners!

The date is 21st March 2023. It was a grey and drizzly morning when we made our way over Brilley Mountain, and the first port of call was the churchyard of St. Peters. This is where our Mr Wood lies in isolated splendour and Dem was going to film our encounter.

From the dream I had no doubts he'd called me over. So provocative had been his manner, I was more than well-up for the fight. Although what was going to happen exactly, I had no clue, only that I wanted to have it out with him – and he also seemingly with me.

As a cock-a-snook gesture I took Demelsa to see Rees and Elizabeth first.

Yes, Mr Wood had my attention, but we would be paying out respects first to the other people caught up in this whole saga of muddy waters and questionable parentage.

What must they be thinking from wherever they are now? Probably glad to be out of it. Indeed, it's possible they never wanted to be a part of it!

And then so onto John. John Wood.

'Sacred' servant . . .

Faithful unto death.

After taking some pictures of me at the grave. Demelsa began filming as I began talking.

I think it's fair to say I was calm at first and firmly called him out. Anyone passing would have thought that we'd gone mad, but not only did I feel that this had to be done. I also wanted to him to know that I knew and that nothing less than 'face-to-face' would do.

It was the nearest I could get. And yet . . . I felt nothing.

Absolutely nada.

Inwardly I cast around. But nothing was happening. All was calm and unmoving on the clairsentient front.

'I feel nothing,' I said turning to Demelsa in some confusion.

She did though.

After she'd stopped filming, she said she could see a tall, dark figure several feet behind me and to the right seemingly watching. Or to use her words, "observing".

And did she think it was him? Was the silent watcher our man?

Yes.

By now I'd left the graveside and was back on the path, but hearing this made me want to see if I could draw him out further. I began filming and sensed a low-key presence, but he seemed to be keeping his distance.

As I tried to bait him into some kind of reveal, I distinctly felt a word, two words, in fact, two, and could scarce believe it!

F**KING BASTARD!

What. . ?

Then the anger came, like a tidal wave. F**king bastard?

How dare he!

Still filming, I recorded my response to what wasn't just blatant disrespect, but the fact he was goading me now and goading me like a good 'un! And now, I felt him.

Oh yeah, all the aggression, all the anger, all the menace of a man who had wielded so much power. He had been bold, brutish, and violence had been no stranger to him.

What a horrible man! The worst kind. And in that moment, I hated him.

The fury was still rising and the language, 'choice', as with the camera now off, we made our way down towards the gate.

I was still chuntering when suddenly, Demelsa paused and looked back the way we'd come.

I turned around and followed her gaze.

'What is it?'

There was just the slightest hesitation before she said, 'He's come out on to the path. He's still observing us.'

I could see nothing, but I responded nevertheless and with no small amount of vigour.

He still wasn't having it, however, and I had enough faith in Demelsa to know she wasn't imagining this figure. But why he should be making himself so evident to her and not me only served to aggravate my frustration.

It wasn't until we left the confines of the churchyard that I began to cool down.

'What was all that about?' I said starting up the car, 'I was so angry. Or was that Mary, channelling her anger through me?'

As we speculated and went over the visit there was another call I needed to make before Maesllwch. The Railway Garden Centre is one of those places that is always a joy to visit, and besides the need for coffee and the bathroom, we needed space for a proper debrief.

Demelsa is self-deprecating at best, and I was intrigued to know what else she might have picked up, and as always, she surprised me!

'When I was filming you,' she said, 'Every time you said about him killing the baby, I had an image in my head . . . When I was young, we lived on a small holding and had a dog that was quite old. Somehow, she got pregnant and had a litter of puppies. Because of her age, my father put two of them in the bucket. I can remember him telling me afterwards and the look in his eyes when I became upset. By putting them back in the water, was like putting them back to sleep, he told me, and it was that look in his eyes I kept seeing when you talked about the baby.'

I lifted my shoulders.

She went on.

'It was a look of regret. Quiet regret. It was there, and I could see it. He had to drown the puppies to give the others a chance. It was just the way of the countryside, the way of dealing with things. He didn't want to do it, but he did what he thought was the kindest way by putting them back to sleep . . .'

She paused, and we gazed at each other in silence. It was busy in the café and noise all about us, but we could have been the only two people in the room at that moment.

I didn't know what to say. This was a disclosure I hadn't been expecting, and something told me there would be more.

I look back now and realise that the look Demelsa was giving me was like that of one about to break bad news. Or in this case, a revelation that was not going to go down well.

She was measuring me up, the sense of anticipation all but bristled between us.

'Okay,' I said eventually, 'So what does this mean? What are you trying to say, Dem?'

'I believe that he is sorry. I feel that he did what he had to do . . . he didn't want to, but he had to do it.'

I felt my eyebrows shoot up.

'What . . .'

Dem waved her hand and seeing a quiet determination in her eyes, respect held my tongue.

'When I was filming you at the grave, I could sense his remorse. But he had to deal with the situation. He had no choice. It was a job that had to be done.'

'What, killing an innocent baby?' I burst out.

'Yes,' said Demelsa, this lovely, gentle mother of three, 'He had to do it. He had no choice.'

As the import of this statement sank in, I could only marvel at the calmness of her tone. Not to mention her obvious understanding. Such natural wisdom. Such inner grace.

I sat back in bewilderment.

'That wasn't the vibe, I was getting, Demelsa. The man was a bully. He swore at me. Sneered at me in my dream. The man I've seen is not the man you are depicting; I can't believe you're sticking up for him!'

Completely unruffled Demelsa continued to do just that and mighty was the inward struggle, I can tell you! Especially when she said she thought I should go back to the graveyard.

What?

No way! There was nothing more I wanted to say to the ghost of a man who I believed had killed Mary's baby. Are you kidding me?

But this lady who usually wouldn't say boo to a goose, quietly persisted and made the argument.

This woman, however, wasn't for turning. No. Nope! No siree! Ain't going back! He can stew in his own juice! Not interested!

Dem then said something that gave me pause to reflect, and as we made our way out to the car, I just couldn't shake it off.

'He was a servant as well, you know . . .'

And so, he was. I'd forgotten about that.

And it resonated.

A servant. Paid to do a job. Expected to perform one's duties without question or . . .

What?

What was the worst-case scenario in those days other than to be sent packing in disgrace? Sent off without hope or references, condemned to a life of destitution.

But what if you sat on secrets? What if you knew things that could compromise the good name of your employers? What happened then?

The saying, 'He who pays the fiddler calls the tune', came to mind and refusal to dance could invite all kinds of trouble down on your head, could it not?

I had absolutely no intention of going back yet found myself pulling over outside the church.

'Okay,' I said to Demelsa, 'Let's hear what he's got to say.'

Once again, I went over to the gravestone and hunkered down as Dem started filming and started to talk.

This time I did feel him. He was still keeping a distance – or was he being kept at bay?

But one thing was for sure, the vibe was different, and I sensed regret.

I want to atone; he kept telling me.

That's between you and God, I told him inwardly.

He was glad that I'd come back, he added, and strangely so was I, and I would be lying if I said any different.

There was nothing more to say. On either side. As far as I was concerned, I'd done my bit, and as we made our way out from St. Peter's for the second time that morning, something still troubled me.

'He presented so differently in the dream,' I said to Demelsa, 'Very arrogant, and was quite belligerent during our first encounter. I don't get it.'

As we reflected on this for a few moments I had a sudden thought.

'What if he did it deliberately? The dream, I mean. Goaded me into coming over because he knew I wouldn't otherwise, at least not to see him! Was it all a ruse so he could say sorry? Because if so, he has you to thank for that!'

And it was true. Demelsa had been the deal-broker, the peace-maker.

I still felt bemused at the sudden turn in events – and attitude on both parts! Had I/ we been played by a ghost? I kept thinking 'good cop, bad cop'. Had this been a case of, 'bad man, good man'?

John Wood, courtesy of Demelsa Hopkins whose sketch is a very good interpretation of the man I saw in my dream.

Who knows, but he had been with us, alright. This time no figure had been detected, but Dem did pick up some phenomena as she was filming. With random focus and intermittent shades of light and dark. Very odd, but then again, could anything be deemed 'normal' since this project began?

I recalled a dream on 22nd December 2022, and seeing men gathered around a girl lying in the snow. The girl was deceased and had long fair hair. One of the men was the character, Hudson, from the 1970's TV series, 'Upstairs, Downstairs.'

I knew that the dream was showing me Mary. As I knew the snow on the ground was representative of the coldness of the men. What I couldn't understand was why the 'Hudson' character was there. I'd said as much to Rebecca the following morning.

For authenticity, I'd started logging any dreams of significance with her via messenger. Now, having discovered John Wood and his commendations so adoringly set in stone; it made sense he would have been at the execution.

I mean, who else could be trusted with such a delicate task than the good old butler? Not just as a first-hand witness, but to ensure all went smoothly in case Mary had any last-minute ramblings before they broke her neck!

Seems feasible, does it not?

As does the idea that poor Mari bach has been drowned in a bucket.

No need to have taken her down to the river to do it, as I'd been told. Just another unwanted puppy. Let's pop her in the water. Won't take much and then we can slit her throat afterwards. Job done.

How does that sound as an alternative version to the one we've got?

I'll leave you to mull that over as I move on next to Maesllwch.

CHAPTER 7

I'd been waiting a long time to a pay visit to 'the scene of the crime'. I knew I'd never be invited into the inner sanctum, but just to get close to the castle and its secrets would be enough.

I'd always wanted a conversation with Walter de Winton and in light of recent developments, today was the day.

It was with a steely feeling in my heart that I drove along the endless drive and pulled up in front of the steps. How ever this was going to unfold, I wanted Demelsa close enough to hear everything.

I rang the bell and waited. It's a big old place, so patience kept company until the door was finally opened and by none other than Walter himself.

'Remember me?' I said.

As it happened, he didn't. But I soon reacquainted him and the reason why I was calling.

I'd uncovered information in relation to Mary's story, significant enough to challenge everything we'd been led to believe and more. The book was still going ahead, I told him, but as a courtesy, I thought I'd just let him know.

Was there anything he wanted to add?

Would seem he did not. But he was certainly keen to know what I'd uncovered. Indeed, he was quite persistent!

It soon became clear to me that Mr de Winton was not going to parley in the way I had hoped, but to be fair he did offer something;

he told to me that Walter Junior did not sit on the Jury that day. That old trial anomaly that had always plagued historians and for my part, I believe him.

I'm so glad Mary was spared the sight of him, although I believe his absence was more out of cowardice than consideration. Besides, why risk a melt-down in court for all to see. Much better to 'box clever'.

Mr de Winton also stated that his ancestor, as he called him, would have married Mary had he been the father, which brings me on to that very allegation. Because this is one of the many things reportedly said at the time. A noble offering I'm sure, but where's the proof?

My response was that it's just hearsay and I don't think he liked that very much. But if you look along the path of Mary's journey to the noose, you'll see snippets here and snippets there of what she said; to the Judge - or was it the Reverends?

Yet no real records exist to countenance these allegations.

In case anyone is wondering, I have no quarrel with Walter de Winton. What happened in the past is not his fault. But it would have been great to have had his side of things. A chance for him to have his say.

He made it quite clear, however that in his view, the official version was exactly that and he had nothing further to add.

To be fair, we did talk for about ten minutes. But then, he did say at the opening stages that he would give me that - after I mentioned John Wood.

Within the first couple of minutes, I put the name to him to which he replied, 'I've never heard of him' before dropping his eyes.

Make of that what you will, but I asked the question to see the reaction, and suffice to say, Mr Wood never got another mention. Despite heated demands to disclose what I knew; suffice to say I am no Mary Morgan.

With no small aplomb I held my peace and was politeness personified before taking my leave.

What I'd forgotten to ask – and more fool me! – was about an extraordinary condition in Walter Junior' will that begs the question: Why was the entirety of his estate to be left to a William and Thomas Morgan of Glasbury should any of Walter's children die without an heir?

For what possible reason could that be - why? A most generous gesture as to be almost beyond belief!

John Wood must be turning in his grave; his assets seem almost paltry in comparison!

I guess we'll never know now, but here is the segment for your perusal. The names of James William Morgan and Thomas Morgan are halfway down the centre of the document.

Feel free to speculate at will.

A section as taken from the last will and testament of Walter Wilkins (Junior). James William Morgan and Thomas Morgan of Glasbury approx. halfway down the mid-section of the document.

I also meant to ask about a snippet I saw in Patricia Parris' manuscript that intrigues me to this day.

Apparently, some Wilkins from America came over and visited Glasbury in the hope of tracing their roots.

This was in 1970's and they had no idea that the family name had been changed. Allegedly they left a sealed envelope to be opened in fifty years' time.

Well, by my reckoning the time is nigh, but who knows.

Tick tock . . .

As I turned and shook off the dust of Maesllwch, it was with conviction in my heart. I had done what I needed to do.

I came. I saw. I spoke. I listened. Not even the slam of the door in my wake could shake the triumph of the moment.

And as I slowly descended the steps, I could all but feel Mary skipping beside me, because the whole reason of the visit was for her.

But then, you already know that don't you . . .

Every conversation, every foray out for clues and connections, every feeling, every word written.

For her.

And for *Mari bach.*

A less robust encounter was when I spoke with a former school teacher called Barnaby. He's the organist at St. Andrews and we met in the precincts last year.

So, when I happened to bump into him again and his lovely wife, the conversation, as usual, turned to Mary. We were in the excellent 'Rose Cottage Café', a popular venue on the High Street, when a man came in.

Turned out his name was Tony Wood, formerly of Kinsham Hall, (and no relation, that we're aware of, to John)! I couldn't believe my luck and all but jumped on him!

So, what is the connection here?

Well, Kinsham Court isn't far from Presteigne and had come up on Rebecca's radar in the early days when we were looking for the servants. Kinsham Court had been home to the Evelyn family, and after finding Ms Meredith aka Mrs Browne, our eyes had alighted briefly on the questionable identity of the Cook, Mrs Evelyn.

And come on, you can't blame us! Every stone unturned so far had given more ground for suspicion, and now here before me was a direct descendent of the Evelyn's!

His grandmother has been an Evelyn, he told me, but his family didn't purchase the estate until some twenty years after Mary's demise.

Based upon this information, I didn't pursue my line of thought any further. But what is interesting, is that his family had bought the property from Lord Oxford. The Harleys, Reverend Scott, remember them?

There has never been a dull or uninformed moment during the writing of this book, and as Mr Wood was moving from the area within days, our encounter had been fortuitous at best!

Less fortuitously for him and his family, the estate has only recently been put to auction. Another casualty of the modern age, but he did acknowledge Mary and express his sympathies.

Poor Mary, it's not sympathy she wants, but closure and disclosure and not necessarily in that order. I'd hoped to have the book finished in time to mark the anniversary of her passing, but the appearance of John Wood had put paid to that! Interestingly, it was about this time, I dreamt of him again.

Rebecca and I were stood on the drive of Maesllwch just before the entrance to the courtyard. Someone was talking to us and how the place was haunted. At that moment, our attention was directed toward two pairs, possibly three, of disembodied hands and feet that crossed from the castle over to the woods.

We were then told to look up and to our right, where high up in a copse of trees stood a tall dark figure. He was watching us and immediately I knew it to be John Wood.

As I came to out of the dream, I had the sense that this man's spirit still watches over Maesllwch. His appearance at the graveyard was a one-off meet and greet – although Demelsa thinks that a night time visit would probably be more forthcoming.

I don't doubt her for one moment, but what I do feel is that Maesllwch is his patch; he continues to keep vigil in death, as he did in life.

But why? And what was all that with the ghostly hands and feet? What did it all mean? And who was the person talking to us?

All of a sudden it came to me in a flash.

Oh my God . . . the baby!

The baby's buried in the woods?

The baby is buried in the woods?

I couldn't wait to tell Rebecca and called her up in a babble.

It was plausible, was it not? A kindly gesture from the House? An act that would go a long way in appeasing any heightened feelings, and surely there must have been some. And what better way to keep the lid on things? Imagine the scenario, I said, just hear the words for a moment. . .

Such an awful tragedy, and under our own roof! Here, let us find a quiet spot for the baby. We have ground aplenty and more than enough to spare. It is the least we can do. John, take some men and see to it, please . . .

Was this how it went? Was this what happened? A quiet word with the coroner? A nod here and a few guineas there? Better to keep the baby close, methinks, because we wouldn't want anyone coming to visit little Mari bach, now, would we? And where better to quietly tuck her away than on the Maesllwch estate!?

Was this what the dream was saying? And was John helping us? Had the unfailingly faithful servant turned rogue and jumped camp?

He told me he wanted to atone and what better way than showing us where to find the baby?

After running my thoughts past Rebecca, she agreed it wasn't beyond the realms of possibility. The idea was in my head now and it wouldn't go away.

With this new information in hand, I put in a call to St. David's Cathedral and spoke with a lady called Judith who very kindly passed me on to their equally helpful librarian, Mari James. There then ensued a conversation about the will of John Wood. Mari agreed it was a substantial sum and that she would take a look in their extensive archives. (Subsequently, Mari could find nothing but who knows what may pop up in the future!)

I then raised the subject of the baby's burial place. Cousin Mary particularly wanted to know, as once again, I found myself amidst another Universal idiosyncrasy of asking a lady, also called Mari, if she can help find our Mari bach. You just couldn't make it up!

So, what happened to victims of infanticide? I asked because no one seemed to really know! The general consensus of opinion was that they would be put in the coffin with the next person due to be buried.

On the same day of the inquest, 25th September, the records say a William Gittoes was laid to rest. Had Mari bach gone into the earth with him? With no known burial location for this gentleman, we can only speculate. Perhaps a better bet would be an Elizabeth Prosser who was the next person to be buried on October 1st, respectively.

Oh, what wouldn't we do to find that baby!

Mari's next words were like music to my ears.

'They kept records,' she told me, 'Every baby, whether they were stillborn, illegitimate or had died in infancy, had to be recorded. Some didn't bother and records can go missing. I'll have a look but there's no guarantee.'

It didn't matter, the fact she was willing to look was a gift in itself. If I could have reached down the phone and kissed her I would've! This was an amazing development and without further ado I just had to tell her about my dream.

Could Mari bach be lying somewhere on the Maesllwch Estate? Would the Wilkins have had enough clout to facilitate such a manoeuvre? As we know, there was never any 'room at the inn' when it came to illegitimate children and consecrated ground.

To my delight this learned lady did not disagree. Neither did the Buftons' when I ran the idea past them.

'Yes, it's credible,' were Heather's words and that was good enough for me! By now it had become more than just an odyssey for the truth; I couldn't have been more committed if Mary had been my own flesh and blood.

Love is such a powerful thing, and it was blowing away the shadows that had so shrouded this case for over two hundred years.

The knowledge that somewhere deep within St. David's Cathedral, lies a dusty old ledger that would not only reveal the resting place of Mary's baby, but would also endorse the validity of my dreams, was an exciting prospect. Because let's face it - if it wasn't for John's largesse, we would never have turned to St. David's. Was he, too, leaving a trail?

Was this his deal with God?

A chance of redemption?

Dear Lord. Take this money. Allow me into heaven and I will leave a clue . . .

John Wood: Devoted butler, sacred servant, who I believe took the life of *Mari bach*. Has led us full circle, and if this was his idea of atonement – then he was playing a blinder!

But oh, the irony. Indeed, the whole saga, if you look at it from a different perspective, for it is as bizarre as it is baffling, and it is the identity of the under-dairy maid that holds the key.

Either Mary (Ann) was the illegitimate daughter of William Meredith and had been given a start at Maesllwch. Not unusual, and an easy way of alleviating responsibility with food and a roof far from your own back yard; scandal averted, love-child sorted, it's business as usual for clever Papa. Job done!

Or . . . the role of under dairy maid was manufactured.

A duplicitous, well-planned, charade designed to ensure the downfall of an innocent girl, because . . .

Because?

Perhaps Mary Morgan was no 'ordinary' servant. Lest we forget, this girl was raised by a woman old enough to have been her grandmother. A woman married to a man twenty-seven years her junior who just happened to leave a fortune in his will.

But it is also the date of their marriage that tells a tale.

Rees Morgan didn't marry Elizabeth Beavan until 13th September 1795.

That's seven years after Mary was born.

So, what does this tell us? What does it suggest?

That Mary was a love-child herself? That Rees and Elizabeth adopted her?

Did this mean her birth-mother had perished when Mary was seven years of age, because . . .

At sixteen years of age, Mary had the great fortune to land a job at Maesllwch? But not anything as lowly as a kitchen maid or some scullery drab. Oh nooo . . .

A good position, an envied position, a role that will set her up for life, because all big houses need a Cook, right? And if reports of Walter Junior taking care of his love-children in later life are to be believed, was this something that the Wilkins did?

Had Walter Junior taken his cue from his father once he was in a position to do so?

I ask the question because of a stipend in Walter Senior's will that leaves an annuity of twenty pounds to his 'servant', Jane Stonehewer, to be paid for the rest of her life.

This little nugget came to light during a reading of Patricia Parris' manuscript and what a find!

So, who was the lucky lady?

Without further ado I started a tree. Originally from Kent, Jane, who was born a Wicks, got wed in Dover to an Ormond Stonehewer, from St. Clears, Carmarthenshire. Ormond's family had been innkeepers at the Blue Boar, Jane perhaps from more humble beginnings.

After their marriage in 1791, Ormond takes his bride back to

Carmarthen where their first child is born about a year later. Their next son comes along in 1795 in Breconshire, so from this we know they are either working in Maesllwch or living nearby.

Ormond, who was a leather worker, dies in 1805, just a few months after Mary, leaving Jane a widow with two small sons to support. This is a terrible predicament to find herself in and her options are limited; face starvation or . . . you can see where I'm going with this.

Second line down.

Far from me to be presumptuous, but the fact we find her youngest, Ormond in India at the end of his life, is further compounded by his three daughters beginning theirs in Bengal! Whatever the truth of the matter, one thing's for sure; it paid to keep on the right side of the Walter Senior, which neatly brings me on to the million-dollar question:

Was Mary his illegitimate daughter?

Is this the reason why she was conspired against because of shared blood? An unknowing victim of incestuous love that couldn't be denied once the baby was born with red hair?

Was this why both mother and child had to die?

To avert what would have been one hell of a scandal and blown Walter's forthcoming marriage right out the water? Not to mention the family name!

The appearance of a love-child could have been smoothed out before Walter's bride even got wind of it. A child born to half-brother and half-sister, however, is a whole new animal and simply not to be borne.

This notion came to me during one of the (many!) 'brick-wall' moments. And it's a reasonable supposition, is it not? Possible, thought-provoking, and would certainly explain a lot.

Or else we have the alternative; the promiscuous undercook who couldn't keep her knickers on. That lying, scheming chit of a girl who had the audacity to plead 'not guilty' and don *'gay apparel'*.

Who'd stood before the Judge with a heart of stone as the charge of murder was levelled against her. A girl with no concept of God and religion; stupid, sly, ignorant, and guilty, oh so, guilty, she even confessed to it!

"I determined, therefore, to kill it, poor thing! Out of the way, being perfectly sure that I could not provide for it myself."

So, when did she say this, then? There is no record of it from the court – the prisoner was not allowed to speak once they entered their plea. There would have been an opportunity after sentence was passed, and yet we have . . . nothing but the word of the Judge. She said it to him apparently.

How opportune . . .

In his letters to the Bishop of St. Asaph afterwards, Judge Hardinge had plenty to say about Mary and her guilt. Her beauty and her tragedy. His justification for hanging her, his obvious attempts to seek approval for these actions through a man of God.

Sound familiar?

Poor old Bishop was getting it right in the ear!

There's also another part where Judge Hardinge's pious outpourings included a reference to Walter Junior. As follows:

'The young Squire, though her favourite gallant, was not the father; but she did him justice in reporting, that, when he was apprised of the pregnancy, he offered to maintain the child when born, if she would only say that he was the father . . .'

A few things here if I may. Firstly, when did she tell him all this? Again, nothing bearing this 'key' information exists in the court records, so where exactly did this conversation take place?

Did the Judge take a turn down the Gaol to have a private conversation with Mary? Or did he pop down to the Shire Hall cells for a word before her trial?

Neither seems likely, does it? Yet, we are expected to believe that she poured out her heart out to the Judge before he passed the sentence of death.

Really?

Secondly, the content is quite telling. It touches on Mary's integrity whilst magnifying Walter's with the assertion he would have stood by her – if she declared the baby was his. Which in turns implies Mary must have been putting it about.

Just those two words *'her favourite gallant'* is fully loaded and infers that there were others.

Rather an ambiguous statement it has to be said. Mary; good girl, bad girl. Walter Junior, however, coming up smelling of roses and firmly off the hook!

Just to touch on my conversation with the current Walter, when he asserted that his ancestor would have married Mary if the baby was his, may I also assert, at this point, that Mary was not Cinderella and pigs still don't fly, that I'm aware of.

But back to the Judge and his written ramblings. His poems to Mary and his obvious guilt.

Because there is guilt there, right? This is the man who'd visit her grave. Who alternated between sentimentality and mercilessness for what she had done. And for why? She was a creature devoid of religion, remember? An absolute heathen who deserved to die.

I wonder if she was thinking along the same lines the day he collapsed at her grave.

Take that for a twist of irony, although a sucker-punch may be more apt!

Stricken with pleurisy, they said. Carried him back to the old Bradshaw Manor on St. David's Street, (St. David's — see the pattern?) before death claimed this judicial giant of morality.

This grand old building where Hardinge croaked his last is steeped in history, and thanks to the owners, I was allowed a peep inside earlier this year.

Much has changed since it was the Judge's Lodgings, courtesy of a renovation project in 1824.

When the new Shire Hall, 'The Judge's Lodgings', was completed in 1829, Bradshaw Manor became the vicarage for a while, and has been lovingly restored by Mr and Mrs Kendall.

The hallway is marked by the most stunning woodwork, with the ceiling, as far as they know the only existing part of the house.

But it gives some idea of how grand it would have looked when His Nibs ate, slept, and died there - as to where that room is exactly, I will hold my peace.

But just as a footnote that only adds to the whole Mary Morgan saga; why isn't his final resting place public knowledge?

Despite an extensive search, all we could unearth was where he drew up his last will and testament in 1815.

At the time he was in Esher, Surrey, residing in a property called Milbourne House, but who knows!

Talk about shrouded in mystery and one can only wonder why.

But back to Mary and her alleged confession that neatly ties everything up. Walter wasn't the father, the Waggoner was, she killed the baby, and for that she will hang, she'll take the rap when all the time it was the butler!

He did it and no one will convince me otherwise No man, woman, fancy historian, or member of the nobility.

Not one.

He acted on orders. I also have no doubt of that. But he wasn't alone in his collusion. Oh no! Which now brings me on to the Morgans.

CHAPTER 8

Ahhhh, the Morgans. . . So many of them; sheep farmers, drovers, exporters of wool and in deep with the de Wintons as far as the eye can see.

Shocked?

Weren't expecting that, were ya!

We weren't either, to be honest, but we found them – or rather Rebecca did, and once again she exceeded herself.

We'd always imagined, as you do, that had Mary been a member of such a large and widespread family, there would have been some kind of outcry from her kin. Yet we hear not a peep. Not one word. Except for an extraordinary statement that had come from one individual and passed on to another.

What wouldn't I have given for a one-to-one conversation with this man, but sadly he had passed away to pastures new some years before. Indeed, it was months before I learned of his identity. My source, despite having shared the initial disclosure, understandably, was loath to start naming names. I was a complete stranger, after all, and keen to know more. But over time, we built a rapport. I kept in touch and kept him abreast of all new developments.

By taking him into my confidence, eventually, he returned the favour and revealed the identity of our man. I'm not sure what I was expecting, but it wasn't a Morgan. The man had been a Morgan! I all but fell off the chair!

So, who was this character?

And what a character he was! George Morgan, local man, a well-known figure around the farming fraternity, had kept sheep and was well known for his love of horses! And what's more, he still had family in the area, hence the delicacy of the situation.

Wow! A direct link, a Morgan and with living relatives who, as you can imagine, I couldn't wait to meet. George had a son and a sister still living, but first the family background and despite painstaking research, I couldn't definitively connect George's line to that of Cousin Mary. This is something I will continue to investigate. But what both families do have in common is a story that was passed down word of mouth. My cousin, a skeleton in the cupboard. The other, a member of the household drowned the baby in the river. Did this mean that George's family were also 'in the know'?

I needed to find out, because as far as I was concerned, where there's smoke there's fire and here was a veritable funeral pyre that simply smouldered with secrets!

But back to George Morgan and where life began for him.

He was born in Painscastle, a small but spread-out community that sits some three miles from the Welsh/English border. It is also a few miles from Llanstephen, Llowes and Glasbury respectively. Steeped in local history, Painscastle, remains home to many local families and is a tightknit community.

George had been born in the 'Maesllwch Arms', now called 'The Roast Ox', an establishment that would have seen a steady stream of Drovers and their livestock passing through almost constantly. Here his father was both inn-keeper and blacksmith, and as such would've been more than privy to gossip from near and far. Indeed, as main host he would have been more informed than many. So, was this how George's allegation came to light? Had a passer-by shared this snippet with his father? Or had it come from someone closer to home, like a servant from the castle, perhaps?

I just had to speak to the family!

Back to my source but he was reluctant to divulge further details. Equally I was keen to make contact. I just had to know. This was incredibly important, and once again, the trust-factor won through, but it had taken months!

I can't describe my joy when the Morgans of Painscastle finally agreed to meet with me. What made this encounter all the more remarkable, is that it was one of the 'love-children' who facilitated it.

Liz Smith, née Anthony, of Clyro, whose Great Grandfather is descended from Walter Junior, has been a huge help throughout this project. Along with her niece, Gill, they even came up to Presteigne to visit Mary's grave. We have been united in the search for truth; for them the definitive identity of their great grandmother, who we think we've found, a servant from Knighton by the name of Sarah. But of course, like much of what's been uncovered, there remain gaps and guess work. Frustrating but not always fruitless, like myself, they have persevered.

As I've mentioned, there has been some serious peculiarities throughout this project and meeting Liz is just one of them, for it turns out that her best friend, Iris Morris, is none other than the niece of George Morgan! A possible descendent of Mary's family, best buddies with a descendent of Walter Junior! On the wrong side of the basket, admittedly, but a descendent of, nevertheless. Once again, you couldn't have made it up!

We all got together around Liz's dining table in early Summer, and I think it's fair to say the mood was tinged with apprehension on both sides. Here we were, with the exception of Liz and myself, complete strangers to each other, about to address an allegation that was as controversial as it seemed fantastical.

They listened intently as I introduced a bit about myself and the reason for drawing them into this two-hundred-year-old mystery. Primarily, my focus was on Derek. As the son of George, he was the obvious choice for any first-hand information, but he was as nonplussed as everyone else: No, this was news to them. George had never said a word!

I looked around at all their faces. They met my gaze openly and with genuine confusion. They hadn't a clue.

Life-long best friends Iris Morris, formerly Morgan, and Liz Smith née Anthony.

But they were certainly intrigued. Brian especially, who is a keen historian and in the local 'know'. They were au fait with their family history but had never considered any direct links to Mary herself. If anything, the mere possibility was met with a kind of bemused wonder. Besides, their links were in Painscastle, and despite a myriad of Morgans, Mary's branch were from Glasbury, some eight miles away.

Interesting that we could find the connection between their clan and my cousin, but not Mary's Morgans, which only served to deepen the mystery.

I was no further on, but it was so good to meet George's family and be allowed the opportunity to ask the question. It wasn't the answer I'd been hoping for, but they struck me as honest people and we will remain in touch. Indeed, Brian even asked if I'd give a talk to his group once the book was published. Would I ever!

From left: Derek Morgan (George's son), with his cousins Brian Morgan, Iris Morris and her daughter, Nerissa.

As we parted ways it was with a warmth and an insight for them into my world of dreams and unexplained phenomena. It was an experience I'm sure they won't forget, as I won't their faces when I recalled seeing Walter Junior in my bedroom!

And was Mary present?

I have no idea. But if she was, she kept well to the background, as did the subject of our meeting - if he was there at all. My meeting was with the living that day, and to this one, I still marvel at the connections that bind us all. I wonder at all the things we can't explain but take on faith, no matter - for without the latter; where would we be when the Universe speaks? How can we turn a deaf ear when voices call from beyond the grave? And should we discount the power of dreams when they point us in the right direction?

Truth be known; if it hadn't been for all of these things, as other-worldly and impossible as they may seem – this book would never have been written. Not one word. Because if we go with the accepted narrative, then the alternative version remains hidden. The very idea that Mary Morgan had been set up from start to finish, forsaken and left to wander in eternal darkness.

But back to George; had he been telling the truth?

As mystified as they were by his revelation, the family have no reason to believe he'd plucked it from thin air. For what purpose?

With all of them living in close proximity to Maesllwch, had he not taken them into his confidence so as to protect them? What you don't know, you can't speculate upon, can you. Ignorance is bliss and the shadow of the local Squire just a little too close to home to make waves by repeating unfounded allegations.

Better to remain the proverbial mushroom, methinks, but Derek, George's son, suggested I might like to speak to another family member, Les Pitts who actually lives in Presteigne.

With the help of Glenys Millichamp, I contacted Les who was intrigued with what I had to say.

He also knew nothing of George's allegation but did say that as much of a character his Uncle was, he didn't think he would make such a thing up. I didn't know the man, but for what it's worth, I feel the same. He had absolutely nothing to gain, but possibly much to lose had he gone public. Who knows? One or two, I believe, but they ain't talking!

With that line of enquiry out of the way, there was still the question of the 'Morgans' and as you can imagine, as the main movers and shakers of the wool industry back in the day, they were legion.

They were also traceable in areas of interest notwithstanding 'Treble Hill' a thriving woollen mill built in 1800 by a John Morgan.

What's left of the property is now a listed building that sits in Gwernyfed on the fringes of Glasbury. With the absence of certain records, nothing could be found to link in to Rees, but it's highly likely they knew each other. And if the Morgans weren't busy with the wool, you could find them pulling a pint!

In addition to the old Maesllwch Arms in Painscastle where George was born, we also have another establishment that went by the same name in Glasbury.

Sadly, this business also goes under another name these days, but back in Mary's day it was the Maesllwch Arms and managed by Morgans.

Oh, and let us not forget 'The Harp Inn' that has kept its original name and much of its old charm to this day - also ran by Morgans. A lovely little pub that serves great food, it's a friendly place and popular with locals. I met a couple who had worked on the estate, but due to the close proximity of Maesllwch, they were reluctant to divulge anything further.

Then there were the Morgans Rebecca found living on the Maesllwch estate in a property called 'The Gas House'.

Morgans, Morgans, everywhere, and not one willing to put their head above the Maesllwch parapet!

Tenants, workers, landowners, innkeepers. All would have been known to each other, all possibly related, and all connected to Rees Morgan and his only child, a daughter called Mary. A large, industrious, well-connected family who, to a man, and woman – had turned a blind eye to the terrible fall of one of their own.

And said nothing.

What does this say to us?

That Mary wasn't a Morgan? That she wasn't one of them? Had she had been farmed out, adopted, by the kindly Rees, who forewent his chance for his own family by marrying an older woman? It certainly seems feasible, don't you think?

So, let's look again at Rees, the man named as Mary's father and what Rebecca had to say about his family and their holdings.

"*Headstone in Llandefalle shows Rees's relative William and Ann. Their son Rees also has a headstone. Cousins listed in William's will as having land in Llandefalle and William's land can be seen on the Tithe Maps. I suspect that William is an Uncle of our Rees and Tithe Maps show he had a lot of land near St Stephen's church in Llansteffan and south of the church. Some properties were listed in his will which he passed to his sons. It should be noted that much of the land was later De Winton Land (after Mary's death)*

. . . It seems that the majority of Rees's family are in Llandefalle and Llanstephan. Mary's Aunts and Uncles on the maternal side are in Glasbury."

Then one night out of the blue, I had a dream about these two and actually woke up crying.

Elizabeth was in some kind of barn and was preparing a feast with other women of the village. I got the feeling of Llowes, even though she and Rees lived and died in Glasbury. Or so 'they' said! But after this lot, can we believe anything 'they said'?! Maybe they were visiting, but anyway, back to the dream. It was getting dusk, the end to a chilly damp day and the menfolk were expected shortly when suddenly Elizabeth collapsed.

One of the women ran to fetch Rees who hurried back, and I watched as he lifted Elizabeth from the ground and carried her to a house.

She couldn't speak but she never took her eyes from his face as he laid her down with great tenderness. That there was genuine affection there, I had no doubt, I could feel it! And as I watched he kept vigil with her. A small man with a quiet manner. His wife, I saw more clearly. A figure smaller still with a heart-shaped face and pale blue eyes.

Despite her age, she looked almost elfin with grey hair cropped close to her head and a downy soft complexion. But it was the look in her eyes and the love therein as all they could do was regard each other as she slowly passed away.

Powerful stuff and an insight I hadn't been expecting. I don't often wake up in tears, but I felt blessed to have witnessed her last moments. And let's be honest, by the standards of the day, she lived an exceptionally long life. I'm not sure what took her off, illness, perhaps or a stroke. But what we do know is that Rees followed six months later. Reunited and at rest together.

But what about Mary? She's not at rest, is she? And is it any wonder! Just what was going on with the Morgan's and the Wilkins and more pertinently yet, who was Mary's mother?

Mary's real mother?

Had she been an undercook, too? Or maybe an under-dairy maid? And where did she go? Mary was baptised under the 'parentage' of Rees and Elizabeth, so can we look at the possibility that her real mother died in childbirth?

Perhaps it was Sybil, the younger sister of Elizabeth. Born in 1742, that would have made her forty-six years old, an improvement admittedly on Elizabeth's fifty-four, but still stretching it. But let's just say for a moment that it was Sybil. That somehow, she had managed to conceive and go full term only for the birth to kill her. The latter not unusual, and in those days at that age, almost certain. So, Mary comes into the World as Sybil leaves it. A child, without a mother.

In steps the father, who has money and power and the perfect solution.

Elizabeth, older sister, spinster and knocking on, only too grateful to help out the master and of course, her niece. Cue then, potential father. What about mild-mannered Rees Morgan, who at thirty-four, still hasn't found a wife?

Perfect. Problem solved and neither will go hungry, especially Mary, who is given a job at the castle when she's of an age, but more importantly a trade for life.

So, if this isn't the scenario, or similar – just what is?

And if Mary's mother wasn't Elizabeth's younger sister, then who was? Suffice to say, we never found out what happened to Sybil, but I'd give my left arm to find out!

We also wouldn't mind finding out more about another servant also buried in St. Peter's of Glasbury. His name was Michael Lynham, and he was a Head Gardener at Maesllwch.

Note The inscription on his grave below is pretty bog standard compared to John Wood's. No ringing plaudits for Mr Lynham, but then, he was just the Head gardener . . .

Sacred to the memory of MICHAEL LYNAM who was many years
Head Gardner to the late W. WILKINS Esqr. M.P. of Maesllwch Castle.
He died 14th of June 1856 aged 79 years
Right side Sacred to the memory of MARY wife of MICHAEL LYNAM Gardener of this parish.
She died March 16th 1843 aged 60 years . . .

It's possible he and his wife were working on the estate when Mary was there. Both were within working age at the time of the scandal, but we have no way of knowing.

In her summary, Rebecca said, *"Evidence shows that they provided memorial stones for servant families, suggesting that Mary's being a servant was part of something much bigger, a close-knit community of the wealthy despite her status as a servant girl. There was no breaking free as it reached every part of her life."*
She added.
"From birth to death, Mary is part of a community that is of two halves, the rich and the poor, the tentacles of the rich permeating her everyday life and most certainly affecting her sentencing . . . Also curious is the tale that Mary was of no religion. Evidence suggests that she was baptised in Llowes church and not part of any Quaker or alternative religious movement.
Mary is painted badly and as mentioned there is no real

reference to her family.

A Morgan grave in Llowes does have Lawrence Beavan listed on it which suggests the family intermarried at some point but difficult to trace due to such a common name. Another Morgan grave in Llowes does have Lawrence Beavan listed on it which suggests the family intermarried at some point but difficult to trace due to such a common name."

We also found an Eckley buried with a Morgan!? Interestingly, Prys, who had compiled the graveyard list of St. Cewydd's, Aberedw, shares the same surname. Something I only recently discovered that quite blew me away. But upon further investigation, we couldn't tie it in.

But the most poignant graveyard find had to be that of Rees and Elizabeth. There wasn't much of the inscription left but enough to know that it was them. This is all thanks to Phil and Heather Bufton of The Powys Family History Society, who spent hours rubbing graves to reveal their secrets. A feat for which I will always be grateful.

To the memory of ELIZ... ... of REES MORGAN of this parish who died Nov. 15 18.. aged 8... Also the above named REES MORGAN died March 14th 1828 aged ... years
"And as it is appointed unto men once to die, but after this the judgment"

As we know, Elizabeth died first and at the grand old age of ninety-three. The 'aged 8...' is because the date of her birth was given as 1742, which was that of her sister, Sybil.

A slip of the stonemason's chisel? It happened, but as I remarked to Rebecca at the time, to mix up the numbers 34 and 42 would be pretty extreme. Like any skilled artisan, a stone mason would take a pride in his work, surely getting the dates right would be fundamental.

But one thing I do feel sure about, is that whoever did dress their stone was not the mason Thomas Ravenhill. As weathered and as flaked as it is, unlike the second stone at Mary's grave and that of Rees' family in Llandefalle, this is much darker, and just the hint of foliage climbing up the sides of pillars. Here Rebecca was more cautious and had this to say.

"The only subtle evidence of her family are the matching Gravestones, one of Mary with the urn and foliage and one of Rees' uncles in Llanstephan...all we suspect were made by T. Ravenhill of Glasbury...would three branches of the same family pick the same design?

It was not T. Ravenhill's only design although could potentially have been a cheaper option?'

What we can agree on, however, is the verse that seems to denote that Rees and Elizabeth Morgan were certainly not without religion.

"And as it is appointed unto men once to die, but after this the judgment".

The psalm in full is taken from Hebrews 9:27 and is as follows. **'And as it is appointed unto men once to die, but after this the judgment. The fixed order for all men is to die once only, and to be judged after death. When they die, finality is stamped on their life work.'**

I find the reference to 'judgement' of interest. It seems to me they might also have been apprehensive of coming before their Maker. They had been compliant, after all, in the whole Mary Morgan debacle - not that I'm blaming them in any way at all.

The Fiddler calls the tune remember, and at least they would never have had to look starvation in the face!

The fact Elizabeth lived to such a ripe old age clearly demonstrates they had both lived a long and comfortable life.

Rees died at the age of sixty-seven. Not bad when life expectancy at that time was about forty-odd.

But back to the question of religion and how it had been wielded against Mary like the Sword of Damocles. I was also interested in what Rebecca had to say about this, and again just to highlight, as taken from her summary.

"Also curious is the tale that Mary was of no religion. Evidence suggests that she was baptised in Llowes church and not part of any Quaker or alternative religious movement."

And it's true! Even the Archdeacon of Manchester wrinkled her smooth brow at that one! So, come on, let's face it, every and any argument had been marshalled into place to ensure a conviction. And religion – or in this case, a lack of, would have been a strong playing card at a time when religious belief was so prevalent. A sure-fire was to play to the crowd and win sympathy.

It also would have gone a long way in salving the Judge's conscience. He was not a stupid man. Vain, pedantic, worlds apart, but not stupid. This is a man who penned two poems to the memory of the girl he sent to the noose. Went by her grave regularly and wrote to a Bishop all but trying to justify the terrible thing that he did.

Below is one of the letters he sent to 'The Right Reverend Dr Horsley, Lord Bishop of St. Asaph.'

Note the opening lines; not so full of himself now, is he . . .

'With many apologies, and with trembling hope that you will honour the enclosed with your attention. I lay them before you and have nothing more at heart than to obtain a few hints from you upon so awful and so alarming a subject. In our part of Wales it is thought no crime to kill a bastard child. We had two cases equally desperate. One of the culprits (and perhaps the worst of the two in a moral view) escaped.'

By that you mean the noose, Judge. Spit it out!

'**In the case of the girl at Prestiegne, circumstances transpired which are of a most affecting and peculiar nature. Her countenance was pretty and modest; it had even the air and expression of perfect innocence.**'

Maybe that's because she was, Your Honour.

'**Not a tear escaped from her when all around were deeply affected by her doom; yet her carriage was respectful, her look attentive, serious, and intelligent. Short as the interval before she perished, her use of it was most wonderful.**
It appeared she had no defect of understanding and that she was born with every disposition to virtue, but of her crime she had not the faintest conception; and there was not a single trace of religion to be found in her thoughts. Of Christianity she had never even heard, or of the Bible, and she scarce had ever been at church.'

Quite a sweeping statement there, Your Honour! Hadn't realised Justices of the Law had access to a person's private thoughts, much less their soul. Your psychic abilities are staggering!

'**A servant in a most profligate family . . .**'

Dang, Judge, you're talking about the Wilkins here! The very same people whose hospitality you have availed yourself of when overseeing the Brecon Assizes. Your distant relatives. Profligate? Wow, bit of a love/hate thing going on here, methinks. Families, eh . . .

'**. . . (she) attracted the attention of her young master, who was intrigued with her. Her office was that of undercook and she killed her child the moment after its birth with a penknife, nearly**

severing the head from the neck. It was the same knife and the same use of it, which had been her implement and constant habit in killing chickens.'

The knife that Miss Marple, more commonly known as Mrs Evelyn, the Cook, retrieved from Mary's bed the following morning? Bit pat, don't you think, Your Honour . . . don't suppose you considered the possibility that the knife could have been planted? But hey-ho.

'This murder it appears by her confession (the most ingenious and complete imaginable) that she committed in mercy to her child . . .'

Wait up, Judge! Rebecca would also like to interject here with a few observations of her own.

First up, Walter Junior; 'How did he know he was intrigued with her . . . was he told? Had this happened before?'

Rebecca also says of you that, *'He tells the court that the confession is what he has to go on however early newspaper reports suggest that a confession 'was obtained' when Mary was in prison...being visited 'almost daily'. . .*

Hmmm, don't think we need to spell that one out, do we, Your Honour . . .

'The young squire, although her favourite gallant, was not the father of the child . . .'

Quite a definitive statement to make there, Judge. Old psychic powers still standing you in good stead at this point, obviously . . .

'but she did him the justice in reporting that when he was apprized of her pregnancy, he offered to maintain the child when born if she would say he was the father. Such was her sense of honour, that although it would have saved her child's life and her

own, she would purchase these two lives with a falsehood.'

Aww, good old Mary, godless one minute, taking a hit for the Wilkins the next. What a gesture, your Honour, what a gal! But even you have to admit that this doesn't add up! All seems a bit 'contrived' to me.

Why would she fall on her sword? You yourself said she looked 'intelligent'. Make your mind up, Judge, can't have it both ways . . .

'The father of the child before its birth (admitting the fact) refused in pre-emptory terms to maintain it when born. I determined to kill it, poor thing (she said), out of the way being perfectly sure that I could not provide for it myself. These were her words and the substance of them was often repeated.'

When was this, then, Judge, and where? In her prison cell being attended to by the likes of Mr Browne and the two Reverends? Was it their presence that helped 'obtain' this confession, or did you dream it perhaps? Once again, you assert the case so emphatically, one reasonably suspects you were trying to convince yourself never mind the Bishop!

'Before she was tried, she solicited her young master's help in the gift of a single guinea to her, for a Counsel to do the best for her could but her prayer was refused and she would have been undefended if the High Sheriff himself had not, in compassion to her desolate situation, fee'd the Counsel himself.'

Well, thank goodness someone was looking out for her! Good old Charles Rogers! But even you have to admit he may as well have saved his money for all the good it did her!

'She took it for granted that she would be acquitted; had ordered gay apparel to attest her deliverance and supposed the young gentleman (whom I know well) would save her by a letter

to me.'

Nicely played, Your Honour. A damning insinuation and you fell for it!

'**She embraced the Gospel Creed and its mercies with enlightened as well as fervent hope; took the sacrament with exemplary devotion; marked a perfect sense of remorse and met her fate in a most affecting manner with calm intrepidity and with devout resignation. The Minister who attended her told me that a feather of religion would have made an angel of this girl.'**

Well, bless me, make your mind up, Judge! Godless creature to potential angel and in record time. I'm impressed! What a glowing account of her 'transmutation' – how did the Minister concerned do it? Dang, you'll have her walking on water next!

'**To wind up the Characters in this Provincial Tragedy, through to the end of her life she spoke with romantic affection of her young master (whom yet she indirectly accused of seducing her) when she was no more, he gave the lie to all she had asserted and without a shadow of interest.'**

Oh, come on! You'll be saying she skipped to her death next, Judge!

'**It must not be forgot that her fellow servant, the father of the child, when she complained of her sufferings from pregnancy, gave her a herb which he told her that he had gathered and advised her to take it; which she could never do, believing that it was intended by him to kill her child in her womb.'**

Oh, you mean the 'Herbalist Waggoner Extraordinaire' your Honour! Had to get that one in, eh? Seems our Mary had a lot to say about the father and the child, yet where is the record? To whom did she address these matters? Seems to me you're speaking for her in more ways than one . . .

'As the law stands, concealment of a pregnancy and birth is punished with two years imprisonment at the most though it is in that concealment that all these murders originate. I have never heard of a Divine, Philosopher, Statesman, Judge, Moralist or even Poet who has written professedly upon this topic. There is, I believe, no illusion to it in Scripture. It never happens in high life, is the vice of the poor, and generally in the pale of domestic servitude.'

Oh, so it's the fault of the poor, is it, Your Honour? Well, fancy that!

'I believe that in every instance of the kind, a total want of religious conceptions or habits will be found one of the features and a neglected education the other. I proportion to the undisciplined and savage characteristics of the poor; this offence is more or less prevalent.'

Yup, definitely the fault of the poor! Get back to the fields you barbarous beasts and know your place! Dang, Judge, going straight for the jugular there!!

'There has not been a conviction at the Old Bailey for this crime for a period of twenty years and cases of trial for it have been very few. In Wales they have been twice as numerous and very often fatal. In Ireland I am told the habit of exposing children to the elements, most of who die, rages like a pestilence.'

Like the poverty that 'rages' and is at the heart of ALL this, Your Honour! But you can't see this from the lofty heights of your pedestal, of course; you lot never do . . .

'I wish to have your Lordship's opinion how you would correct the law upon that subject and what expedients you would recommend for prevention of the mischief.'

The mischief? We're talking about lives here, Judge, peoples' lives. Poor people. Wretched people. Plunged into poverty from the moment they are born. Condemned to struggle and squalor, and all because they are at the mercy of the likes of you!

And you refer to the calls they had to make over life or death as a 'mischief'!?

There for the grace of all that's sacred, go we all.

All of a sudden, I have no more desire to address you with even the slightest modicum of respect . . .

There is no honour in sending a girl - little more than a child, to face strangulation at the end of the rope anymore than your efforts to appease your conscience.

'I will do myself the honour to wait upon you whenever you will appointment me. It will be my turn at Brecon to deliver the charge in the summer; and I wish to do as much good as I can, by admonition from the bench.

I remain with highest respect my Lord,

Your Grateful and Obedient Servant,

George Hardinge.

Well, Judge, you sure are going for gold here. Appealing to a man of God to help assuage the troubles of an afflicted mind.

The gall of it!

But he wasn't that fussed, was he? Either with you or your flowery prose.

That's what I heard, Judge, because not everyone was a fan of the 'Great Judge Hardinge', were they?

And as for these poems of yours, let it go, man! Only you couldn't, could you, and that was the problem . . .

'Flow the tears that Pity loves
Upon Mary's hapless fate.
It's a tear that God approves:
He can strike but cannot hate.

Read in time; oh beauteous maid!
Sun the lover's poisonous art
Mary was by love betrayed
And an arrow stung the heart.

Love the constant and the good
Wed the husband of your choice,
Blest is then your children's food,
Sweet the little cherub's voice.

Had religion glanced its beam,
On the mourner's frantic bed,
Mute had been the tablets theme,
Nor would Mary's child have bled.

She, for an example fell,
But is Man from censure free?
Thine, Seducer, is the Knell,
It's a messenger to thee.'

Ahhh, if ever a man knew what lay at the rotten heart of all this, it was you.

That one was entitled *'On Seeing The Tomb Of Mary Morgan'*.

The next one was originally written in Latin and called, **'An Epitaph on Mary Morgan'**.

Dang, but you had it bad, George, the need to keep justifying yourself as the guilt kept gnawing away . . .

'Deserving of our sorrow, let righteousness prevent our weeping.

She was born into virtue, but lacked religion. In the flower of her youth, she was corrupt,

a sinful mother, wielding the unholy weapons of the crime she undertook.

She was betrayed, and the frightened victim of a secret lust.

Hoped not to keep the child she had begun. Vengence fell upon the witness to her crime, the child died.

Mary, who deserves our tears, had died, by the punishment she deserves.

By her death, she has humbly paid the penalty with modest expression, flying high on the wings of hope, and strong in her piety.

You women like her, proud in your beauty, weep for her.

Her ghost, in the shadow warns.

Beware of men.'

Finally, Judge, we can agree! Beware of men indeed, including men like yourself and those who betrayed her. Wise words but then you had to spoil it with **'the punishment she deserves.'**

Still battling there, I see. Indeed, methinks the Judge doth protest way too much, but then I guess that's what happens when you send an innocent girl to her death - which now brings me on to her ghost.

So, did she show herself to you, Judge Hardinge? Was she a ghost in the shadows which was why you kept visiting her grave in a bid to make her stop? Was that the reason? Coming to you in your dreams, was she?

I bet she was! In fact, I'd put money on it!

Oh, poor, tormented man that you were. Haunted and harried to the very grave.

Well, as you had so much to say about the poor people of Wales, here's a word in our Mother tongue; bechod. It means 'pity'.

And guess what? I find it very hard to have any for you. You may have been a man of the times. I just hope your idea of God was as understanding to you as you were to Mary, and that the very same mercy was shown your soul . . .

I'm not alone in my sense of outrage, and believe me, there was plenty expressed back in the day. Indeed, the subsequent outcry may have had something to do with his bid for approbation from the Bishop.

People were shocked and the story made the newspapers.

> At Radnor assizes, on Friday se'nnight, Mary Morgan, a girl of 17, was convicted on the clearest evidence of the wilful murder of her female bastard child by almost severing the head from the body with a pen-knife, which was afterwards found under her bed. The wretched young creature, during her trial, did not manifest any symptoms of alarm at her unhappy situation; nor was it until the dreadful sentence of the law was pronounced by Mr. Justice Hardinge, in an address which suffused every eye in the Court with tears, that she evinced any apprehensions of the fate which awaited her; and even after she left the bar, she entertained hopes of a reprieve. On the following day, convinced that mercy could not be extended to her, she acknowledged her guilt. She was executed on Saturday last, and her body delivered over for dissection.

From the Chester Chronicle April 1805 courtesy of Roger Bragger, descendent of the Stanton line who sent this to me. My thanks!

Besides these articles marking her fate, there also remains a reminder of Mary's stay in 'His Majesty's finest' that set me off on a whole new search.

There is a bill to the prison from a local baker by the name of John Stanton.

Images courtesy of Powys History Project

This is interesting because it is a direct connection to Mary. Stanton: the name wouldn't go away, and I wanted to know more.

An unexpected link came from an article in the *'Cardiff Times and South Wales Weekly News' July 1898* that flagged up a chap called Stephen Coleridge.

Entitled **'THE STORY OF MARY MORGAN'**, it went as follows:

"Mr Stephen Coleridge sends the following letter to the 'Westminster Gazette' in reply to 'Radnorian's' letter that we

published at the time: -

Sir, - Absence from London prevented my seeing the letter from your correspondent 'Radnorian' till today. If he inquires, I think he will find that the name of the father of Mary Morgan's child is perfectly well known at Presteigne, and that he will readily understand that, his direct descendent in the male line being a well-known living person of high character and blameless life, it would have been very unseemly of me to publish more than I did..."

Unseemly? I have no such problem. He is all but naming Walter Wilkins Junior as the father, and if you care to ask the people of Presteigne today, you'll find opinion has changed very little.

And what of the 'Radnorian'?

Who was that?

A member of the Wilkins family perhaps, or an advocate of?

The piece went on;

"The other details of the story I learnt from an old man two or three years ago, who detailed them to me as we stood over the grave of Mary Morgan. I took him to be the sexton, and he (told) me that his Grandmother was the matron of Presteigne Prison in 1805 and had had the care of Mary Morgan between her sentence and execution.

This seemed to me authority enough for my purpose, which was to raise at least, a passing sigh of pity over this long-closed grave – Your obedient servant, STEPHEN COLERIDGE.

Rhannoch. Perthshire."

Wow, a couple of things here! Firstly, who was the old fella, and was he the sexton? As for the Grandmother! *She had looked after Mary?* This was dynamite and I just had to know more.

There had to be a connection, but with no names it would be tricky.

A search in the burial records of Presteigne led me to a William Stanton whose inscription says,

"To the memory of WILLM. STANTON who died Feb 1 ... aged 88 years He was Clerk and Sexton of this parish upwards of 54 years".

Could this be a link? Was the chap Coleridge spoke to in the churchyard a Stanton? Which of course would mean that the matron of the jail would also have been a Stanton.

If this was the case, were they related to John, the baker?

I began a tree and looked closely at the dates. William had died in 1809 and it would have been a hard push to expect a man of eighty-five years to dig a hole!

He left behind, however, a large and industrious family. Had the role of sexton carried on down the Stanton line?

I then focused on William's wife only to discover he'd had two, and that both had passed away before Mary's demise. With them now eliminated as the potential matron, I turned my attention to his children – all twenty-two of them!

Here I found a 'John' and it's possible that he was the baker. He had married a Mary Page but upon closer inspection, with half a dozen kids to look after, I thought it highly unlikely that she was our 'matron.'

There were a lot of Stanton's, but I could find nothing definitive. I got busy on Ancestry and found a whole plethora of descendants who were kind enough to get back to me.

*With a special mention to Brian Woodward, who recently made The Oban Times this year with a lovely moment of fame!

Unfortunately, there were no snippets they could share, but Rebecca found an interesting item from a London newspaper called the *'Oracle and Daily Advertiser'* dated 20th April 1808.

DEATHS.

At Knutsford, Cheshire, Mrs. Legh, relict of the late H. C. Legh, Esq. of High Legh in the same county.

In Brompton-row, Mrs. Osborne, relict of N. Osborne, Esq.

At Penzance, Mr. Joseph Whicher, aged 70, having for 50 years practised Medicine at that place.

At Presteign, Radnorshire, aged 83, Mr. William Stanton, who had served the office of parish clerk 54 years. He was blind latterly, but lived to know his great-great-grand-daughter, who had living (previous to his death) her father, grandfather and grandmother, great-grandfather and great-grandmother, and the above-mentioned great great-grandfather, all of whom resided within thirty yards of each other. What is remarkable, his immediate predecessor in the office of parish clerk (Richard Bebb) held that office forty years, and was grandfather to one of the present Directors of the East India Company.

The East India Company – again! And a reference to Richard Bebb. Could the latter be related to a certain John Bebb who provided Mary's death garb, including the coffin?

Most likely. They all seemed closely-knit, especially when it was established that the Gaelor during Mary's time was a 'Robert Lewis'. But first the Stantons' and Rebecca came back with this: -

"With regard to William Stanton. His Granddaughter was Ann Harriot (father was John Stanton). She married Robert Lewis in 1808 and her birth is registered in St Andrews. She married an Astley of Presteigne however, I'm yet to find the marriage."

What this seems to establish is that the man Coleridge spoke to in the churchyard was indeed a Stanton. More interesting yet, is the direct connection between the Stantons' and the man who held

Mary firmly under lock and key.

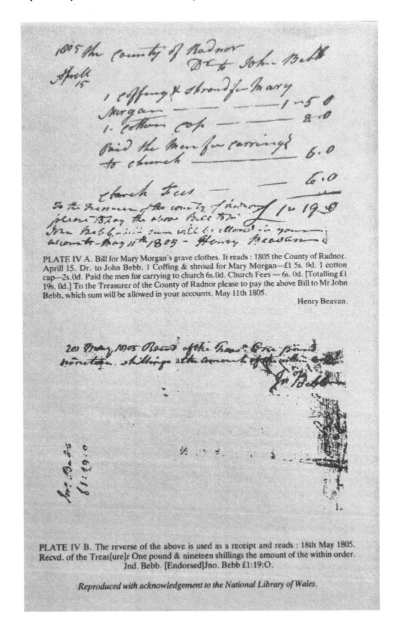

PLATE IV A. Bill for Mary Morgan's grave clothes. It reads : 1805 the County of Radnor. Aprill 15. Dr. to John Bebb. 1 Coffing & shroud for Mary Morgan—£1 5s. 0d. 1 cotton cap—2s. 0d. Paid the men for carrying to church 6s.0d. Church Fees — 6s. 0d. [Totalling £1 19s, 0d.] To the Treasurer of the County of Radnor please to pay the above Bill to Mr John Bebb, which sum will be allowed in your accounts. May 11th 1805.

Henry Beavan.

PLATE IV B. The reverse of the above is used as a receipt and reads : 18th May 1805. Recvd. of the Treas[ure]r One pound & nineteen shillings the amount of the within order. Jnd. Bebb. [Endorsed]Jno. Bebb £1:19:0.

Reproduced with acknowledgement to the National Library of Wales.

Image courtesy of the National Library of Wales

Rebecca went on to say: -*"Robert Lewis was listed as the Gaoler of Presteigne Gaol in 1808 and confirmed by Powys Archives. He married his wife Anne Astley in Presteigne 1808, both listed as Widow and Widower.*

Despite an extensive search I am unable to discern who his first wife was; however, Robert seems to be on the board of guardians and lived in Broad Street Presteigne and Hereford street for some of his life.

He is recorded as being a Timber Merchant on most documents and he has a memorial to himself and wife Anne on the wall of St Andrew's Church in Presteigne..."

Mary's gaoler was obviously a man of clout, but it is this next section that got the old mo-jo going and not just my own . . .

"When looking for evidence of his wife I encountered an interesting individual on the 1841 and 1851 Census living with him. Francis Evelyn. Francis was born in 1829 in Camden and was the son of the MP Lyndon Evelyn of Summerhill, Dublin.

The Evelyn family were prominent in the area and Francis' son would later own Kinsham court.

Francis came to Presteigne following the death of his father in 1839. It remains unclear what connections he had to Radnorshire prior to his living with Robert however it seems as though he had taken him under his wing."

This seems to strongly suggest that the Evelyns' were already known in the area and had associations that perhaps went back further again?

I'm talking about 'Miss Marple of Maesllwch' the intrepid Cook who gave evidence against Mary before disappearing off into some unknown life. I ask the question because Francis' grandmother was also an 'Elizabeth Evelyn'.

Coincidence or pure conjecture? Either way, with all that's been uncovered it's worth referring to Hamlet here when he said, "There are more things in Heaven and Earth, Horatio, than are dreamt of in your philosophy." And on that note, I cannot help but most mightily and heartily concur!

As a little pointer to the shenanigans before Mary's time - it would be 'criminal' not to share this little nugget. For here we find a member of the Pyefinch family, no less, and well in cahoots with Robert Lewis, the Gaoler!

At the time of this hearing Mary would have been taking her first steps.

First name(s)	Henry Patte
Last name	Pyefinch
Birth year	-
Year	1789
Date	30 October 1789
Offence	Neglect of duty by allowing Robert Lewis, keeper of the gaol to remain in office after allowing Daniel Jenkins to cohabit with Jane Jones, sentenced to solitary confinement.
Prosecutor	Thomas Caldecott, esq.
Accused status	Under-sheriff
Accused parish	Presteigne
Accused county	Radnorshire
Accused country	Wales
Court	Court of Great Sessions
Place	Presteigne
County	Radnorshire
Source	Court Of Great Sessions In Wales 1730-1830
Reference	4/530/1 - 6
Record identification	5799
Series	-
Record set	England & Wales, Crime, Prisons & Punishment, 1770-1935
Category	Institutions & organisations
Subcategory	Prison Registers
Collections from	Great Britain, Wales

In the meantime, back to the newspaper article and Stephen Coleridge.

Who was this dude and what was he doing so far from Perthshire, Scotland!

And why the interest in a mere serving girl.

He was no less engaged in the next article from **'The Kington Times'** 1934, entitled.

"LOVELY MARY MORGAN"

Presteign'* Tragedy Recalled

The Hon, Stephen Coleridge contributes an interesting note to the "Western Mail" on the subject of the "Betrayal and Execution of lovely Mary Morgan" and complains that her headstone in Presteign Churchyard has been moved. He writes:

It is not often that there is a criminal case at Presteign for an Assize Judge to try.

But Friday last week, there being a case to try, my duties took me there and I had an opportunity to visit the churchyard, where, to my astonishment and sorrow, I discovered that the headstone of the luckless and lovely Mary Morgan had been moved away from her grave and placed leaning against a wall.

Those of your readers who do not know her sad story may be glad to be reminded of it.

In 1805, then a beautiful child of 17 Mary Morgan was betrayed by a man of importance in the county who prompted her to destroy the infant of which he was the father. He took her for his pleasure and abandoned her for his convenience.

HANGED AT THE CROSSROADS.
HE SAT ON THE GRAND JURY THAT RETUNED A TRUE BILL AGAINST HER FOR MURDER.

She was hanged at the four cross-roads outside the town and buried in what was then unconsecrated ground, but which is now incorporated in the churchyard. There she lies under the grass, her broken heart long mingled with the dust. I trust that she was forgiven and received in the sweet Heavens.

The headstone, in the religious accounts of the time, records that the benevolent judge brought her to "unfeigned repentance."

But someone subsequently put another smaller stone at her feet with these words on it:-

In Memory of Mary Morgan,

Who suffered April 13th, 1805,

Aged 17.

"He that is without sin among you,

let him first cast a stone at her." – John 8, v 7.

Forty years ago, when I was at Presteign, I heard from the aged sexton his grandfather had dug the grave for Mary Morgan that there was one gallant gentleman in the court when she was sentenced who instantly took horse to London to procure a reprieve if he could.

REPRIEVE TOO LATE.

It must have been a generous heart that prompted him, and though with relays of horses, he galloped back with a reprieve through the night, alas for Mary Morgan, love and death had been the same to her for two hours before he reached the awful gibbet at the four-cross roads.

There can be nothing on Presteign so interesting, so full of poignant sadness and helpless regret, as the stone which stood at the head of that pitiful grave.

Are its inhabitants so lost to all promptings of sentiment, all stirrings of heart, all feeling of compassion, as to make no protest when that stone, with its awful record, is taken from the grave and put against a wall to suffer the indignities and obliterations of Time?

I'm guessing that this article is the source of Mary's would-be saviour who rode to London to seek a pardon but didn't get back in time. This tale still abounds in Presteign to this day.

*Presteign (sic)

Pretty powerful stuff, eh? Mr Coleridge still throwing punches after thirty-six years, and once again, referencing his conversation with whom he now definitively identifies as the sexton.

Again, no actual name given but how many grave-diggers did Presteigne have? My money is still on the Stanton's, but not so the story of Mary's would-be saviour. What I can agree with Coleridge, however, is that indeed the tale still thrives today.

But did it happen?

To all intents and purposes, no.

Despite an extensive search, there is not a shred of evidence to support that such a reprieve was sought, but it certainly makes for a fantastic tale, does it not? A story built up, perhaps, by wishful thinking and noble intent as the good folk of Presteigne came to terms with the gravity of Mary's fate.

But as this book has clearly shown; 'never say never' and so I'm happy to leave it at that.

Just as intriguing is Stephen Coleridge. Who was he? And why was he so set on Mary being accorded so much respect?

Soon I was in contact with the descendants of this wonderful man, and despite no further information on a personal level, publicly there's plenty and he had many strings to his bow.

Author, barrister and obviously a man of compassion as a key campaigner against vivisection and founding member of the N.S.P.C.C. His talents with the pen extended to poetry and he even wrote verses for Mary.

His family were rather illustrious; his grandfather the nephew of one of the founders of the Romantic Movement, Samuel Taylor

Coleridge. His father was the Lord Chief Justice of England.

So, it's safe to say that Coleridge had a good grounding in Law before he became a clerk of the Assizes, and during a visit to Mary's grave in 1898 his interest was piqued. He was particularly rattled about her headstone being moved, not to mention her case. One cannot help but wonder how much he knew, and with it the wish he'd been around during Mary's darkest hours. Not just because of her tender years, but because no mercy was given. Not a jot. Walter Senior could have stepped in and saved her from the dreaded noose, yet he stood by as the law of the land took her all the way to the gallows.

This young girl, just turned seventeen-years-old . . . his own daughter?

Will we ever know for sure?

CHAPTER 9

I can only go with what's in my heart, and as for the ol' spidery senses . . . Well, they've served me well up until now, and I have to say, the Universe keeps giving.

Which brings me on to 'Horton's Elegy'

If you read anything about Mary Morgan, you'll have come across this. It's a piece that was written by a chap who came to Presteigne with travelling performers thirteen years after Mary's death.

His name was Thomas Horton, and he was a comedian, although he wasn't laughing when he saw Mary's grave!

So struck was he by the tragedy of her story, he penned a poem he then went on to publish and distribute as a small book.

I'm not going to share his work here. It can be found in other areas, but it did come to me, or rather a copy did after a fortuitous encounter in the Rose Cottage Café.

This lovely establishment is at the heart of the community and serves the most delicious home-cooked food, and after ordering my usual toastie, I got into conversation with the W.I. book club.

Once again it seemed the Universe was at play when one of the ladies told me she had a copy of 'Horton's Elegy' in her possession, and what's more, she was more than happy to gift it me.

What an amazing gesture, and true to her word, she dropped it off to me. It isn't an original copy, but it doesn't matter, I was thrilled to receive it and it gives some idea of how Horton's book might have looked.

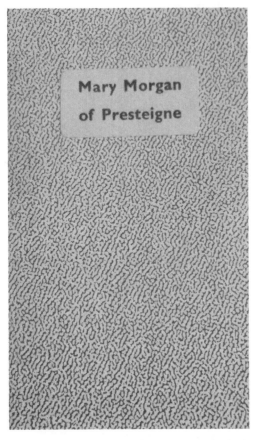

So, thanks again, to the lovely lady who found it in the Hospice Shop tucked inside another book. What an absolute gem of a find!

Thank you also, to Andy Leavis of Courtyard Antiques on the High Street, who put another book my way, 'The Folklore of Radnorshire' by Roy Palmer. An absolutely fascinating insight into this part of the World and suffice to say I bought it!

This is how it's been throughout this project. Little gifts here, various snippets there, people helping, peoples' time, open doors and hidden messages coming to light; and all for Mary Morgan whose story still resonates and has never gone away.

It seems a lifetime ago since that day I stood in the clearing on Gallows Lane and called out to a girl who'd been dead for over two hundred years.

Gallows Lane is more than a place of execution, and the clearing that lies further on, a place of historical interest within itself and who better to tell me, than someone I will refer to as the 'Landman'. Like the lady of the Hospice Shop, he wishes to remain anonymous, but he is worth mentioning for what he passed on to me.

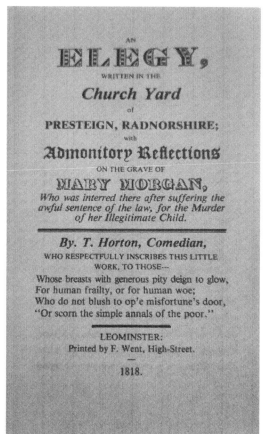

AN

ELEGY,

WRITTEN IN THE

Church Yard

of

PRESTEIGN, RADNORSHIRE;

with

𝔄𝔡𝔪𝔬𝔫𝔦𝔱𝔬𝔯𝔶 𝔕𝔢𝔣𝔩𝔢𝔠𝔱𝔦𝔬𝔫𝔰

ON THE GRAVE OF

MARY MORGAN,

Who was interred there after suffering the awful sentence of the law, for the Murder of her Illegitimate Child.

By. T. Horton, Comedian,

WHO RESPECTFULLY INSCRIBES THIS LITTLE
WORK, TO THOSE---

Whose breasts with generous pity deign to glow,
For human frailty, or for human woe;
Who do not blush to op'e misfortune's door,
"Or scorn the simple annals of the poor."

LEOMINSTER:

Printed by F. Went, High-Street.

—

1818.

I'd been trying to pin this individual down for some time and finally got lucky in November last year. I'd first heard about him from Demelsa's partner and that his local knowledge is second to none, with the exception of Keith Parker, who he knew well.

Unfortunately, due to failing health, Keith was unable to meet with me, but I managed to get hold of his excellent book, 'A History of Presteigne' (Logaston Press) from the local library.

By this time, I'd learned two things; firstly, sites of execution i.e., the gallows, would commonly be found just outside towns and villages on the crossroads.

The other, that the tree through which I'd captured the footage, was not where Mary had kicked out the last of her life.

The clearing itself is quite a bit further on, so how could this be?

I especially wanted to know more about what happened to the hanging tree. Apparently, it had come down in a storm some years ago, but no one seems to know any more than that.

Poor old Landman, I absolutely bombarded him with questions, but he was able to confirm, on behalf of Keith's knowledge, that a stump is all that is left of the tree.

Demelsa and I visited a couple of times and took many pictures. Here I am with my right hand on the overgrown stump of the old hanging tree. We're not sure what the strange light anomaly is all about. Quite possibly it is a trick of the light or a camera aberration - or, as someone suggested, a rather large orb! Whatever the explanation, I will leave you to be the judge of that!

So, how was it I picked up on Mary so far from the site where she passed from this world into the next?

As I mentioned previously, Demelsa and I have visited several times, but have usually been interrupted by passing traffic.

The mystery remained, however, of the hollow further up and

why I'd captured phenomena there, not once but twice!

This, the Landman took in his stride with the remark that he harboured no particular stance on the supernatural. And I in turn, was more than intrigued by his response.

'It was a meeting place,' he told me. 'It's where people would meet who were up to no good before slipping into town.' Immediately, I envisaged shifty-looking characters huddled beneath the trees as they made their plans and couldn't help but wonder if Lynn's ghostly highwayman had been one of them.

The Landman also explained how the Holloway had been much wider before it was used as a dumping ground during the Victorian period.

Old pottery shards and pieces can still be found, and he himself had also found a large number of sewing thimbles.

Thimbles? That threw me, I have to say!

'Yes,' he said, 'Well, you have to imagine that an execution was much like a fair. It was a big day out and there would be stallholders and all kinds of tradespeople selling their wares. I made my finds in the field next to the site. It wouldn't have been very different then, and there would have been lots of people.'

A day-out to watch a hanging, now there's a thing!

Poor Mary, strung up like a piece of meat as people made merry about her. I wonder where Judge Hardinge was that day?

Tucked up in his cosy rooms, no doubt, as she prepared to meet her Maker.

I walked the site again some months later with Demelsa, who told me she could hear voices murmuring within the clearing and not for the first time. Whispers from the past?

I heard nothing but remained intrigued as to why Mary had come through at that location, and not the execution site itself.

The answer, I felt, lay in the Holloway and the trees.

I came to this conclusion after coming across a fascinating snippet that read:

'Biologists say that trees are social beings. They can count, learn, and remember. They nurse sick members, warn each other of danger by sending electrical signals across a fungal network and for reasons unknown, keep the ancient stumps of long felled companions alive for centuries by feeding them a sugar solution through their roots.'

I don't know where this information came from, it was an anonymous meme I just happened to find, but it resonated deeply. Not least because the stump of the hanging tree is now a veritable hub of life. It has all kinds of shoots and foliage striving for a new life as Nature does its stuff.

So, going on the basis that trees communicate and connect; could the angst and death throes of all those who perished on the hanging tree, be translated down to the roots that would then transcribe all along the trees that border the Holloway?

Was that how Mary was able to communicate that day – via the memory trails of the trees? The concept certainly gives some serious food for thought and cannot be discounted.

Supernature at its best!

Less impressive is the fact that even at this stage of the project, we are still struggling to find Mary's mother. As Rebecca remarked more than once; the records are there, but the people are not.

I'm talking about the family members listed in Rees' will, namely, Jennet Beavan, who he refers to as 'his sister'. In the will, Jennet is mentioned as 'deceased', yet she has a daughter, Elizabeth who is named as a beneficiary. What makes this so intriguing, and bizarre, is that despite Herculean efforts, neither can be found!

Can we assume that Jennet was a sibling to Elizabeth Morgan, or had she married into the Beavan family? Maybe she was an unmarried mother which in turn leads us back to Mary.

We've stepped back from Sybil; a double-check in that direction ruled her out. She is not our woman, or in this case, Mary's mother.

Jennet, however.

So, with nothing else to go on, I asked for a dream: Was Jennet the real mother of Mary?

And got an answer!

The dream opened with me sat in a court building. I was waiting to be called in to give evidence. The hearing had something to do with a child, but I didn't – and haven't – got any. I'm sat on a bench; there is no one else present except for my sister who sits next to me. She, too, is waiting for her case to be called up only she does have a child. A tiny, and I mean tiny, toddler – not a baby, that is looking out from a large black handbag.

The mood is very off-key. I'm decidedly tetchy at the delay and my sister is quietly aloof. There is no conversation between us, so I get up to go to use the toilets.

As I open the door, I realise the tiny child is behind me, so I scoop her up and hold her to the basin so she can wash her hands. When I return my sister seems oblivious to the fact her child had just been missing. I pop the child back into the bag saying, she should be more careful in future. I am struck by the complete lack of care and obvious disinterest in the baby.

In real life, nothing could be further from the truth.

So, what is the significance of this?

My sister's name is Janet, of which Jennet is a derivative. To my mind, the dream couldn't have been any clearer.

As I fired up the search-engines a few Jennets popped up, but only one was a real possibility. She had been married to a 'James Morgans' of Llandefalle.

This is the same parish where we found the graves of Rees' kin. Jennet is also buried there, and the inscription makes for interesting reading – not least because it is in Welsh! Not that is unusual, we are in Wales after all! But it is the fact the rest of it is in English.

So, what does the inscription say?

Yn Cymraeg – In Welsh:

'Gwel rybydd heunydd mewn byd
Tro gallu cais wella dy bywyd.
Fel to ddewi yn ddiwid
I'r bed gorweddfa fud...

My Welsh is rusty, but I got the gist, it seemed to be some kind of admonishment. I needed a more concise translation, so I ran the message past Tim Lynn, friend and former S4C director whose encouragement saw me write my first book. He came back with this and the observation of 'Cheery!!!'

I couldn't agree more!

'See the constant warnings in the World
Always trying to improve your life,
Like me you work hard.
In the grave you will rest in peace...'

So, what's the story here? And was it her?

We decided to explore deeper and the reason why her husband wasn't buried with her. We couldn't find him in St. Mathews until Rebecca found him some miles down the road buried in Brechfa Chapel.

He'd been interred with his daughter, Martha, who died at the age of seventeen. It turned out that James had married again after Jennet passed away, but the maths also said there would have been an age difference of 41 years between them!

But was this Mary's mother? If so, what on earth was going on!

On the gravestone it cited that she and James had lived at a place called 'White Hall', and so I spread the net further afield.

I have to say, I've had a lot of dealings with farmers throughout the writing of this book. The Morgans of Nantmel, namely Howard, whose brother Llewelyn prefers to be known as 'Joey'.

Mike Lewis of Llanbadarn Fawr, whose family are buried in the churchyard. The Eckley's of Glasbury and the Havard's of Pengwern, of course!

Now I was about to descend on another poor sod, no doubt enjoying a quiet evening after a hard day's graft in the never-ending quest for Mary Morgan.

As usual, the initial bemusement was replaced by a willingness to assist. The farming fraternity has never been less than helpful with my enquiries, but Mr Price was about to go over and above.

Not only did he share names and family details. But he also put me on to his sister Diana, who lives in Devon.

As the iron was still hot, I called her up immediately. She was out walking the dog but equally happy to help. And the link?

Their grandmother was a Beavan who had links to Glasbury! This was dynamite and a lead too important to miss. Could this be the connection we'd been looking for?

Diana had already compiled their family tree, and to my amazement, invited me into the inner sanctum of her family ancestry to see for myself. An unbelievable gesture of trust and support!

It was with great anticipation that I went into this other tree. It almost felt like going into someone's living room when they're not there! As I checked out the Beavan link, imagine the intake of breath as I spotted a Havard!

Unfortunately, upon further investigation Diane and Nigel's connections were not our own, but what a truly memorable experience, and once again, such unmitigated faith in a complete stranger!

Having investigated that avenue, I was still perplexed as to where Jennet may be – or more questioningly yet – what happened to her? By now, I'm harbouring the belief that she might actually be Rees's sister. In view of the Morgans' close ties to Maesllwch and the benefits they'd been reaping – would the notion be so far-fetched?

It would certainly explain why the Llandefalle records are

missing, and the mention of Morgans in Walter Junior's will. Remove the evidence of any family links and a handsome reward for doing . . . what exactly? Are the two men, Thomas and William, related to Rees? And more pertinent yet – would we ever know?

I'd had that dream about her of course, that seemed to confirm to me that her name was indeed, Jennet. But with nothing else to go on, once again, I put the question out to the Universe . . .

It is late evening and I'm making my way across the grounds of Maesllwch towards the castle. I have been invited to dinner. I'm very wary, and as I draw nearer, I decide to check out the lay of the land first.

Dusk has descended and there are lights on in the nearest tower. I know my host awaits me here, as I do that the meal, which is pie and mash, is already on the table.

Something isn't right. I can feel it. For some reason I suspect a trap. Suddenly a hundred yards in front of me, a brown horse bolts out of a small copse of trees with a woman clinging to its neck. Her long, flowing hair, is also brown, and streams out behind her, but there is no fear that I can sense. If anything, she seems exhilarated, and I can hear her laughter as the horse takes off.

Behind her then come two men on horseback and in obvious pursuit. But unlike the runaway rider, their shouts are of concern.

I stop to take in this extraordinary scene as the trio gallop off into the growing darkness. I don't understand why they would be riding at night, and I am suitably distracted when a figure suddenly rises before me from the long grass.

I cannot see a face, but I 'know' he is 'security' and that I've wandered too far.

As he flexes towards me, I brace for a fight before the dream then switches location.

I now find myself stood on a street in Cardiff where I went to Primary school. The man is still before me, and even in the dream I find this bizarre. Why are we outside No. 66 Stacey Road that sits next door to that of the old school caretaker?

The details are specific, and I remember the house well.

Back in the early seventies the house was occupied by a Mr and Mrs Carne. They were a very nice old couple. She would reward local children with sweets for attending Sunday School at 'The Church of the Nazarene'. Suffice to say I wasn't one of them, although I did try my luck on one occasion when my ignorance of a certain scripture saw me sent packing!

That dear old lady was kind, but she wasn't a pushover; a psalm for a sweetie and nothing less!

Mr Carne had a cobbler's hut at the back of the house which kept him busy, but when he wasn't repairing shoes, you'd find him tending the front garden.

I asked on a Facebook page if anyone remembered them and hit gold!

A former resident of the street got in touch and found them on the census. It is down to him I have the number of the house. A lovely gesture after a forty-year hiatus, so thank you, Mark Lucas, and yes, I remember you!

So, there I was outside the green-painted house with its garden full of flowers about to do battle with an opponent that I knew in my heart would never go down. I felt he'd received some kind of specialised combat training, but we went at it, nevertheless. What other choice was there?

It had been some time since I'd brawled on this particular street, so I'm pleased to report that no one was hurt in this instance!

As is the way with dreams, I woke up mid-scrap, unhurt and with the thought What the hell was all that about!

That I was being blocked off from the learning the truth, I had no doubt. But who was the woman on the horse, and why was she so reckless?

I was intrigued as to her identity and I was sure as damn it, it wasn't Mary. Older by a few years at least, so was this dream showing me her mother?

271

My mo-jo said 'yes'.

What also came to mind was 'loose cannon'.

Horses in dreams denote our self-will, and hers was seriously out of control. It is worth noting that there was once a breed of horse called a 'Jennet' that originated in Spain. It was often used as a light riding horse by medieval ladies. Apparently, they are now extinct. Suffice to say, this 'Jennet' was more Mustang and no, I'm not talking about the horse!

So, what was the dream trying to tell me?

That Mary's mother was unstable and had to be reined in?

Did she have mental health problems and was a danger to herself? Perhaps she was averse to the prospect of motherhood and did a runner. Or maybe she didn't want to be beholden and loved another. Decided to take off in a new direction. Wanted to be free.

Not all women of the time were without spirit.

And what about the meal in the castle? Nothing fancy, more comfort food; good old pie and mash. An unexpected offer of hospitality that for some reason, filled me with dread. Not to mention the man hiding in the undergrowth waiting to intercept anyone who got too close . . .

To what exactly?

Information that had to be protected at all costs?

And why on earth did we end up outside 66 Stacey Road, Cardiff, that has connotations with both religion and of all things, a cobbler!?

I'm asking you, and believe me, I asked myself - a dozen times! But like all dreams there is often a hidden meaning; you've just got to find it.

When I ran it past Rebecca and the reference to the cobbler, her answer all but blew me away.

'Rees' brother, David, was a shoemaker,' she told me, 'it's mentioned in the will.'

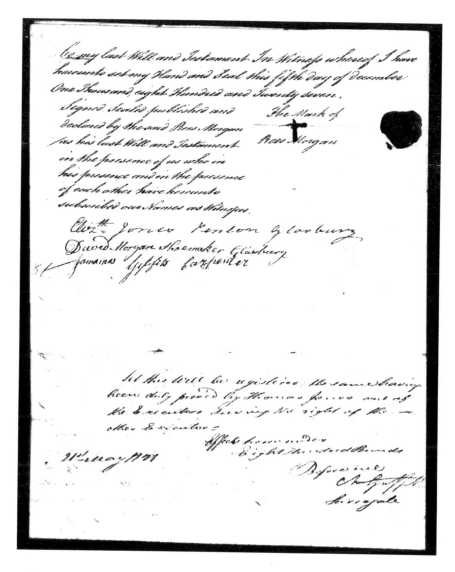

The will of David Morgan the Shoemaker. Note the mark of his brother Rees Morgan

Yowser, the connection! Now, we know that Rees had three brothers and a sister, but thanks to the missing records we know little more than that.

So off I went on a hunt for David Morgan in a veritable sea of them. But after much searching and cross-referencing, I finally found him my man.

He'd married an Elizabeth Griffiths, in St. Peter's, of Glasbury - the very same church as his brother. But once again, anything else was thin on the ground. Records were not showing the people; yet the people had been there.

Indeed, with so many family members listed in Rees' will – and let us be clear, there were a lot of them – you'd think there would be a copious forest of trees!

Not so.

Now why would that be? Where are they? Where have they gone? How has such a large family evaded detection?

Maybe they all left the area after the Mary Morgan scandal . . .

It is a mystery. As is the reference to David Morgan, the shoemaker – did he know something? Did he and his wife have any children? Has anything been passed down, like it had in Cousin Mary's family?

Maybe this book will bring something to light, because I don't know about you, but thus far, this whole business of a entire family disappearing by chance is a complete load of cobblers!

Meanwhile, after months of silence I get a call from Mary. It is the evening of the Coronation, and as the great and the good celebrated across the country, I found myself at her graveside as dusk deepened into night.

So, what did she have to say?

Quite a lot as it happened.

Initially, she talked about the baby, which came as something of a surprise. And she spoke with great fondness as she recalled her quiet joy of this new life growing in her belly.

She was 'my lambkin', Mary told me. And I felt the love. I felt the love of a long-lost girl to whom motherhood had been denied, and instead of the expected ire, I felt only a wistfulness and a heaviness in my heart.

We all assumed so much with this girl; her horror at finding herself with child. Fear in the face of destitution. An overwhelming sense of shame as the scandal unfolded around her like a vengeful beast, and what a beast it was! A merciless creature of such power it would crush you like a fly than risk the tarnish its name.

The fate of many a poor girl, raped and seduced into a life of misery, robbed of all hope and, in this case, left to their own devices – or was she?

My mind went back to something else Demelsa said to me that day when we went over to Glasbury. We were driving back and discussing the whole Mary/John Wood saga, when she surprised me (once again!), with another revelation.

She alleged that Mary's condition had been common knowledge within the household, and that she had been beguiled into a false sense of security right up until the moment she gave birth. That's when everything changed and 'they turned on her'.

They turned on her . . .

I remember, even now, the chill that filled my being as Demelsa spoke those words. That tingle you get when something resonates – but not in a good way.

So, was that what had happened?

Had Mary been led to believe that all would be well? That she and the baby would be taken care of? In-house management. Damage limitation. Perfectly feasible but was this the case?

I didn't have to ask Demelsa how she came by this information, she is a 'feeler' just like me. She has nothing to gain by making such an allegation. I took it onboard with no small bewilderment and no less respect for her remarkable gift.

Of equal wonder was her next statement; that John Wood and Mary had actually, to use her words 'got on together'. That he was fond of her in a paternal way, which almost makes it worse.

As head honcho of the understairs, I think we can safely assume that he would have had dealings with Mary, in her role as undercook. And if she was – and I believe she was – the illegitimate daughter of Walter Senior, then it would make sense the squire's most trusted servant would keep an eye on her surely?

Was this why I felt such anger in the churchyard when John appeared to insult me? Or was it a ploy to draw Mary out for an age-old confrontation?

If so, it would explain the absolute fury I felt. Such a betrayal would be off the Richter scale. 'Uncle John' turning into the 'Bogeyman'.

The sense of hurt would have been phenomenal, but as Demelsa had said: What choice did he have . . .

Much food for thought and then some, which brought to mind to the story of the Witches of Belvoir. Like Mary, there is a lot about them out on the web, and after scrolling through I came across a book.

Entitled 'The Witch and the Priest', it was written by Hilda Lewis, an author I'd never heard of, and I was intrigued. The reviews were good. Very good. I searched for a copy and got stuck in.

She writes an imaginary tale of the haunting of the priest by the mother-witch, Joan Flowers, and it made for an interesting and at times, disturbing read.

With an insight that often had me wondering, she chronicles events that culminate in the witches' arrest and ultimate demise. As I said, the story is fictionalised, but the baseline for much of it is true, and it was only towards the end of the book I felt I got the message.

We all know that 'wise women', or witches were persecuted terribly throughout history, but this book pulls no punches and highlights the cruelty used to obtain a confession. Indeed, I don't mind admitting there were parts that readily brought me to tears, especially the case of an innocent young woman with the mind of a child.

Sleep deprivation was just one of the methods used to break a subject down. Couple this with almost constant interrogation and the mind begins to crack.

Mary, as we know, had been locked up in the castle for two weeks after her alleged crime. It was said that she needed the time to recover.

Based on what Demelsa had said to me; had sleep deprivation been used against Mary to coerce her into compliance?

Was this why she had guided me to the Belvoir witches, knowing my search would lead me to the book and the message therein? The thought struck me like a thunderbolt and wouldn't go away.

As I stood at that grave these thoughts ran through me as the ghost of a young girl reminisced a love lost. Tender, loving, heartfelt Mary; ill-used and demonised unto death.

On impulse I began recording on my phone. Not because I expected to pick anything up, but more as a means of recording my impressions rather than doing it from memory when I got back to the house. Besides, to have been called out after months of silence was highly significant, so I hit the button as she gave me the word 'Croft'.

I had no idea who or what she was referring to, but I asked her to repeat it as I start recording. She was quite forthcoming, mentioning 'Robin' and 'Arrow' (River Arrow?). She also kept referring to the Pyefinch family. Something about one of the sons.

There is a story, unsubstantiated, that as she thrashed on the rope, a young man was paid a shilling to pull on her legs. An oxymoron of kindness, but she was as light as a feather and slow strangulation could take up to twenty minutes or more.

Such an act showed pity for her plight, but who was the boy, and who paid the coin? No one knows. No one has ever come forward with a name. You'd think such an act of mercy would have been recorded by someone – not least the boy's family and passed down?

Going on this proviso – what would be the reason for them not to? Why wasn't the identity of this knight in dubious armour made public?

Delve into Pyefinch family history and the answer may lay there. Besides accommodating our Mr Browne and having links to the coroner, the family were large and powerful enough to be influential locally. Whilst Cooksey went bust and lost everything, they thrived. Having already an interest in the Pyefinch's, the possibility that they, or at least younger members of the family may have attended the execution cannot be discounted. It was a big event after all and on their doorstep, so to speak.

What I'm speculating is what if it was a Pyefinch who made that fatal pull, ensuring not just merciful release, but also a swift end, should anyone get any ideas. She was barely more than a child after all and there may have been strong feelings.

According to reports, the good folk of Scottleton Street drew down their blinds as Mary passed by to her death.

Equally, much has been said about the popularity of the Wilkins amongst the townspeople, and that this wasn't in any way affected by the case. Maybe that was propaganda, or perhaps it was due to the fact that when funds for a new Gaol were urgently needed, it was Walter Junior who came up trumps.

The old clink was in a sorry state and inmates had been breaking out at an embarrassing rate. Unfortunately, Mary didn't get the chance, despite 'the report' that a plan to spring her out had been thwarted. Just another reason to keep her under close lock and key, eh? This aside, the prison was falling apart, nevertheless.

By 1819 it was clear that something had to be done, but who was going to pay for it?

Over to an extract from Keith Parker's excellent book, 'A History of Presteigne' (Logaston Press), page 20.

'The project was financed by borrowing £2,000 on the security of the county rate. Walter Wilkins advancing £1,500, and he duly obliged with a further loan of £500 when it proved impossible to borrow this from any other source.'

Not a problem. The Wilkins weren't short of a bob or two, but you can see the irony; it is hoped!

By this time, Walter Senior had passed away and Junior was now in the driving seat. Lest we forget, there was also the family bank!

'This private bank was established in 1778 as Wilkins, Jeffreys, Wilkins & Williams. It was also known as Brecon Old Bank. Of the four original partners, Walter and Jeffreys Wilkins had worked abroad with the East India Company. The firm largely served the local agricultural community and opened branches throughout South Wales: Merthyr Tydfil (1812), Haverfordwest (1832), Carmarthen (1834), Cardigan (1835), Llanelli (1837), Aberdare (1854), Cardiff (1856) and Dowlais (1875). It was acquired by Lloyds in 1890.' (Courtesy of Archives Hub)'

This is important because it also brings us directly back to the Morgans. They were, as we know, busy on the Drover roads that would take them from Wales to Hereford and Gloucester before hitting the Big Smoke! London was the final destination and where the money changed hands.

The money was then in the hands of the Drover men themselves who, besides as acting financiers for farmers, also played an important role in moving deeds, promissory notes, and money all over the country. By doing so, they helped put banking in Wales on the map.

Indeed, in 1799 the drovers themselves opened 'The Black Ox Bank' in Llandovery, before, like the Brecon Old Bank of the Wilkins, it was merged into Lloyds in 1909.

So, can we assume that the Morgans, who lived, travelled, and traded on the Maesllwch estate and beyond would have dealings in the same way?

As from 'On the Trail of Welsh Drovers' by Twm Elias (of Gwasg Carreg Gwalch) I felt I found my answer!

Besides being an informative and thoroughly enjoyable read, there amidst the pages I came across a direct reference to the Old Brecon Bank under the section, The Post and early drovers' banks (page 88).

'Wilkins Bank in Brecon...was well known for servicing drovers and dealers from a wide area...'

So, did the most lucrative wool traders in the whole of Wales avail themselves of these services? In truth, methinks it would have been rude not to . . .

Onto Croft Castle just outside Leominster now under the care of the National Trust. It was the only Croft I could think of that was close by, and after a quick search I found a previous resident of interest.

His name was Thomas Johnes and he had stood against Walter Wilkins Senior in the elections. I had the sense there had been no love lost between these two and decided to make some enquiries.

The phone was answered by a lovely girl called Claire, who also happened to be from Presteigne. As a child she recalled being taught Mary's story in school and visiting the grave. This was great for me as I could cut to the chase; was there anything in the family papers pertaining to Mary Morgan and her trial?

Within an hour I received an email from their senior archivist Kim, who was happy to explore my query further.

Unfortunately, nothing turned up, but it is my hope that someone reading this book may know or will have something that'll tie in the link.

I did come across an interesting snippet however when reading up about its history.

According to *Wikipedia,* Sir John Croft married one of the daughters of Owain Glyndŵr, 'The Last Prince of Wales.'

Her name was Janet.

Another hint?

For anyone who works with spirit and is a dreamer of note, will know; nothing is ever given on a plate. Playing detective is often the way, especially with dreams as you build up a language that is unique to you. But sometimes messages are more succinct, and up to this point, I have to say, the Universe had been nothing less than direct.

So, with another possible connection to Mary's birth-mother, I looked at what else she had given me that evening but have yet to expand on 'Robin' and 'Arrow'. I don't always have the answers but perhaps something else will come to light as these things often do.

On the subject of dreams my cousin, Geraint, had two about Mary, that he is happy for me to share with you.

In the first one he was driving a car and in the passenger seat was the silent but unmistakable figure of a young female figure. They were following another vehicle with steamed up windows that contained, he sensed rather than saw, two male figures. There was no conversation or emotion from his mystery companion, but he remembers his shock as the car they were following suddenly careers off a cliff.

Make any sense?

Here is the second dream he had the night before the anniversary of her death whilst staying at the Radnorshire Arms. Here, you will find, a link between the two.

In the dream Geraint is stood on an old, cobbled street watching as two men load a large sack into the back of an old vehicle. It's dark, but he sees a hat on the head of one of the men, and sideburns on the face of the other. They are at best, sinister. Indeed, Ger likened them to the child-catcher character from the old classic, 'Chitty, Chitty, Bang, Bang...'!

If you're familiar with this film - and I have to confess, it was one of my childhood favourites! - the portrayal of the 'child-catcher' was chilling. Indeed, the actor Robert Helpmann, "and his terrifying personality caused him to win the award for the "Scariest Villain in Children's Books" in 2005"! (As taken from CBR.com).

Interestingly, Roald Dahl, who wrote the screenplay, invented the character.

But back to the dream!

As soon as the two men leave the scene, Geraint makes his way over to the vehicle and pulls open the two doors. He reaches in and opens the sack. Coiled up inside he's stunned to find a huge green snake, that despite its size, poses no threat. He woke up at that point but with the strong sense that the dream was in some way connected with Mary.

In esoteric terms snakes have always been a powerful symbol of healing, rebirth, and wisdom. The colour, and the absence of menace would suggest that despite the efforts to make her disappear off the edge of a cliff.

Mary is no longer the 'green' girl and like a snake, has simply shed her skin and remained, just in another form. The attempt to depict her as sinful and a trickster, is reverberant of the serpent in the Garden of Eden.

The child-catchers may have thought they'd 'put her to bed', but her soul has other ideas.

It's worth pointing out that my cousin is very down to earth and not given to flights of fancy. If anything, it took some doing for him to open up about something so personal, but I'm so glad he did. The Universe speaks in many ways, and in Geraint's experience, a reflection of his obvious connection with Mary, and hers with him.

Would seem we weren't the only ones who had dreams of Mary, for in her manuscript Patricia Parris records a dream she had during the course of her research.

She was in the graveyard with W.H. Howse, (author of 'Presteigne, Past and Present' 1945 and who had an interest in Mary). It was dark and pouring with rain. Howse was shouting and pointing to where Mary was standing on her grave.

'There are your sources! There!' He cried.

Patricia described the figure as wearing a long, white dress that had no sleeves, her arms held up and covering her face as she cried inconsolably. It made for a sorry sight as Patricia noted the long dark hair streaming over her shoulders as she did the tears that intermingled with the rain.

Wow, what a powerful dream! Yet Ms Parris freely admits she had no idea of what it meant despite Mary's pleading waking her up. She did say, however, that Mary was a silent source but not anymore, eh!

There have been so many strange and at times amazing quirks and encounters throughout this project. Like the time I got lost looking for Stanage Park on the back roads above Knighton. I stopped to ask directions only to find myself talking to a Mr Morgan, who happens to be a grave-digger.

Or the time I met Janet Gardiner, who lives in Llowes. I was wandering around in the hope of picking something up when an enquiry to one of its residents led me to this lady's door. Her face was a picture as I explained my reason for calling.

'I've been looking at photographs of her grave just this morning,' she said, 'How strange that you should now knock at my door!'

How strange that your name should also be Janet, I thought, but held my peace.

I asked if I might take a look. They had been left in the possessions of a lady who had recently passed away and had obviously been taken many years ago. The quality was still superb, however, and were kindly donated for the book.

Another chance encounter was with former horse-breeder and jockey, Graham Lloyd, who I fell into conversation with at Hay Castle. An interesting man, not least for the fact his mother had been a cook at Maesllwch!

Then there was the Gas engineer, Steve Smith, from Talgarth whose Grandfather had been Head-Gardener. Diane of the Yorkshire Building Society in Hay, (blink and you'll miss it!), whose grandparents had also worked on the estate. Mr Greenow of Glasbury who used to work on the farm. All with stories, all with snippets, and - for the most part, loyal to the de Wintons and so we'll leave that there with my grateful thanks for sharing.

One of the photos courtesy of Jan Gardiner

There have also been moments of great poignancy. A chance meeting in the graveyard early this summer saw me read out Mary's testimony just yards from her grave.

An impromptu rendition before an equally impromptu audience that consisted of Nicky Evans, Jeremy Price, and Julian O'Halloran, former BBC World News Correspondent. One minute they're going about their business, the next, absorbing the passion of a long-lost voice.

Suffice it is to say they listened with the greatest of respect. Mary had found her voice, alright.

Another occasion involved a more recent addition to the community. Belynda Johnson Carranco-Maclean and her husband Andy, recently moved into Cemetery Cottage on the outskirts of Presteigne.

We'd met over fried-egg sandwiches in The Coffee House, the home of hearty breakfasts, and Columbian coffee beans. It was Belynda's birthday and I'd invited her over for lunch.

Post-pasta, I read her the opening chapter as a cool wind suddenly blew past me and in her direction.

Mary.

And did she feel it?

Yes, ma'am, she drawled in true Texan style before dissolving into tears. In her experience a sign of 'spirit', more definitively, when she 'feels God'.

Belynda is a Mormon, and obviously more receptive than I would ever have anticipated. Religious people have often been hostile to the face of my unearthly gifts. That has often been my experience, which makes it all the more remarkable when presented with an open mind.

Mary has had a propensity to make her presence felt whenever she, or her situation, has been the subject of conversation. Not always, but often enough to have been noted.

She manifests, as many do, as a tingle at the back of the neck, accompanied by a soft wind and s drop in temperature. Not everyone will experience such phenomena in their lifetime, as some will never believe in life and after death.

But before I move on from this section, let me say this; electricity exists yet you can't see it. Energy doesn't have to be visible to 'be there'. Science doesn't have to have all the answers because Man demands it.

Some things are meant to stay hidden.

Long may the veil between Worlds remain a mystery, but we are given enough to know that life doesn't end when the lights go out. We shine on, just in another place.

Yet, for souls like Mary Morgan, who have never known rest; it is literally, a case of unfinished business. Injustice has kept her in the shadows all these years, but it is love that will finally set her free.

Love and acknowledgement for a very great wrong.

And how do I know this?

A shared encounter with Demelsa earlier this year when a conversation about Belynda's experience saw Mary come rushing into the shop, and with an energy I'd never felt before.

Instead of the usual heavy sense of grief and loneliness, I felt joy. In abundance. So much joy in fact, when I turned back to Demelsa there were tears in her eyes.

'Oh my God!' I exclaimed, *Can you feel her? Can you feel that!*'

'Yes,' said Demelsa, her face breaking into a smile. 'She's happy.'

'Happy!' I echoed incredulously. For the first time in all of our encounters I felt the girl, not the ghost. The essence, the personality, her personality and what a lovely, lively little cricket she was!

Suddenly Dem cocked her head up to the ceiling.

'What?' I said.

'I thought I could hear footsteps running around upstairs.'

By now I'd joined Demelsa with a few tears of my own. The sheer joy of this young girl as she whizzed about was as uplifting as was the knowledge that she had shaken off the shadows and risen like a beautiful bird freed from its cage.

Then I felt her on my lap, an act so natural yet so surreal I thought my heart would burst. I've experienced some physical phenomena in my time. I've been brushed against, poked, tapped and had my bum pinched, but nothing could prepare me for what she did next.

With a delicacy as to be almost imperceptible, I felt what I can only describe as a gentle peck on my cheek.

'She's just kissed me!' I said in wonderment, 'She's just kissed me on the cheek. To say, thank you . . . '

It was an incredible moment as it was unexpected, and the message had been delivered, loud and clear.

No more suffering for Mary Morgan. No more banishment into enforced silence. Heard and heeded. Suffused with happiness and as light as a feather. Finally, she was free.

And that was good enough for me . . .

It seemed fitting we mark the anniversary of her passing and I wanted to do something special. As Karen had played such a powerful part in Mary's story, it seemed more than apt that she performed the blessing.

Despite an extremely busy diary, April 13th was set aside to celebrate the short and tragic life of a stricken soul who had suffered a great injustice.

With Mary's approval I organised a get together that would coincide with her final moments. It would be private, intimate, and attended by those who kept the faith and believed in her innocence.

Of course, Cousin Mary and her family were top of the list. For them, the journey had been the longest since word of a family skeleton had stirred their interest.

In spite of Herculean efforts, we could not find a direct link to Mary, but as Geraint and Karen have stated on many occasions, maybe there'll be another book. Maybe there will.

But only if people are honest. If people come forward, and – more importantly – if the Universe wills it. Nothing has been by accident throughout this project, and if there is more to be told, then it will happen and back into the fray I will go.

But for now, and for the family, the day of redemption had come, and it was good to see what it meant to them. A quiet joy marked by a sense of vindication. They are Mary's kin, whether by blood or marriage; they are her people, and I am proud that they are mine.

Present also was Rebecca, who had played such a pivotal role in bringing Mary's story to life.

Then there was Demelsa. Dear, gentle, Demelsa, whose confidence in herself and her amazing gifts, I hope, will continue to grow. She opened my eyes in so many ways; she and her family will always have a friend in me. As will Jan Matthews and Roger Millichamp, Nicky Evans, the most dapper man in Presteigne and the kindest. As a close friend of Jenny Green, he had witnessed firsthand the storm of her foray into Mary's story and is a loyal advocate of her work to this day.

Jenny rocked some boats, I know, but she had sailed into uncharted waters and found mysteries in the hidden depths. Now having sailed those waters myself, I appreciate the amount of research she had undertaken without the benefit of the internet. Having Nick there in her stead, however, was the closest we were going to get, and I was grateful for his presence.

As Karen began the service, I looked across to where the Reverend David Thomas stood quietly with his wife, Davina.

They had been the first to arrive and it did my heart well to see their ongoing support for Mary and the whole ethos of this project. There were several faces missing, but it didn't matter. I understood that many of the clergy, to quote my vicar, 'take off for the hills', once Easter is over. Which made the presence of Karen and David all the more consequential.

We were all there for Mary, and as the Archdeacon of Manchester spoke of those who stumble in the dark before love reaches out and catches them. We could, all to a man and woman, relate to the frailty of human nature and the importance of forgiveness.

It was a beautiful speech that resonated deeply on all levels. Mary would have been pleased. Karen did her proud, as did David. He had been nothing but supportive in helping Mary to find her voice.

From left: The Venerable Karen Lund, Archdeacon of Manchester. Demelsa Hopkins, Rebecca Eversley, Jan Matthews, Roger Millichamp, Davina Thomas, and the Reverend David Thomas. Cousins Becky, with daughter, Lillie Amber, Geraint, Ken, Cousin Mary, and Nicky Evans.

As you'll see from the photo, the primary headstone that marks her grave has been removed from the picture and this has been done deliberately.

Refer back to Mary's testimony and you'll see why. We have no room here for the pompous posturing's of an entitled class who stood by in judgement and let her die. We have only respect for the lesser stone, that sits, slightly tilted, but strong, nevertheless, in its condemnation of an act ill-done.

How far we've come since that fateful day on Gallows Lane. How much has been roistered out of centuries-old sleep and revealed in all its tell-tale glory.

Mary Morgan, little more than a child, but with a tenacity that defied her years, refused to lay down and acquiesce to the charges that had been brought against her.

At her trial she had pleaded, 'Not guilty', remember? The only reference of anything that came out of her mouth; a spontaneous and desperate bid to save her skin? Or maybe she was innocent all along.

We know the truth, as we know that Mary is now at peace, and it was a lovely and love-filled service of acknowledgment and remembrance that drew a line beneath the journey.

Mary's journey.

From an unknown womb to working the kitchens of Maesllwch, to standing trial and being hung from a rope. Her road was cruel and pitiless, not least for the fact she had been driven to her death – and all for whispered words and a misguided love.

Poor Mary. How the heart weeps. But how the spirit soars as we bid her board that train and to reconciliation, finally, with her beloved Mari bach.

On behalf of the family, Geraint also read a heartfelt speech that clearly shows how Mary has always been close by; for them as much as for her.

"Firstly, we would all like to thank Mandy for all the very hard work, for all the travelling and for all the hours and hours of research she has put into writing this book.

As a family we have known about Mary Morgan for several generations. Mum was in her teens when she was told – "that there was a skeleton in our cupboard, by my grandmother. She was then shown an aged blue piece of paper, that was dated 1869. On it was an inscription of the larger grave of Mary Morgan.

This began my mum's fascination with the life of Mary.

When mum was in her early twenties, Mum, Dad, my grandma and grandpa all came to Presteigne to see the two graves. They also looked around at some of the local cemeteries in the area looking for other graves with the Morgan name, but as there were so many they had to give up.

Then in 1984 Mum heard on the radio about Jenny Green writing a book about Mary Morgan. However, it wasn't until 1988 that mum and dad came to Presteigne again, this time with me and mu brother Ed, to visit and pay our respects to Mary.

I have a vague memory of being in a village shop at the time and Dad asking the staff about Mary. The response was pretty cold, they did not want to talk about her.

Since I first found out about Mary, I have been interested in all aspects of her story, so much so, that I have had her grave incorporated into my ink sleeve. I am always more than happy to explain the story to people when they ask about it, in particular, the wrongful punishment that was dealt out to her on this day over two centuries ago.

Our grateful thanks again to Mandy for putting right the wrongs of what we have been led to believe about the deaths of Mary Morgan and her baby all those years ago."

As I bring this story to its conclusion with tears in my eyes, I had word back from another Mari, the lovely librarian of St. David's Cathedral. Despite an extensive search, she could find no record of her namesake's burial. The final resting place of the little mite that had paid the ultimate price remains a mystery, as does the true identity of Mary's mother.

I have my own thoughts on this, as you know, based on a dream and what's in my heart. But for now, I will hold my peace in the hope that one day I may be allowed to walk in the place where I believe, a baby, who was once nameless, now sleeps.

We have come to the end of what has been an incredible journey of twists and turns, dreams and drama, lingering echoes and long-lost voices that have reached out and allowed Mary to rise

from the ashes of her terrible fate and demand that she be heard.
My job now done, her will is done. And to that end, a few lines
from me to join all those who felt her injustice and decried her fate.
With love and the most sisterly of hands, I bid her to the light.
May she finally find her peace . . .

When grief permits the stole of sleep and stillness dulls the
pain, the sun will rise and bless your eyes to see her face again.

For in the light beyond our dreams, beyond the realms of Time.
A state of grace, a lovely place that words cannot define.

Where angels walk and brave men cry, where softness curves
the sky. 'Tis but a veil, love will prevail, beside you she will lie.

And as the gentle dawn unfolds and cloaks the furthest star,
be sure to know, that whence you go, your baby's never far.

Amanda Aubrey-Burden (16th September 2023)

BIBLIOGRAPHY

COURTESY OF REBECCA EVERSLEY
PGDIP BA(HONS)
'HISTORIC DOCK PROJECT'

https://www.historicdockproject.co.uk/

Bowen, H. V. Wales and the making of British India during the late Eighteenth Century. *Honourable Society of the Cymmrodorion.* 2017.

Burke, Sir Bernard. A genealogical and heraldic history of the landed gentry of Great Britain & Ireland. 1814-1892. London. Harrison

King, Peter & Ward, Richard: Rethinking the Bloody Code in Eighteenth- Century Britain: Capitol Punishment at the centre and on the periphery. Past and Present, Vol 228. Issue 1, Aug 2015, Pg 159-205

Southwood, John. The Meredith Family of Presteigne and Kington, 1391-1940. *Kington Family History Society.* 1988.

Wood, Thomas.1904.The Registers of Glasbury, Breconshire:1660-1836; Transcribed by Thomas Wood. London. Parish Register Society

Powys Family History Society. Monumental Inscriptions: Presteigne, Llowes, Llandefalle Glasbury, Crossgates.

Howse, W H. Presteigne Past and Present. 1945. Hereford. Jakemans

Parris, Patricia. Mary Morgan, Contemporary Sources. *Radnorshire Society Transactions*. Vol. LIII. 1983.

Internet resources

https://www.Ancestry.co.uk

https://www.Findmypast.co.uk

https://www.apothecaries.org

https://www.crimeandpunishment.library.wales/

https://www.NaomiClifford.com

https://www.historyofparliamentonline.org

https://www.ucl.ac.uk/lbs
https://www.highsheriffs.com

https://www.Journals.library.wales

Unpublished

Patricia Parris, unpublished manuscript, Powys Archives.

Newspapers

Brecon Gazette
Chester Courant
Hereford Times
Hereford Journal

Printed in Great Britain
by Amazon

33117367R00163